BEST SELLER

Timothy B. Sagges

Also By
Timothy B. Sagges

FINAL RESPECTS
(A Two-Act Comedy for stage)

TAPE
(A Screen Play)

Dedicated To
The Ill-mannered People in the World,
who have driven me to the solitude
necessary to write this.

And to Joseph Sirak,
for his
open heart
and
steady shoulders.

ONE

His eyes fixed on some unknown distant spot in space, twelve year old Stewart Clark slowly closed the novel in front of him and placed it tenderly on his lap. He sat for a moment, motionless, waiting for the familiar sound of the bathroom door closing from down the hall. Finally alone, his mother locked away in her customary 7 PM bubble bath, he could think straight. He ran his fingers through his kinky orange hair and took a deep breath, exhaling with resolve. As he stood, he tightened his grip on his novel then headed for the dining room window, flung it open and let himself bathe in the warm August breeze. The dread of starting seventh grade in the morning evaporated like the sweat on his forehead as he leaned into the gentle wind wafting up from the ground fourteen floors below.

It was always windy and ten degrees cooler up here. But tonight was somehow different. Tonight the air seemed to be beckoning him.

He closed his bright blue eyes and let his thoughts drift to his new friend, Cassandra. They had been through so much together in such a short amount of time, and staying with her now would mean the ultimate sacrifice. He shivered a little and leaned slightly more into the wind. He was secure in his belief, pure in his thoughts, as he tucked his book inside his blue jeans and plummeted to his death on the sidewalk below.

SEVERAL MONTHS EARLIER

As Rich took one final glance at the clock on the wall behind him, his mind strayed just long enough for the steam from the cappuccino maker to find its way to the back of his hand. The jolt of white hot pain pierced his skin and the Vente Mocha Skinny with the double shot of vanilla flew from his grasp, landing squarely on his Kelly green apron. His screams of agony sliced through the din of the coffee house like a machete as he bolted for the sink. "Dammit!" he cried. "Sonofa bitch!"

But scalded or not, progress stopped for no man. The other baristas went into double time and within seconds, it was as though he didn't exist. As the pain began to subside he reached under the sink for the first-aid kit, grabbed the half squashed tube of burn salve and slathered it on. As the throbbing commenced he yelled into the air, "Where's the gauze?"

Terrance, the shift supervisor emerged from the back office with a fresh roll, "Here you go. Why don't you just go ahead and split. It's almost nine anyway."

He snatched the gauze and began to wrap his greasy right hand and with as much sarcasm as he could muster, looked over his eyeglasses and snapped, "Ya think?"

In less than a minute he had tossed his apron over the counter and stormed out the front door, leaving a line of customers behind him.

Stepping into the cool Manhattan night, he made his usual sharp left turn and headed for the liquor store just two doors down. He had a good mind to quit that place once and for all, and just as his resolve reached its peak, the tiny bell above the liquor store door tinkled, jarring him awake from the notion of beautiful freedom.

A squat old Arab man greeted him with a toothy grin, "Hello, Mr. Richie. The usual?"

Rich forced himself into a state of affability and reciprocated with a smile of his own. Why, he thought, should poor old Adnon bear the brunt of my bad fortune. "Yes, Mr. Adnon. But tonight I would like the 100 proof."

"Yes Sir, yes Sir," the gray haired old man offered as he struggled off of his stool to reach the pint sized bottles on the bottom shelf behind him. "Difficult night tonight?"

Awkwardly counting his money with his left hand, "You bet. Everybody and their brother is jonesing for their caffeine fix all at the same time tonight." Relenting, he placed a wad of cash on the counter top and waited for Adnon to count it.

"Did Everybody Jones do this to your hand?" he asked, bagging the bottle and straightening the dollar bills.

Hesitating for a moment, then chuckling a little, "Yes, Adnon. Yes, Everybody Jones got me good tonight." He wadded up the remaining bills and tucked the bottle under his arm, turning for the door.

" 100 hundred proof is good for Mr. Jones."

The bell again chimed and, relieved, Rich made his way alone through the park to the Q line at 57th and 7th. Alone on the platform, save for an Asian family at the opposite side, he cracked open his Southern Comfort and took a refreshing gulp straight from the paper bag. Its warmth coursed through him and by the time the train barreled into the station, his right hand had stopped throbbing.

He made his way from the 31st Street stop in Astoria to his apartment just a block away. It was unusually quiet for a Friday night. Everyone, he thought, must be in the Upper West Side buying coffee. Entering into the courtyard of his building, he found the same group of young children playing on the cement, their parents nowhere to be found. He navigated through the melee and into the hallway to the mailboxes.

Months of routine rejection letters had taken their toll on him, but each night before turning the mailbox key, a faint glimmer of hope sprung forth from the ever waning well within him. Phone bill, electric bill, a coupon from Macy's and a postcard from the new dry cleaner on the corner. No news was good news, he thought, as he trudged up the marble stairs to his third floor apartment.

As if on cue, the music from the next apartment began to blare just as he settled into his office chair in front of his computer. Finishing the pint of Southern Comfort, he lit a cigarette and closed his eyes, letting his thoughts meld with the music from next door. Just then the phone rang, snapping him back to life.

Knocking over his ashtray as he reached for the phone, "Hello? Dammit!"

Hearing his sister' s voice on the other end of the line he resigned himself to another 45 minutes of preaching. When are you going to settle down? Why don't you look for a real job? You're letting your degree go to waste. He would sit and listen, playing his part in this weekly dance they had done since he moved to the city from West Reading, Pennsylvania over a year ago. As she took a breath, he was finally able to inject a sentence and change the subject all at once. "I burnt the shit outta my hand tonight."

"Maybe it's a sign," she said. "Maybe someone's trying to tell you to go look for a real job."

He was silent as she went on for another ten minutes. Finally, he managed, "Is it Tommy's dad's weekend?"

"Yes," she answered, "He's taking him to Six Flags. Why?"

"Well, you seem especially chatty tonight." He took a long drag of his Marlboro and waited for a reply. "You there?"

"I'm here," she snapped. "I'm just trying to be less chatty."

He opened the top drawer to his desk and retrieved his baggie of pot and the rolling papers. "You know what I mean. Don't be bitchy."

"I just get a little lonely when Tommy's out of the house."

"I know," he offered, placing the receiver between his jaw and his shoulder. He contorted his body, then repositioned himself. Rolling a joint with one good hand would be a bit of a challenge.

"Any news?" she asked, hoping to change the subject.

"Nope."

"What's that noise?"

"It's the next door neighbors. They're having another party." He licked the edge of the paper and wrapped it tightly.

"You should go over," she instructed. "You might meet a nice girl."

Firing up the reefer, "I don't want a nice girl. I want a mean girl who can hump like a dog."

"You're a pig. I'm gonna hang up now."

Holding in the smoke, "Are we still on for next week?"

"Yes," she replied. "And yes, you can bring a date. But no skanks."

Finally exhaling, "Okay. Love you Rachel." He hung up the phone and took to the business of cleaning the ashes from under the desk.

An hour later, the party next door was in full swing. Laughter, screams and the unmistakable sound of general roughhousing emanated through the paper-thin walls. As he stuffed himself with Doritos, he flipped through his mail and found a piece belonging to his neighbor. Veronica Hall, apartment 24. Interesting, he thought, talk about your signs. He stuffed the envelope into his pocket, went to the bathroom mirror and patted down his disheveled hair. Satisfied with his natural good looks, he threw on his Chucks, grabbed his keys and went next door. After politely tapping yielded no results, he pounded with his full fist, causing the number four to fall off of the door. Finally a short, heavy-set blond in her twenties opened the door.

"What are you knocking for? Just come in." She disappeared into the crowd as the door began to swing shut.

Realizing the apparent informality of the situation, he pushed open the door and stepped inside. When his eyes adjusted from the obnoxious fluorescent light in the hallway to the smoky darkness of the room, he could finally see what the noise was all about. Packed, wall to wall, reeking of marijuana, the apartment resembled a twenty-first century adaptation of Studio 54. As he scanned the room he marveled at the sights. A gigantic drag queen with neon green hair. A midget, arm wrestling a guy in a wheelchair. Siamese twins, actual Siamese twins giving a piggy back ride to a Labrador Retriever, and a man that came in at over seven feet tall giving random shotgun bong hits to everyone he passed. Rich stood dumbstruck for a few moments, not sure if he had landed in Hell, or Heaven. Only when a gorgeous, six foot tall black woman handed him a Heineken, did he stir from his awe.

"Thank you," he muttered as she floated away just as deftly as she had arrived.

Slightly more emboldened, he drew upon his most nonchalant posture and slowly weaved his way through the crowd. The music, the reefer, the Southern Comfort and the company all conspired, within minutes, to bring him to one of the happiest places he had been to in a long while. As he took in the lay of the land, he noticed that the activities all seemed to center around one spot in the room. Bopping his head to the beat of some forgettable top forty tune, he wended his way closer to the center of attention. Through a break in the crowd he saw a beautifully, thin woman with long, straight, black hair, sitting regally on a chair shaped like a giant pair of lips. She wore a black dress that accentuated every glorious curve of her tight little body, and held an ornate piece of stemware from which she drank white wine. While the right side of his brain urged him to jump upon her and screw the living daylights out of her, the left, more sarcastic side of his brain thought, what's Morticia Addams doing here?

The excuse he needed to approach her was right in his back pocket. He whipped out the cable bill and moved closer to her. "Excuse me," he shouted to her over the clamor, "I'm looking for," he paused to re-inspect the mail, "Veronica Hall?"

"You're talking to her," injected the tall guy, as he passed by with his bong.

"Are you Miss Hall?" he asked, crouching down to her.

She pouted a sexy, inviting smile and answered, "Yes. Yes, I am. Have you tried the olive tapenade?"

"Um," he stammered, struck by the baritone in her voice, "Um, no. I'm your neighbor from next door, and..."

She sat up and placed her glass on the coffee table, "O my God, are we making too much noise?" She jumped from her seat and clapped her hands. "Let's turn the music down some. It's getting late!"

"No!" he held. "I'm not here to complain. I just wanted to bring this over to you." He offered the envelope. "It was in my mailbox by mistake."

"Oh," she chuckled. "I thought I was in some kind of trouble."

Trying not to stare at her breasts, he apologized, "Well, I better get going."

"No!" she insisted, grabbing his arm, "Really, have you tried the tapenade?"

It was obvious to them both that she wanted him to stay, and as a sheepish grin stretched across both their faces, he relented and she led him to the buffet.

By 4 A.M. the crowd had thinned out to just a few diehard revelers. They all sat on the living room floor surrounding the coffee table, from left to right; Veronica, Rich, Rita, Margot, Dan and Dennis, the seven foot tall man. A marriage of wine, vodka, marijuana and cocaine had them all intensely focused on a candle in the center of the table. Rapt in the greatest tale they had ever heard, goose bumps randomly made their way up one neck, then another. Fear, joy and fascination swirled about them like a celestial hurricane as Rich turned the final page of his manuscript and read aloud, *"Battered and bruised, she clung only to the hope that Billy would make it out alive. And as the sun gave way to the unforgiving moon, Cassandra remained steadfast in her belief that she again would one day see her friend."*

Rita let out an audible sob and tried to catch her breath. While the others let out a sigh, Dennis managed, "You wrote that?"

Rich smiled and took a sip of Diet Coke.

"Seriously, Rich," Veronica demanded, "did you write that?"

"Yeah," he smiled, " and I gotta tell you, that's the first time I've ever read it out loud."

Reaching over the coffee table and giving Rich a nudge, Dennis bragged, "And you didn't want to bring it over and share it with us."

Lighting a cigarette, Margo asked, "So, does Billy ever make it back?"

Dan rolled his eyes, mocking, "Hello? That's where the sequel comes in! Gawd!"

Slack jawed Dennis turned to Veronica, "That totally blew my mind!" Turning to Rich, "Have you tried to get it published?"

Rich made his way to his feet and stretched, "It's no use," he answered. "I've sent it out to every publishing company and literary agent in the city and no one wants anything to do with it."

Rita was next to rise. "Ronnie, you should talk to…"

Veronica interrupted, "I'm way ahead of you." She rose to her feet, removing some glasses from the coffee table and headed for the kitchen.

"Ooh, that's right!" Dennis realized, standing and moving toward the coat rack. Pulling on his sweater, he turned to Rich. "Ronnie has a friend in the publishing biz."

Rich straightened his manuscript and took a seat on the sofa. His curiosity piqued, he struggled to remain blasé. "Well, if he's in the publishing business his people have probably already gotten a copy of it."

"Actually," Veronica said, returning from the kitchen, "he's a one man operation. He only takes on projects he feels close to."

She opened up the tiny fuse box door in the dining room wall and retrieved a key on a shoestring. Holding it tight in her hand, as if making a mental note, she added, "But I have a feeling he'd love to take a look at what you have."

Rich straightened his posture, "Wow. I'm flattered that you think it's worthy."

"It's more than worthy," Dan said, grabbing his man purse from behind the sofa.

"Well lovers," Dennis announced, "I gotta get home. Looking this gorgeous doesn't come easy." He opened the door and Margo and Rita slipped past him waving goodbye. "Rich, are you sure you don't want to come home with me?"

Rich smiled, "You're more woman than I can handle Dennis."

Blowing kisses to all, Dennis commanded, "Give a copy of that to Ronnie so she can pass it on. Kiss kiss." And with that, the room became a little more dull.

"Yeah, I gotta split too. You need some help Ron?" Dan offered.

She met him at the door and leaned in, "No, you beautiful person. You've done enough. Go home. And tell Val I said I hope she's feeling better soon."

Rich stood in the doorway and watched as Dan disappeared down the staircase. He turned to Veronica. "Thank you for letting me crash your party."

"Thank you for my cable bill."

He turned to leave and just before the door shut, Veronica peered into the hallway. "Are you going to leave that with me?"

"Oh! This," he hesitated. "I almost forgot." He paused for a moment in thankful reflection, then added, "Do you really think your friend will like this?"

Relieving him of the manuscript she said, "To me, an author reading his work aloud is the only way to appreciate the full impact of the story. Your words. Your voice. They mean everything. You obviously have a talent for this, but talent alone doesn't cut it. It really is true, what they say. It's not what you know, it's who you know." She caressed his bandaged hand and continued, "And now you know someone."

He beamed with appreciation, "Thank you."

Pushing him away, she scolded, "Now get the hell outta here and get some sleep. You look like shit."

They parted company with mutual hushed laughter.

TWO

Monday, Tuesday, then Wednesday passed and not only had he not heard from Veronica, but her apartment had been strangely quiet since the party last Friday. By midnight on Thursday he had lost what little hope he had had in Veronica's friend. He understood that perhaps this person was a busy man and that reading his manuscript was probably not on his priority list. But after months of rejection letters had eroded his hope, these last few days had hung like weeks.

He made his way through the park after his usual stop at Adnon's Liquor Emporium, and took a seat on a bus stop bench next to the subway entrance. A black woman in her forties, outfitted in a white uniform pulled her purse a little closer to her chest and slid a few inches away as he tilted his paper bag and took a gulp. He smiled politely when he caught her staring at him. "Evening, " he coughed.

She smiled and nodded and sat a little more upright.

Lighting a cigarette he added, "Don't worry, I'm harmless."

Again she forced a smile but said nothing.

He held out the bottle and said, " I blame my mother for this." He leaned back and took a long drag from his Marlboro then went on, " She always said, 'Richie,' she always called me Richie. She would say, 'Richie, you can do whatever you want to do in life."

Realizing that he was just another drunk on the street, she began to relax a little. She was a nurse and knew from years of first hand Emergency Room experience that drunks, while they might talk a good talk, were the weakest of the weak.

He persisted, "What a load of crap. Excuse my language, Ma'am."

She shrugged but still said nothing.

"What happens if you're no good at what you want to do? I mean, I spent my whole life doing what I wanted to do." He hiccoughed and went on, "It's not like I spent my entire life smoking crack or anything like that."

The woman leaned forward longing for her bus to arrive.

He took another swig. "I mean the one thing that I've always imagined myself doing for a living," hiccough, "and I find out I'm no good at it."

She could see her bus a mere three stop lights away and, feeling a bit safer finally, responded to him. "Well, Son, what is it you do for a living?"

He turned to face her, appreciative of her concern. "Well, Ma'am, I'm glad you asked. It's a very sad story. I am thirty two years old and I'm a Barista."

"Mmm hmm," she nodded. "What's a Barista?"

"I'm so glad you asked that, Ma'am." He leaned in a little closer to her. "A Barista is one of those losers you see schlepping coffee products at your local Starbucks."

"Oh, I see," she said, now fully engaged. "Well, I would hardly call them losers. I go to Starbucks every morning, and Child, I'm amazed at how they rattle off all those orders and manage to get them all right. But," she said, pointing at his bandaged hand, "I can see how someone might not be good at that job. It looks very difficult."

Rich let out a hearty laugh that quickly evolved into a smoker's hack. "Oh, I'm very good at it," he croaked.

Checking on the progress of the bus, then turning back to him, she asked, "Then why are you so ashamed of it?"

"I'm sorry Ma'am. I think I gave you the wrong impression. I don't want to be a Barista. Christ, sorry, Ma'am, I work with people young enough to be my children!" He gazed thoughtfully toward the sky and continued, "I want to be a writer."

"Oh!," she laughed. "And you say you're no good at writing?"

He nodded in resignation.

"Oh Child, you're still a baby. You've got plenty of time for that!"

As the bus's brakes squealed in protest, she gathered herself and arose from the bench. Rich staggered to his feet as the bus came to a stop. As the doors swung open and the woman took a step, Rich asked, "Do you have children, Ma'am?"

"Why yes I do. Two boys. Fourteen and seventeen."

She took hold of the handrail and Rich grabbed her by the arm. She glared at him incredulously as he spoke, "Don't ever lie to them."

She shrugged herself away from him and in moments the doors were closed and the bus growled its way into the stream of New York's late night traffic. He watched as it rounded Columbus Circle and disappeared down Broadway. Undaunted by her terse exit, he shrugged her off and tottered down the stairs to the subway platform.

THREE

Three days later, Sunday, he found himself once again hung over from another Saturday night's reveling in the East Village. Only this time he sat stoically in his sister's living room, nodding off at the monotony of watching his nephew read.

"Lunch is almost ready. You guys wash up," Rachel announced from the kitchen."

"Almost done here, Mom," Tommy hollered from his overstuffed armchair, snapping his uncle to attention.

Rich sat up and took to the edge of his seat as Tommy turned the final page of the manuscript. He was motionless, waiting for a reaction. Tommy leaned back, crossed his legs and arms and finally spoke. "Well, Uncle Rich," he paused, "how do I put this?"

Rich squinted the scowl that only a relative could get away with as Rachel, leaning in the kitchen doorway, looked on.

Tommy decreed, "You've written better." He hopped to his feet and marched toward the bathroom.

Dumbstruck, Rich could only stare as the boy disappeared into the hallway. He exchanged a disbelieving glance at his sister who could only laugh as she turned back to the oven. He lurched his way from his chair and joined Rachel in the kitchen. "Can you believe that? You've raised a thirteen year old William F. Buckley!"

"Uncle Rich," Tommy offered, emerging from the bathroom, "I believe you're thinking of Northrop Frye, one of the most learned literary critics of the twentieth century. While William F. Buckley *was* a celebrated author and columnist, " hopping onto his usual chair in the dining room, "but his claim to fame was more for laying the ground work for the modern conservatism, you know, the likes of Goldwater and Reagan." Stuffing his napkin into his collar, he continued, "Mom, do we have any juice boxes left?"

Rich came to the table carrying the casserole, then took his usual spot. "Who are you?" he said, mocking the boy with as much sarcasm as he could muster.

Rachel followed, shaking a juice box, asking, "Didn't you like Uncle Rich's little story?" She sat and began to dish out the meal.

"Well," Tommy announced, stabbing his juice box with the attached straw, "I get where you're coming from. I mean, it's a solid concept and a really unique plot, but," he hesitated then stuffed his mouth with noodles. He opened his mouth to continue.

"Not with your mouth full," scolded his mother.

After an audible gulp, "Uncle Rich, it's like you're being a little condescending."

Stunned and nearly choking, Rich countered, "What does that mean?"

"Well," Tommy lectured, "condescending is when someone..."

"I know what condescending means you little turd."

"Careful," Rachel warned, peering over her eyeglasses.

"It's just...it's like you're writing it for babies," sipping from his box.

"Go on," Rich prodded, leaning his elbows on the table.

"Everything about it, the plot, the story line, is quite mature and very concise, but then the characters all come across so infantile. Take the Harry Potter series..."

"Oh God," Rich moaned.

Tommy went on. "It's a children's story but the dialogue is structured in a way that doesn't talk down to kids. It therefore ends up stretching our minds."

"Okay," Rich relented.

"Look at all of the most successful cartoons ever produced," Tommy instructed. "While no one considers cartoons something that adults should be spending their time with, the most successful cartoons, your

Simpsons, your Family Guys, The Flintstones, they all speak in very adult terms. And while the adult masses laugh at them, us children are actually educated by them."

"Imagine that," Rachel chimed in with disdain.

"Granted," he said, "they are for the most part really inappropriate for kids. But you once told me you wanted to make a lot of money writing. Trust me, Uncle Rich, the money is in speaking to children like they were adults."

Rich leaned back in his chair and folded his hands in front of him. "So you're saying to kick it up a notch? Make it more edgy?"

"Exactly!" he cried. "Edgy is the perfect word!" He took another huge bite.

Rachel covered her mouth, tilted toward Rich and, in a stage whisper asked, "Do I need to start censoring the reading material you bring into my home?"

"Mom, I'm sure Uncle Rich won't give me anything to read that's offensive. I'm just saying, I'm your biggest fan, Uncle Rich, and everything you've ever written has held real merit in some way or another. In fact, I can't believe you haven't been published yet."

"Well thank you young man," Rich beamed, finally finding his appetite.

"I guess what they say is true," Tommy concluded, "It really isn't what you know, it's who you know." He pushed himself away from the table. "Mom, can I go play with my Play Station?"

"Yes. Go," she said, as Tommy erupted from his seat. As he left the room, she whispered to her brother, I know I said I'd never get him one of those, but it keeps him away from the matches."

"I think the pyro thing was just a phase," Rich shrugged. "My God, he just reminded me," Rich said, "I might actually know someone now."

"What do you mean?" Rachel asked, clearing the table.

As she washed and he dried, Rich brought Rachel up to speed on meeting his next door neighbor. While he left out the part about the reefer, conveniently omitted anything with regard to the cocaine and never mentioned being propositioned by a man, he recounted with detail the evening's chronology. Especially the part when he was practically begged to give a reading of his latest work. Exhausted by the retelling of the night's events, he concluded, "But I still haven't heard anything."

Rachel dried her hands and cautioned, "Don't hold your breath. For every legitimate human being in this city, there are a hundred assholes that just enjoy hearing themselves talk."

It didn't occur to him to point out her negativity until he was in the elevator, half way to the lobby of the building.

FOUR

Veronica poured two snifters of brandy and returned from the liquor cabinet to her seat at the great mahogany desk across from the decrepit old man. She placed a snifter in front of him and asked, "So, what do you think?"

He turned the final page of Rich's manuscript, looked up and gurgled in a hideous baritone voice, "I can work with this." He sipped his brandy and went on, "The important question is, how bad does he want it?"

"It's difficult to disguise the hope in one's voice. He tried to keep it to himself, but I know he wants it badly. Who wouldn't?"

The old man chuckled and lit a cigar.

Veronica continued, " People and their indomitable hope. Their mothers and fathers instill in them the source of all their longing. From childhood they are taught they are somehow special and that they can achieve anything."

The old man nodded his head in agreement.

"I feel kind of sorry for them, Seth," Veronica went on. "When they finally realize that they're not special, that they're simply mediocre, this hope thing ends up biting them in the ass. This guy," she paused, sipping her brandy, "is exhausted. He's either been very disappointed for a very long time, or he's a complete alcoholic, pot head. Even though he has talent," she sipped, "he's...weak."

"That's where I come in," the old man reminded her. "You think he wants it that bad?"

Just then, there was a tap on the giant office door and Gwendolyn Wright poked her head into the room. Demure in stature and voice she squeaked, "Mr. Volos, if there's nothing else, I'll be going for the day."

He held up a card and motioned for her to approach. "Call this," inspecting the card closely, "this, Richard Rossi, and schedule him to come see me this week"

She took the phone number and retreated to her reception desk.

Veronica waited for the door to click shut and whispered, "I laugh every time I think of how she came to work for you." She stood and rounded the desk as he swiveled his chair toward her. She sat on his lap and continued, "I mean, she's such a sweet person."

Volos laughed and caressed Veronica's thigh, "Her tenure here has worked well for both of us."

Wednesday afternoon finally rolled around and Rich found himself crammed onto the R train bound for Cortland Street in Lower Manhattan. Dizzied by the tight quarters and the idea of meeting a publisher face to face, he fought the nausea with more than one swig of Pepto-Bismol. His thoughts swirled throughout him like a hurricane finally making landfall. He couldn't remember a time when publishing a novel wasn't a dream, and though he had enjoyed a certain satisfaction with the many small articles he had in print, there was no escaping that today could be a turning point in his life.

Before long, he imagined, his mug would grace the inside flap of millions of book covers, his schedule would be stuffed with requests for interviews, book signings and speaking engagements. He vowed then and there to rid himself of his fear of flying. Soon he would be faced with the task of finding a new apartment, somewhere in Murray Hill he thought. An airy, open loft over looking Park Avenue. But what to furnish it with? Surely he couldn't be expected to entertain his new found peers with a Futon, a beaded room divider and Scooby Doo tumblers. But certainly his new assistant would be charged with such minutia.

"Stand clear of the closing doors," the automated voice warned from the speakers overhead. One more station to go.

He allowed himself the luxury of setting adrift once again. The kids at Starbucks would stop in their harried tracks to peer out the plate glass window, craning their necks to see who was riding in the back of the black stretch limo that pulled up in front. Jane, no, Edna his assistant, motherly but gruff, would stride with presence into the coffee shop and announce to one and all, the magnitude of his new success, and that the shop's ownership had been transferred to Mr. Rossi. Then it would be off to JFK and their trek to London, Paris and Madrid for the European launch of his novel.

The subway squealed to a halt and the doors slid open. Finally he could stretch and smooth out the wrinkles in his only suit. Emerging from the station, he paused for a moment to orient himself, then headed toward Broadway. As he rounded the corner, the butterflies in his gut began to migrate farther south, as before him stood the ornate, tan brick building. He found his way to the elevators and readied himself for the ascent. When the doors parted on the twenty-fourth floor, he was spilled out into a narrow, unmarked hallway. Directly in front of him was the only door in an otherwise featureless corridor. His attempt at a deep cleansing breath served only to cause him a sharp pain under his right ribcage. Exhaling, he turned the knob and entered.

He was greeted by a tiny redheaded woman in her early forties. "Good afternoon," she smiled, all the while avoiding eye contact. "You must be Mr. Rossi." She stood and motioned for him to have a seat on one of the leather wingback chairs in the reception area. "I'll let Mr. Volos know you're here."

As she disappeared through a massive set of double doors, Rich glanced around the room, in part, to find a quick escape route should things go badly, and in part, to absorb the details of this new chapter in his life. It was a sparsely appointed waiting room. Devoid of plants, magazines or even a reproduction on the wall, it appeared new and unfinished. He somehow felt a little less intimidated due to the lack of style and effort spent on the room, but quickly worried that this was a harbinger of how his work might be promoted. Hopefully, he thought, this means Mr. Volos puts his energy into his work and has no time for such trivial matters as how to decorate a waiting room.

Moments later the receptionist returned to her desk and offered, "Mr. Rossi, Mr. Volos will see you now." She motioned toward the doors.

As the doors shut behind him he paused and allowed his eyes to adjust to the shadowy gloom of the office. Slowly he could make out the details. He was struck by the oddly high ceilings in comparison to the architecture of the building as a whole. Built in bookshelves lined every wall from floor to ceiling, a window to the right, shrouded by a dark velvet curtain allowed in what seemed to be the only breathable air in the room, and twenty or so feet in front and to the left of him was a gigantic wooden desk lit by a solitary green banker's lamp. Behind the desk sat Mr. Volos, illuminated only from the neck down from the tilt of the lampshade.

Volos touched a switch under the desk and the room brightened just enough to make out the two men. "Mr. Rossi," Volos snarled as he rose from his chair and hobbled toward Rich, "I cannot tell you how delighted I am to meet you."

Instantaneously, Rich's unease evaporated. The tambour of the old man's voice was that of a longing grandfather and not the intimidating publishing mogul he had imagined. He strode over to meet Volos by the edge of his desk, reaching out his hand, "The pleasure is all mine Sir," he gushed.

"Please, sit down," Volos offered, heading back to his side of the desk. "Let's get right down to business."

The first forty-five minutes of the meeting went exactly as Rich had imagined all these many years. Volos spoke of wealth, fame, movie rights and sequels. He regaled Rich with the details of his many successes in the publishing business. And for the first time, Rich felt as though another human being actually "got" him. Every word, every syllable the old man uttered plucked a chord in him that had long been silenced by doubt. A poet couldn't have written a script more tailor made for boosting his confidence in the old man.

A while later the conversation turned toward the topic of Rich's writing style. Fanning through the pages, Volos said, "You've got a lot of raw talent, young man."

But as quickly as Rich began to beam from the praise, his face clouded over as Volos continued. "But that's just it. Raw."

Puzzled and speechless, Rich leaned in, waiting for some almighty words of advice.

"Don't get me wrong," Volos continued. "This is something that I can definitely work with. But you need to consider making a few changes."

Hanging on the old man's every word, Rich nodded in agreement.

"I can help with that too," Volos offered.

Rich mustered his thoughts and asked, "What kind of changes?"

Volos thumbed through the manuscript, scanning the pages, then stopped and pointed to a single line. "This, for instance." He read from the story, "Billy said to the King, but sir I haven't a horse to ride." Volos looked up from the page and went on. "There are lines like this throughout that just need to be," he paused, groping for the right words then carried on, "more edgy."

Rich smiled and chuckled to himself.

Noticing, Volos asked, "Why is that funny?"

"No reason," Rich lied.

Volos leafed through the rest of the manuscript and said, "Your story is one of the most original I've seen. The character development is fantastic and the plot is impeccably formulated." He stopped there.

"But?" Rich anticipated.

"But," he gazed up to the ceiling, then down again, "let me ask you this. Who is your intended audience?"

"Excuse me?"

"Who do you want me to sell this book to?"

"Well," Rich guessed, "everyone?"

"Good answer, but not the right answer. Your audience, if I'm reading it correctly, will be children under sixteen or so."

"I suppose so," Rich answered.

"Have you read what kids that age are reading today?" Volos pressed. "They aren't reading children's books like they were thirty years ago. Kids today are far more sophisticated. The quote, unquote, children's book is for babies learning to read. That is what you have here."

Deflated, Rich sank back into the brown leather chair, longing for the conversation to revert back to one rife with glowing compliments and assurance building.

Volos went on, "But, I'm telling you that with a few changes, your idea and my expertise will elevate you and this story to a completely new plane of literary status." His voice became clearer and more enthusiastic, as he brought himself to his feet, "Young man," he asked, as he rounded the desk and approached Rich, "If you want it badly enough I will make you wealthier than you have ever imagined."

Again, like a child with a bag of peanut M & M s dangling just in front of him, Rich took to the edge of his seat.

Volos paced behind Rich, leaning in one ear, then the other. His tone, far more animated now, rose with the passion of a newly elected Presidential candidate. "Son, you know of J. K. Rowling and her Harry Potter series."

Rich nodded.

"And the Chronicles of Narnia, by C. S. Lewis?"

Again, Rich agreed, turning to face the ranting old man.

"Well fuck Harry Potter!"

Stunned by the curse word that issued forth from someone who reminded him of his grandfather, Rich froze, waiting for something terrible to happen.

"And fuck C. S. Lewis!" Volos raised his walking stick into the air as if to curse the heavens above. His gait quickened as he continued, "That shit'll seem tepid at best, next to what I have in mind for you!"

Frightened and exhilarated all at once, Rich clung to every word and watched as the old man paced around the desk.

"It'll take a lot of work on your part. Once we release this thing, it'll take on a life of its own." He turned to Rich, "You won't get much sleep after that."

"I'm up to it," Rich interjected.

"Are you?" Volos spun around and peered down at Rich from across the desk.

Like a cadet coming nose to nose with his drill instructor, Rich shouted, "Yes Sir!"

"Do you understand that how badly you want this is directly correlated with how successful we'll," he corrected himself, "you'll be?"

"I do," he answered, like a groom standing before a preacher.

"And how badly do you want this, Mr. Rossi," Volos leaned in still closer.

Rich felt the sting of tears begin to fill his eyes. Pulling himself together, he paused and answered, "I've never known a minute of my life when I did not want this."

Satisfied, Volos returned to his chair.

Rich continued, "Mr. Volos," he moved in closer to the desk. "As long as I can remember, nothing has felt as right to me as when I was witnessing the expressions on the faces of those who were listening to me tell a story." He paused for a moment, looking down at his hands. When he again lifted his head to speak there were tears streaming down his face, but he soldiered on, "I will do anything it takes to spend what time I have left on this planet feeling that joy."

Save for the hum of traffic on the street below, the room became completely shrouded in silence. His pitch complete, Volos opened a small wooden box atop the desk and retrieved a cigar, then offered one to Rich. They sat in peace, sharing in the afterglow of a most fulfilling exchange, smoke dancing above their heads.

Volos broke the calm and commanded, "You'll be here Monday at noon. I'll have all changes made and the paperwork ready for you to sign."

Overcome with exhilaration, Rich remained glued to his seat for fear of fainting.

"Now, get out of here!" Volos barked, "And for Christ's sake go celebrate!"

"Yes, Sir!" Rich whooped as he tripped over himself to shake the old man's hand. "I'll see you

Monday!" He practically danced toward the office doors.

"You won't see me on Monday. My assistant, Ms. Wright will take you through everything."

"Yes, Sir," he said, bowing his way out of the room. It never occurred to him to question the changes that might befall his work.

FIVE

For the next three days and nights, Rich partied like it was 1999. He had dug through every suitcase, dresser drawer and closet salvaging every old stash of pot he could locate. His checking account plundered, he used what little available credit he had on his charge cards to make cash advances. Single, wasted and pockets full of cash, he trekked from Flushing to Harlem, Coney Island to Yonkers, hitting every conceivable watering hole he could find.

It was Friday evening and he found himself in the East Village at a bar called, The Rooster. Empty, except for the bartender and two regulars, it was as dark and seedy a place as he had ever been. He sat, hunched over the bar, nursing a Southern Comfort on ice while murmuring along with a song by Katrina and the Waves that crackled forth from the jukebox in the back. For Rich, time always seemed to stand still whenever he graced such an establishment. High, and alone with his thoughts, he found himself in the rare circumstance where no one knew his name nor had any expectations of him. And he imagined Heaven to be something like this, only with less sticky floors.

About six or seven dollars worth of songs later, he glanced around the room to find that a modest crowd had gathered without his knowledge. Upon closer inspection of the others, he realized that he was sitting smack dab in the center of what had to be one of New York's most notorious gay bars. Men clung to one another, some like brothers, some like lovers, but he was too drunk to care. He remained glued to his bar stool, looking up only when his drink needed topping off. To each his own, he thought.

Becoming more comfortable with his surroundings than a straight man ought to, he permitted himself to swivel his stool around and take in the sights, leaning his back against the bar. Every nook and cranny was filled with groups of men, some making out and a few snorting powder from their finger nails, but all of them bopping their heads and churning their bodies to the music. He took particular notice of how happy they all seemed to be. He had known a few gay people back in West Reading, but they had all seemed to be driven by an undercurrent of misery and self loathing. Not these guys. While many of them might have come from places like West Reading, it was obvious that they had long ago broken the bonds of such oppressive hometowns.

Having put it off long enough, he finally admitted to himself that he could no longer hold his bladder, and that he must brave the crowd and make his way to the men's room. With intermittent staggers, he navigated his way through the throng to the relative serenity of the single stall in the restroom. He had barely tucked himself back into his briefs when the door swung open to reveal a tall and menacing Latino man. Backed into the corner and dumbstruck, he was frozen in fear. Before he could utter a word, the man produced a tiny brown bottle, dipped a cue tip into it and offered Rich a clump of snowy white powder. In a nanosecond he reasoned, do I say no thank you and risk having this behemoth make short work of me, twisting my defenseless body into a soft pretzel? Or do I graciously accept his offer and hope that he doesn't expect anything in return? Giving in to his fatigue and blood alcohol level, he smiled and leaned into the cue tip, allowing the man to plant it deep into his nose. When the powder had been completely inhaled, the man stepped politely aside and permitted Rich to pass unabated.

By three-thirty in the morning, Rich found himself on a first name basis with the bartender and a small group of men that seemed to approve of his intrusion. Just before closing time, a late-comer approached the bar next to him and ordered. Before Rich could focus on him, Dennis stooped from his dizzying seven foot height and giggled, "Well, hello, Stranger! I knew it! I just knew it!"

A few moments later Rich realized who was speaking to him and beamed, "Hey Lady! Dennis! From the party!"

They laughed and shared a toast while Dennis settled into the stool next to Rich. Sipping his drink, Dennis said, "Don't worry, you're secret's safe with me, Mate."

At first confused and then realizing, Rich countered, "Oh! This! Me! Here?" he laughed heartily, "No, it's not what you think. But then again, I don't give a shit what anybody thinks. These are great guys." Pulling on the arm of a new chum, Rich went on, "Do you know Larry?"

Larry wasn't his name and, insulted, he pulled away coalescing with another group of men.

"I get it, Mate, but pretty soon you're going to have to give a shit what people think," Dennis warned.

Rich sat silently, only grimacing.

Dennis continued, leaning in, "From what I hear, you don't have many more nights of anonymity left."

Confused and scratching his nose, Rich shrugged.

"I hear you're going to be doing alright for yourself pretty soon."

"Not in here, I'm not," Rich answered in a feeble attempt at a quip.

"I'm talking about the book, Mate," Dennis insisted.

Rich nodded, finally getting it, "Ohhh! Yea, that." Puzzled, he went on, "How'd you know about that?"

"Ronnie told me." Clarifying, "Veronica. Your neighbor? The one you owe all of your future success to?"

"That Veronica, she's one great girl," he slurred.

"She is indeed," Dennis said. "Just keep your eyes open around Seth."

"Who's Seth?" Rich squinted.

"Seth Volos. Her friend?"

"Ohhh. Yeah, he's gonna make me rich."

"He can definitely do that," Dennis offered. "Just keep your eyes open."

With that, Rich raised his glass and finished his drink. "Will do, my friend. Now I gotta split before I pass out and these guys all have their way with me."

As he steadied himself on his feet, Rich reached out and shook hands with Dennis. As he turned to face the door, Dennis stopped him, "Take my phone number," he said, handing him a business card, "in case you get into trouble or need anything."

Rich, now dwelling in a very happy place, leaned over and planted a kiss on Dennis' cheek. He turned and headed for the door and hollered back, "Don't get any ideas, Lady!"

Just before dawn, Rich fell into bed naked and exhausted. As the sweet sting of sleep pierced his soul, he floated, weightless on an unseen cloud, hovering just inches above a lush, green landscape. A cool and comforting breeze tousled his thick black hair as his body gently swayed. As he lapsed deeper into unconsciousness, he could hear a distant rumble approaching from beneath him. Content though, with the uncommon sensation of complete relaxation, he paid no attention to the sound. But as the ground began to shake and growl, the humid perfume of dread enveloped him, and despite his trepidation, he turned his body around to face the noise. The moist blades of grass that had moments ago tickled the back of his neck now heaved upward against his face as the Earth began to split apart. He flailed his arms and legs fighting against the dirt, sod and debris that pelted his body, but could not escape the onslaught. As the tear opened into a gaping maw, a steamy, fowl smelling stench assaulted his senses. The center of the Earth seemed to open up and his body, once supported by an omnipotent pair of hands, suddenly began a descent into the awaiting pit below. He opened his mouth to scream but could only groan in muted protest as he sank deeper and deeper into the unknown.

The trip down was agonizing. As he fell, he saw a thousand faces of disappointment and despair embedded in the tunnel wall. They wailed in anguished cries of disapproval and fear, but reaching for them to claw his way back upward was futile. The salt of his sweaty brow stung his eyes as he squinted in search of a final destination below him.

Inexplicably, he came to a deliberate, yet gentle landing on his own bed. He turned quickly to face the room around him and found brief solace in the familiar atmosphere. Almost immediately though, his skin began to tingle. Inch by inch it was as though his entire body was being assailed by a million tiny gnats. As he flinched and swatted, the tingling grew into stings until he was utterly consumed by an excruciating invisible bombardment. In moments the barrage escalated into a violent bludgeoning, until finally he could see the assailants. Helplessly, he ducked and weaved as three dimensional letters of every font, color and pica ricocheted off of him, the walls and the furniture. Strings of entire sentences eddied wildly above him, morphing into paragraphs and unfamiliar symbols. As the mêlée strengthened, the words and symbols seemed to suck the air out of the room into their vortex. Gasping for breath, Rich clung to the sheets waiting to die. With his final, hard fought lungful of air he let out a shriek that severed him from the nightmare and left him lying cold and awake upon his sweat drenched mattress.

SIX

Noon, Monday found Rich rearranging his hair in the ornately framed mirror in the reception room of the office of Mr. Volos. It would be hours later until he would realize that the mirror was a new addition to the office's décor, and that perhaps the old guy had finally decided to chip in a few dollars for a presentable waiting room.

He sidled over to the window and gazed out upon the city, pondering how long it would be until they all knew him by name. The secretaries that scampered about, the window washers a few stories above, the bankers, the lawyers, soon all of them would want his autograph. Just then, Gwendolyn Wright returned from a back room with a red folder.

Keeping her eyes on her work, she began, "Everything's in order. Mr. Volos himself has highlighted everywhere you need to sign." She opened the folder and retrieved the paperwork.

Rich stood across from her and scanned the contract. Puzzled, he asked, "This paper. Is it parchment?" He gently caressed it, "It feels like parchment. What's up with that?"

Averting her eyes and dismissing him, she replied, "Oh. Mr. Volos," she hesitated, "he has an impeccable sense of style." She glanced up at her reflection in the mirror and went on, "He feels that this kind of detail adds," she paused, wringing her hands, "a certain measure of class to the transaction."

Satisfied with herself, she handed a pen to Rich and pointed to the bottom of the first page. "First, sign here."

Annoyed, he smirked, "Do you mind if I read through it first?" He took the stack of papers and made himself comfortable in the chair next to the window.

"Not at all." She took another nervous glance at her reflection then sat, busying herself.

Finally, Rich returned to the reception desk with the paperwork. "Everything looks okay," he said. "I just have a couple questions."

Gwen smiled and stood, keeping her eyes on the contract.

Rich continued, "It mentions here on the second page," reading from the contract, "...Party of the first part has seventy-two hours from the date of ratification, to disapprove of any changes to the manuscript made by the party of the second part." He looked up at her and said, "I haven't seen the changes he made yet. Am I going to get a copy of them?"

"Oh, absolutely," she insisted, "In fact, your copy was FedExed on Friday. You should be receiving it by the end of the day today. Then you'll have until Thursday to let us know if you don't like the changes. If everything's fine, you don't have to do a thing. It'll go to set up and press on Friday morning."

"What if I don't receive it?" he pressed, "I mean, what if it's late or gets lost?"

Reaching into her top drawer, she retrieved a slip of paper and handed it to him, "If you don't receive it by the end of the day today, just call this number and it will be tracked for you. What was your other question?" she said, changing the subject.

"Oh this," he pointed to the fourth and final page of the contract, "at the very bottom here. This is Latin, right?"

She chuckled a nervous laugh and answered, "Oh, that's sort of Mr. Volos' tag line. It's on the bottom of all of his contracts."

"Hmm," he grunted, "My Latin's a little rusty. I can make out the words, eternity and Lord, but," he asked, turning the page around to Gwen, "what's the rest of it say?"

She wiped away a tiny bead of sweat that had formed on her temple, glanced at her reflection and said, with a giggle, "Oh, beats me. I've been after him for years to translate it for me. But something always comes up. So if everything looks in order, just sign here first," she pointed.

He scribbled his name on the lines on every page just above the signatures of Mr. Volos. "Do you mind if I keep the pen?" he beamed. "It's kind of a big day for me."

"Not at all, Mr. Rossi," she answered, making eye contact with him for the first time.

With the sound of the door latching shut, she collapsed onto her chair, weakened by her deeds.

SEVEN

It took an unusual sum of effort just to raise his sticky, weighty eyelids. Finally, though, the garish fluorescent light that shone above him like a thousand suns, found its way into his eyes. As the murky world around him came slowly into view, his sense of hearing reawakened as well, letting in an incessant beeping noise. Soon, distant voices could be heard and finally, one that was familiar seemed to be shouting, "He's awake! He's awake!"

He painfully turned his head in the direction of the kerfuffle and saw the silhouette of a person, a woman, hopping madly about from a doorway, to his side and back again.

"He's awake!" the woman, his sister, bellowed.

At last, his surroundings came into full focus. Lying in a hospital bed, wholly confused, he peered about the room. A clock on the wall read 3:35. Upon a table, to his right, sat an enormous spray of yellow daisies topped off with a silver balloon that read, 'get well soon'. Above and in front of him, a muted television set was tuned to the local news, and his sister, Rachel dodging maniacally between an onslaught of nurses. One nurse held his hand, another wrapped a blood pressure cuff around his upper arm. A doctor leaned in and shone a light into his eyes. And they all spoke in discordant tones to him and one another.

"Rich!" Rachel cried from the foot of the bed.

Confused and disoriented, he could only manage, "What's going on?" from his parched and craggy throat.

For what seemed an eternity, the doctor spoke to him in what might as well have been Arabic, as the crowd of nurses and orderlies slowly dissipated. Finally, more alert to his situation, he called out to his sister, "Rachel?"

By now she was at his side holding his hand and thanking the doctor as he made his exit. "Oh, my God! Thank God! You scared me to death!"

Sitting up, he dizzily turned to face her. "What the hell is going on? Why am I here?"

"Oh my God, you don't remember." She pulled a chair closer and sat, still holding his hand. "When they called me I freaked out!"

"Who called you? And can I get something to drink?"

"The nurse said she'd bring you something." Rachel moved in closer and got back on point. "They found you unconscious on the sidewalk downtown! The paramedics said that witnesses saw you get hit by a tool bucket! Apparently if fell from a window washer's scaffolding! Don't you remember?"

Squinting, he groped for a memory, any memory.

"It was downtown," she persisted, "in front of the Mercury Building. On Broadway?"

At last it hit him, "Oh my God! I was signing my papers!"

"Papers?" she questioned.

All at once, new found energy coursed through him. "I didn't even get a chance to tell you!"

He spent the next few minutes filling her in. She sat dumbfounded as he outlined in detail how the old guy had come through, how easy the whole thing had been and how it really is who you know and not what you know. As he wrapped up his story, he turned to climb out of bed. "I gotta get home!"

"What? Stop it!" she commanded as she stood and shoved him back against the mattress. "Are you out of your mind?"

"I gotta call work!" he belted, as he fought her presence. "I should've been there and hour and a half ago!" he insisted, pointing at the clock on the wall.

"Stop it!" she yelled, punching him in the chest. "I already called them on Monday!

He froze, giving up the fight. "Monday?" he quizzed.

"Yes!" She paused and then realized, "Oh."

"What's going on?" he demanded.

Resignation set in as she explained to him that today was Friday and that he had been unconscious for four days. She spelled out for him that she had made all of the necessary arrangements for him to take a leave of absence, and that she had not only stopped his newspaper and collected his mail, but she had cleaned his apartment and had arranged for home health care, should he need it.

"Now just relax. The doctor just got finished saying that you could go home tomorrow if everything looks good overnight."

The next afternoon he was discharged and finally found the comfort of his apartment. It smelled of Pine Sol and Clorox, the laundry had all been done and all of the ashtrays were emptied, but still, it felt like home. After Rachel got him settled in, she took her leave and made him promise to call her the next morning.

A few hours into a well deserved, voluntary nap, there was a knock on the door. Pulling himself to his feet and tying shut his robe, he checked the peep hole and welcomed Veronica.

"Hi stranger," she said poking her head into the foyer, "Haven't seen you in a while. I signed for this for you." She handed him a white package.

"Oh, great. I was expecting this. Come on in."

"No, you look like this is a bad time."

"It's been an interesting week," he explained. "Maybe we can have coffee tomorrow?"

As she made her way back to her front door, "You bet."

"Oh!" he added, "Thank you for hooking me up with your friend, Mr. Volos. He seemed very encouraged about everything."

"Good. I knew he'd like it. I'll catch up with you tomorrow." With that she disappeared into her apartment.

He closed the door, tossed the package onto his desk, wrecking his sister's freshly organized handy-work and rattled his way back to the futon. It wasn't until the following morning, when he awoke from a fourteen hour nap, that he opened the FedEx package and realized that it was the copy of the manuscript changes he had been expecting.

A fresh pot of coffee in the kitchen and a new pack of cigarettes at his side, he hunkered down and sifted through the pages. And by midnight he had finished and resolved to call Mr. Volos first thing Monday morning to discuss the changes.

"What time do you expect him?" he asked.

"Well," Gwendolyn Wright reasoned, "he's been in and out all day. I'm really not sure what time he'll be back."

"I really need to talk to him about some of these changes," Rich pressed.

Volos stood at her side and pointed with an ancient arthritic finger to a page in the contract. "Well," she hesitated, "I'm not sure what good that will do at this late hour." She nodded self-assuredly at

Volos and continued. "When he didn't hear from you, he assumed you were alright with everything."

Volos smiled confidently and waited for the next response she would give.

She went on, "No, Mr. Rossi, it's already gone to press." She nodded, Volos smiled.

After a few moments she explained, "Mr. Rossi, I understand what you are saying, and I'm so thankful that you're okay, but your contract with Mr. Volos is quite clear about the time frame. You had seventy-two hours," she smiled at Volos, "and like I said, since we didn't hear from you, it was sent off to press."

"Well, I still need to talk to him as soon as possible," he demanded, snuffing out a cigarette. "Will you please have him call me? I just need to get my head around his reasoning for such a drastically different ending than the original."

"Indeed I will, Mr. Rossi. But let me assure you, Mr. Volos is a very wise man and I think you'll come to realize that his changes will only add to the success of the project."

They said their goodbyes and as she hung up the phone, Volos cradled her face in his primordial hands, and as she froze with fear and uncertainty, he praised, "You are magnificent".

Her expression lifted in relief as she came to understand that she would live to see another day.

EIGHT

Rachel read to herself from the manuscript, quoting aloud the edits that appeared in red ink. *"And whosoever, for millennia to come, would tread on these hallowed grounds would know that the royal family had suffered a devastating loss here."* She shrugged and said, "So the good guys lose?"

"Keep reading," he scowled.

She scanned the pages in silence, at times nodding and at others grinning. And each time her facial expression shifted, Rich interrupted with, "What part are you on?"

Fed up after an hour or so of this, she finally barked, "I'm a slow enough reader as it is! If you keep pestering me we'll be here 'til Christmas!"

Dejected, he left the room to join his nephew in a video game.

For men, regardless of the pressures and woes of life, time flies when playing video games. So, when Rachel called out to him at nearly midnight, he found himself bewildered at the passage of time. He crept out of Tommy's bedroom, careful not to awaken the boy.

"So, what do you think?" he whispered, approaching her from the hallway.

She put her knees together, placed the manuscript squarely on her lap, looked him in the eyes and decreed, "Rich, I think it's very good."

Flummoxed, he found himself without words and took a seat at the dining room table.

Rachel took a seat across from him. "Rich," she reasoned, "whatever he changed," she paused, "you should keep it."

He nodded in feigned agreement.

"I mean, Rich," she stood and began to pace, "it was good before but, obviously this guy knows what will sell! I mean, it's a pretty creepy way to end it, but, my God! If it's marketed properly, people are going to go nuts over this book!"

Tuesday afternoon, as he was hurrying out the door, late for work, the phone rang. On the other end of the line, Volos greeted Rich, "What's this I hear about you having problems with the changes I made? You realize it's too late to do anything about it now."

Rich opened his mouth to speak, but Volos, rattled on, " It's being printed as we speak and I've already invested more money than you'll make in a year on the North American marketing campaign!"

"Mr. Volos," Rich injected, "I just wanted..."

"Look Son, you agreed to let me know if you had any issues, and you never said anything. Do you have any idea how much this whole thing has cost so far?"

Rich was completely bowled over. As prepared as he was to confront Volos, he knew from the man's tone that this was a battle he couldn't win. "Mr. Volos," he interrupted, "I'm fine with the changes. It's just," he used his sister's word, "the ending is a little creepy. I mean for a children's book."

"God dammit Son," Volos barked, "we talked about taking the children's book up a notch! You've got to trust me on this!"

"I do! I do!" Rich swore. "Look, I'm really late for work. I'm sure you have everything under control. I just need to rethink ways to continue the saga, in case we need a part two."

"You're a good writer, young man. You'll come up with something. Now go to work and stop worrying so goddam much!"

Rich heard a welcome and abrupt click from the other end of the line, grabbed his manuscript and bolted out the door.

As he waited for the train, he flipped through the pages until he found the final chapter, determined to read it once more. He resolved to scan it with the eyes, not of an artist, but of a businessman, longing to see the commercial viability that his sister and Volos saw. As the train lumbered along, he pored over the type and read to himself.

It's up to you!" the miserable toad said. "Do you save the kingdom? Or do you save yourselves?"

Billy and Cassandra stood at the precipice with the toad's sword at their backs. The crowd was frozen in fear. Silent dread covered the land. From her perch high above, Queen Julia screamed, "Somebody do something!"

But it was too late. The fight was over and although the key had been won and returned to the Keeper, the poison had already taken effect. The sheep had all died a horrendous and agonizing death, the trees had lost their leaves and turned an ugly wintery brown, and Princess Gabrielle had fallen into a deep sleep.

Billy and Cassandra had given up hope that the King would return. Throughout it all, their last great hope was that King Neptune would find Hag Neltha in time to break the spell. But alas, it hadn't happened. The army, brave and victorious, the masses, devoted and true to the throne, were all helpless in the face of the toad.

"What's it going to be?" the toad persisted.

Billy held tight to the hourglass. He knew that handing it over to the toad meant the kingdom would fall completely under his rule. For generations, the entire royal family and all of their faithful subjects would fall under the rule of the swamp lords. He wished that he and Cassandra had never climbed over the fence to begin with. He longed to be back home, and as he looked into Cassandra's eyes, he could see that she too was thinking the same thing.

"Go ahead," the toad said, "I'll let the two of you talk it over. I've got plenty of time." The toad leaned back against a boulder and sunned himself, all the while keeping the sword at their backs.

Cassandra whispered to Billy, "We can't just turn it over to him."

"I know, but what else can we do?"

"Look," Cassandra said, "We could just drop it and let it crash to the rocks below us."

"No!" Billy scolded, "Remember what Neltha said? The time piece is everything. We can't let it break!"

They both paused in thoughtful silence and in unison, looked up at each other.

"Are you thinking what I'm thinking?" Cassandra asked.

Billy replied, "We are the common denominator!"

The toad relaxed, snacking on grubs from beside the rock, turning a deaf ear to their conversation. He was confident that the two children would make the obvious choice.

Cassandra repeated what they had been told, "Neltha said, 'let go of time and you shall fly!'"

"That's it!" Billy cried. "All of this, everything that has happened is because of us! The drought, the war, everything! Because we intervened."

"That's right," Cassandra interrupted, "If we hadn't met Hans in the forest, he would never have shown us where to get water."

Billy added, "And if he had never taken us to the stream, he would have never found the key next to the tree trunk. And if he had never found the key, none of this would have happened!"

"Let me try something," Cassandra said as she grabbed the hourglass from Billy. She turned around and held it toward the toad.

As he turned his attention from his dinner to her, she slowly and deliberately turned the hourglass upside down. Horrified, the toad was helpless as everything he had done in the past few moments began to rewind. Even the sounds and the movement of the crowd seems to reverse. She quickly up righted the hourglass and stood tall with her new ammunition.

"Give me that!" the toad bellowed as he moved toward her.

Cassandra held out the hourglass once more and turned it, sending time and the toad backward to his spot next to the rock. She turned to Billy, "We've got to erase everything we've done here."

Solemnly, Billy added, "Then let go of time. And fly?"

Cassandra and Billy smiled with resolve, now knowing exactly what they had to do. Billy took the hourglass as he and Cassandra backed their way to the very edge of the cliff. When they could go no further, Billy squatted with the hourglass. The toad's face contorted with dread as he came to understand that all was now suddenly lost. The crowd looked on with a collective hush as Billy slowly turned over the hourglass.

Billy and Cassandra stood for a moment and watched as the prior few minutes rewound. The toad removed grubs from his mouth and unpicked them up from beside the rock. The clouds reversed their direction, once again letting the sun shine through, and geese that they hadn't noticed before flew backward into the horizon. Frightened and a little amused, they could have watched the show all day, but they knew they had to make their exit to make things right again. They turned their backs to the events that were un-happening and faced the open air in front of them.

"Don't look down," Billy said as he took hold of Cassandra's hand.

But neither of them could help it. In unison, they lowered their chins to inspect the landscape below. The mist from the waterfall couldn't disguise the jagged rocks beneath them. They raised their heads and turned to face each other, resisting the temptation to turn around and watch the un-doings.

"Cassandra broke the silence, "Let go of time and you shall fly?"

Billy nodded as they faced forward, tightened their grip together and closed their eyes. They inhaled together and leaned ever so slightly into the cool and comforting breeze wafting up from below.

For the remainder of the evening he mindlessly supplied caffeine to a yearning public, all the while pondering his future.

NINE

Gwendolyn Wright sat curled up in her favorite chair in the living room of her three story brownstone on East 76th Street in Manhattan. The room was dark save for the single Tiffany lamp that sat next to her. Bundles of papers, clipped together lay upon her lap, the arms of the chair and the adjacent tables. With her reading glasses on and a pencil between her teeth, she read through each batch, organizing them into order of importance and chronology, then inserting them into her black binder.

It had to be perfect. There couldn't be so much as a single misstep now that the ball was in motion. She had been charged with carrying out every detail of the book launch; the photo shoot, the interviews, the public speaking and the book signing tour. Volos had laid out every detail, and the last thing she wanted was to disappoint him. She had witnessed his wrath when his projects hadn't lived up to expectations, and could not stomach the thought of failing this late in her tenure. As she paused only long enough to stretch her neck, her daughter's empty wheelchair caught her eye from across the room, encouraging her to steal a deep and cleansing breath and carry on. Soon, with a final click of the binder rings snapping shut, she was at last finished.

Secure with the notion that all was in place and that the real work would begin in the morning, she allowed herself the simplistic luxury of a frosty cold Diet Coke. The full glass of ice, the champagne-like fizz, the ease of the cool effervescence trickling down her throat, permitted her shoulder muscles to glide back into place.

She tightened the belt of her terrycloth bathrobe and strolled into the solarium just behind the kitchen where she plucked a few dead blooms off of her African Violets. Tossing them into the garbage bin as she passed, she headed through the dining room to the foot of the stairs where she caught herself beginning to call out for her daughter before suddenly remembering that she was all alone in the house. Resigned, she made her way back to the living room, caressing a framed photo of her and Casey at last year's Mother-Daughter picnic. She passed the empty wheelchair and pulled back a curtain, glancing at nothing in particular on the street below. As she began to contemplate the loneliness of being without her daughter, the telephone rang and she darted to the kitchen.

Gleeful and relieved when she read the caller I.D., she beamed as she picked up the phone. "Casey?" she said.

"Hi Mom."

She took a seat on the stool next to the refrigerator, "Oh Baby, I miss you already."

"Me too Mom," her daughter answered.

"Are you getting all settled in at Gram's?" Gwen asked.

"Yeah, but it smells funny over here."

Gwen let out a chuckle and said, "I'm so sorry Honey, but I'd be worried sick if I knew you were here all alone while I'm gone." She paused and then continued, "Even still, sixteen is too young to be all alone for that long."

Casey added, "I just hope Mr. Volos appreciates all you do for him."

Gwen's tone darkened abruptly, "Young Lady, we owe everything to Mr. Volos and don't you forget it. Now put your grandmother on the phone, and you do what she tells you, okay? I love you."

A grumble, then a voice came from the other end of the line. "Hi Sweetie!"

"Hi Mom. Don't let her walk all over you."

"Oh, we're gonna be just fine. Your father is in the basement as we speak, setting up the train set."

Concerned, Gwen asked, "Is she doing okay with the stairs?"

"Gwenny, it's a miracle. The last time I saw her she couldn't even feed herself! It's just a miracle! She's up and down those stairs like a marathoner! You tell that boss of yours he's a prince."

"Well, let's not get too cocky. It's only been a little over a year," Gwen cautioned.

"Oh, I know, Sweetheart. I'm watching her like a hawk."

"I'll check in every day. And you have my cell number if anything comes up."

"Gwen," her mother consoled, "I have all the numbers to everyone. The doctor, the pharmacist, the physical therapist. Casey's in good hands. You just concentrate on your work and make that guy famous and come home safe and sound."

Gwen didn't sleep very much that night. Her thoughts reverberated off of one another, from the daunting task ahead of her and the prospect of her early retirement, to the remnants of her daughter's illness and her debt to Volos. As she gazed up at the ceiling she vowed to revive her home and rid it of the many leftovers of the darkest days of her life.

She recounted the events that had conspired to bring her to this point, and wondered if she would ever really be free again. She had sunken to depths that no right-minded person could even imagine, much less be party to. She prayed that early senility would erase the past from her mind, and groped for her only solace, that at least Casey was well again. And after watching her only child disintegrate from a healthy, vibrant ten year old, to a wheelchair bound young lady of fourteen,

Gwen reasoned that, any mother would have done what she did.

She first noticed subtle changes in Casey's personality. Normally light hearted and content, she became withdrawn and easily agitated. When her grades began to suffer and her vision became impaired however, Gwen found herself mired in worry. The clumsiness evolved into seizures and the worsening vision into complete blindness. By the end of the year her daughter was bedridden and had descended into dementia. All the while she had endured batteries of tests of every conceivable body part. Finally, and to the horror of a mother's heart, the doctors unanimously concluded that her daughter was suffering from Batten's Disease. It made no difference to Gwen that it was incurable, and barely treatable, she held fast to her hope just the same. Only after weeks of online research though, did her hopes fragment into despair.

She would spend the next few years alone, caring for her daughter, Casey's father having finally found the balls to be with the woman he had been cheating with for a decade. Blind, paralyzed and demented, Casey needed constant looking after. She lay stupefied in utter sensory deprivation while the apathetic seasons passed callously by. Feeding, bathing, exercising, and diaper changing had tested and pushed Gwen's capacity to hope beyond what any sane person could ever expect to bear.

And tonight, as slumber took its grip, she found herself still thanking God, or whomever, for the extraordinary way Mr. Volos came into her life.

TEN

By that Friday afternoon, Rich found himself at Volos' office standing between the old man and Gwen as the three raised their glasses of champagne. Next to them, three cases of the final product, the hardbound first edition of *The Keeper of the Key, by Richard Rossi.*

Richard beamed as Gwen sliced open a box, retrieved a copy and handed it to Rich. Volos and Gwen looked on, as if their child were inspecting a long sought after Christmas gift, and then shared a wink.

"Excuse me," Rich apologized, "I need to make a call." He made his way out of the office and into the waiting room.

"Well then, Ms. Wright," Volos began as he made his way behind his desk, "Let's have an update."

Gwen opened her bag and recovered the black three ring binder and opened it. "Let's see," she flipped through a few pages. "The photo shoot is taken care of. So the ones being distributed next week will actually have the jackets on them."

"Okay." He lit a cigar.

Turning a page, "Let's see. Everything with regard to distribution is finalized, including the downloadable versions. They'll be released a few weeks after the initial release." Reading from the pages she took a seat across from Volos. "The marketing distribution is fine. Everything has been released."

"What about media coverage?" He asked, peering at her through a thick veil of smoke.

"Well," leafing through the notebook, "Let's see, tonight he's on standby for Letterman. But next week," scanning further down the page, "next week, on Thursday, three days after the release, we've got two minutes on New York One and two minutes on Philadelphia Live." She turned another page and took a deep breath, "Then it gets fun."

Volos sneered.

"Let's see," she continued, "We release Monday, the fourteenth at noon. Press releases are scheduled to go out that morning. This review," she passed Volos a sheet of paper and went on, "will be in the Times on Sunday, the thirteenth and, depending on that week's sales, we're keeping his calendar open for GMA, Today and Live."

"Oh, you don't need to worry about sales," Volos bragged as he puffed on his cigar. "I've got everyone working on it."

She was sure he did, but knew not who "everyone" was.

Meanwhile, in the waiting room, Rich spoke with his sister on his cell phone. He caressed the binding, flipped the pages and inspected the ink as he spoke. "Rachel, you won't believe it! I have one right here in my hand!"

Her pride for him shone through more than he had ever known. Finally, he was all grown up. Her tone, at least in this conversation was bolstered by a healthy air of respect for his accomplishment. "Rich," she gushed, "I knew you could do it! You are such a good writer! I just knew all it would take was meeting the right person."

"Listen, Sis," he said, looking over his shoulder, "I gotta run, but I want to bring the first copy over for Tommy to read this weekend."

"Yikes," she grimaced.

"What?"

"You better make it snappy if you want him to have it this weekend. Ed's picking him up," she checked her wristwatch, "around three-thirty for their camping trip."

"Aw shit!" He groaned, "That's this weekend?"

"Yup."

"Dam, I really wanted him to have it before the Times book review came out on Sunday. Let's see, what time is it now?" He checked the clock on the cell phone. "You know, if I left here now I bet I could make it up there. You know what, I'm gonna try. I'll call you with my progress. If he gets there before me, just stall him."

"You know how Ed is," she said, "always in a hurry."

"Yeah, and that's one of his good qualities. If he wasn't Tommy's dad," Rich gave up, "never mind. Let me try to get out of here. I'll talk to you in a bit." He flipped the phone shut and returned to Volos' office just as Gwen was closing her notebook.

"Pardon me," he said, holding his book close to his chest, "would it be alright with the two of you if I took my leave for the day? I need to run an errand that's pretty important."

Gwen checked her schedule. "I don't see why not." She turned to Volos who merely shrugged.

"Thanks," he offered, and headed for the door.

"By the way," Volos injected, "quit that job of yours."

Rich stopped and turned to Volos, "But I still need…"

"Fuck that. You don't need any goddam money from them. Ms. Wright?" He waved her along to a desk in the corner and continued, "Write him out a check. How much do you need, young man?"

Before Rich could digest the question, Volos barked, "Oh hell, just write it out for fifty thousand. That'll cover you for a while won't it?"

As the blood rushed from his head to his limbs, Rich froze for fear of losing his balance and passing out. Suddenly, as his saliva deserted him, he could smell the deodorant he had applied earlier in the morning wafting up from his underarms. He gathered himself and squeaked, "That'll be fine."

Surely, he thought, they were playing a colossal joke on him, and it would only be a matter of seconds before they would break into stitches, leaving him cold and deflated. But the laughter never came, only the sound of a check being torn from its perforations. He watched as Gwen took the check to Volos for signing, and still no hilarity erupted from them. Could it be for real? As she brought him the check, he stood slack jawed and in awe, mustered a thank you and slowly backed out of the room.

On cloud nine, he sprinted the three blocks to the subway station. As he ran, he tried to recall how he used to imagine this day would feel, but the sensation was so surreal, so foreign that all he had pictured in the past got lost in the here and now. His thoughts became cluttered with the possibilities to come. Would he first look for a new apartment? Hunker down and begin the sequel? Or take a week to just savor this outrageous turn of fate and plot the perfect way to leave his job at Starbucks. As the doors to the train slammed shut, he fought the temptation to announce to the entire carful of commuters that he was indeed a published author. That he had a cool fifty grand burning a hole in his pocket. And that he would like to personally invite everyone out for a drink.

The LED clock built into the ceiling of the train flashed 3:22 PM and when it caught his eye, he tried to land gracefully back into reality and plan his quick escape from the train station. When the doors opened, he bolted, first through the turnstile and up the tile steps two at a time. Adrenaline and delight carried him the first two blocks, but soon, as he weaved his way thru the afternoon throng, his chest became tight and his breathing labored. Sweat flowed freely from everywhere and, panting and coughing, he limped with shin splints around his final turn onto Rachel's street. Through the stinging slits that were now his eyes, he spotted his ex-brother-in-law's red Dodge Ram pick-up truck in the middle of the block, the new girlfriend in the passenger side and a suitcase being thrown into the bed of the truck.

With all his might, he inhaled and let out a bellow that stopped the activity in front of Rachel's building. Having gotten their attention, he checked his watch, 3:33, and stopped in his tracks. He put his hands on his knees and heaved one painful breath after another as Tommy ran toward him.

"Uncle Rich! You made it!" Tommy cried, pulling him along the final fifty feet. "I did everything I could to stall. We're going camping!"

Rich nodded and tried to speak but nothing came out. As they grew nearer, he could see the angst in Rachel's face as her ex-husband lectured her.

"Made it!" Rich managed, waving the book like a white flag, ending his sister's discomfort.

He stopped and handed the book to his nephew and panted, "This is the first copy ever. I wanted you to have first crack at it."

Tommy's eyes widened as he opened the front cover. "Look Mom, it's autographed!" Then, turning to Rich, "Will this make it harder to exchange?"

Rich put his hands around Tommy's neck and gave it a fake squeeze, as Ed chimed, "We have to leave now if we're going to beat the weekend traffic."

"Hello to you too," Rich chided.

"You guys better get going," Rachel said, hugging Tommy. "I'll see you Sunday night."

"Let me know what you think!" Rich yelled as the truck pulled away. As it rounded the corner onto Lexington Avenue, he added, "He's just as big a dick as ever."

Rich and Rachel rode the elevator up to her apartment as Tommy, in the backseat of his father's truck, began chapter one.

Oblivious to the grown up banter coming from the front seat, Tommy sat quietly, engrossed in *The Keeper of the Key, by Richard Rossi*, Uncle Richard Rossi. His face seemed to glow as he drank in every word. By the time they arrived at his father's cabin, around seven o'clock, Tommy was a little more than a quarter of the way through the 346 pages. By bedtime, he was fully captivated, walking in the shoes of one of the main characters and consumed by the events to which he bore witness.

Throughout dinner and well past his bedtime, Tommy remained spellbound in an altogether separate world. Though his head grew heavy and his sight grew dim, he soldiered on, just like the boy in the book.

Lights out warnings shouted from downstairs went ignored, and he only allowed himself to rest his head when Billy, his new alter ego, did so, bombs bursting only a mile away, the castle crumbling stone by stone.

Tommy awoke the following morning, Saturday, to the smell of slab bacon frying in the kitchen downstairs. He wiped the sleep from his eyes and trundled down the split log stairway and into the kitchen where he took a seat at the table.

"How'd you sleep last night?" Abby asked, placing a plate in front of him.

"Okay," Tommy mumbled. "Where's my Dad?"

"He's down at the dock getting the boat ready. Mr. Collins from across the lake came by earlier and said the fish were really biting." She took a seat across from him and continued, "Your dad's not that good at fishing so I'm counting on you to bring back dinner."

Unengaged, Tommy sat quietly and ate his toast while his father stomped up the front steps and through the screen door. "Morning, Son," he bellowed. "After you eat, run upstairs and throw your jeans on. We gotta get an early start on those trout." He poured himself a refill of coffee and kissed Abby on the head.

Soon Tommy pushed himself away from the table. "May I be excused?"

"Of course you can," Abby smiled.

"And don't forget your boots!" Ed yelled as the boy disappeared up the stairs. Turning to Abby, "Things okay between you two?"

She picked at the plate of bacon in the center of the table, "It's a little awkward, but nothing I can't handle."

"You're such a trooper," Ed offered.

"Is everything okay with the boat?" she said, changing the subject.

"I told you before," he assured, "I don't want aluminum. I like the way the wood feels. The one we have is fine." He stood, sipped his coffee and gave her a suffocating bear hug.

"All ready, Dad!" Tommy glowed, appearing in the kitchen doorway.

Ed noticed his son's book tucked under his arm and said, squatting down to him, "Son, can we just have a few hours of you and me time today?"

"But I..."

"Look Son, tonight when it gets chilly and boring, I promise you can read until the cows come home. But the daylight, that's my time."

He tickled his son until he relinquished the novel , then tossed it onto the sofa. They poked and giggled their way down the front steps and over the path to the dock. Abby watched as the two climbed on board and sped into the glistening morning sun, their wake casting shards of light that danced off of the ceiling of the front porch.

Later that evening, his belly full of fish, corn on the cob and homemade potato salad, Tommy bundled himself in a quilted ball upon his bed and readied himself for another exciting night of adventure. As he opened the book the pages gave off an intense yellow glow, lighting up the room around him. A breeze drifted upward into his face mussing his hair and causing him to squint at the words before him. He was not shocked or even mildly disturbed, for even with his above average intellect, it was merely another sign of a fascinating boyhood escapade about to unfold. He accepted it willingly and dove into the text.

Around that same time, back in Astoria, Rich waited outside of his neighborhood bodega for the New York Times truck to pull up and drop off Sunday's paper. It always amazed him how Sunday's news could be told on Saturday night. As he stood, one patron after another came and went. He watched as the young Latino girl behind the counter rang up orders and dispensed change, concluding that she couldn't be more than thirteen years old. With no other adults in sight, Rich worried like a father about her safety, puffing up his chest and exaggerating his presence whenever someone slightly shady would enter the store. This went on for nearly an hour, a price he was willing to pay for getting his hands on an early Sunday copy.

When the truck finally arrived and the papers were checked in, he paid, grabbed six copies and abandoned his post, and the child, like a draft dodger, and scurried back to his apartment.

He tore open a paper and rifled through, tossing the irrelevant pages aside. He had no time or inclination to read about the wars in Afghanistan and Iraq, no desire to catch up on the Mayor's shenanigans and scoffed as he hurled the classifieds across the room. Like a bargain basement shopper bent on finding the deal of a lifetime on an Armani suit, he honed in until he finally reached the Book Review section. The remaining newspaper fell off of his lap and onto the floor in front of him. He scanned each column until he at last came across his objective:

MODERN DAY CLASSIC HITS THE SHELVES TOMORROW
by A. N. Bloom

When I sat down with Richard Rossi, a Pennsylvania native, and asked him what the inspiration was for his debut novel, The Keeper of the Key, *his answer was predictable; It came to me in a dream.*

The story itself, however is anything but predictable. Rossi has managed to reformulate the traditional castle on the hill, good versus evil, flying sorcerer, ill-fated kingdom, children's fable into a delightful and witty tale that corkscrews more gleefully than a Disney thrill ride. He has successfully molded the customary boy meets girl, boy and girl save the world story into what is sure to become a twenty-first century classic that young and old alike will treasure.

Suburban neighbors, Billy Miller and Cassandra Reed, barely knew each other until together they trail a fallen baby sparrow under a junkyard fence. The stricken bird leads them to a dilapidated wooden shed, under which they crawl. From there, things get interesting as they tumble into a hidden cave under the floorboards that spills them into a land called Farthynia.

In their quest to find the baby bird, they lose all sense of time and space and meet characters like, the curmudgeonly, but lovable Neltha. Over three thousand years old, she dispenses wisdom that the children eventually use to save the day. A disappearing King, an anorexic Princess, and a half-man-half-grasshopper named Steve, are only the tip of the iceberg of this cavalcade of misfits that grace every page.

What really sold me on Rossi's work was the courage it must have taken for him to end his story the way he did. I won't give it away, but I will say that my adult friends who were able to get their hands on advance copies were shocked, mesmerized and delighted, and I comfortably predict that every child who reads this book will be changed forever.

He got up from the futon and started for the kitchen, let out a squeak, and turned back, sat down and read it again. After finishing it, he lit a cigarette and made a pot of coffee. It would be a while until daybreak, and hours more until it was a respectable enough time to call his sister, his co-workers, his exes and anyone else who might not mind being bragged to on a Sunday morning. As he sat on his fire escape, sipping coffee, he gazed out upon the city just beyond the East River.

Although known as the City That Never Sleeps, it was certainly calm at this hour, at least from this vantage point. In the stillness he pondered that he may not have many more opportunities for this kind of quiet contemplation. For the very first time, he felt the melancholy sting of success, and with it, the disquieting sense that soon, his life would no longer be his own.

Back at Ed's upstate cabin, Tommy sat quietly upon the dock as the morning sun peeked over the stand of pine trees across the lake. Barefoot and bundled up in a blanket from the sofa, he began by scanning page 191. Once again, completely immersed, he ignored the reality of the world around him and became one with Billy, the gallant and upright visitor in the land of Farthynia.

"Wake up!" Cassandra screamed. "Billy, wake up!"

When he opened his eyes he found himself standing next to Cassandra, confronted by the hounds. Their teeth, sharp and grey, glistened with drool as they snarled and barked. "What do we do?" Cassandra cried.

"Try to stay calm," Tommy advised as he took her hand and they slowly backed up the immense circular staircase.

The dogs, hackles up, heads down, followed them step for step. Staying close to the wall, Tommy backed into an ornate golden mirror and did a double-take when he caught a glimpse of himself. A stranger standing next to Cassandra stared back at him from the reflection. Maybe this was the Billy that she had constantly referred to him as. But at the moment, it really didn't matter. Six hungry, rabid, pissed off Dobermans trumped a little identity crisis any day.

That he happened to appear in the flesh as someone else was a minor hiccough compared to how his weekend had been going. He had traversed a canyon on a vine rope, fought and slew a nine foot tall, three-eyed rabbit and involuntarily eaten nearly a pint of fire ants. Now he was standing toe to toe with a pack of hell bent eating machines that envisioned him and Cassandra as T-Bone steaks making a run for it.

They steadily made their way up the stairs and onto the mezzanine level, their immediate goal, to get to the closest open door and make a run for it into a bedroom, or where ever it might lead. Out of her periphery, Cassandra saw an opening and duly noted it to Tommy, but just as they readied themselves to make a dash for the doorway, a horrendous, metallic rattle emanated from behind them. Ending their retreat from the dogs was not an option so, without stopping, they turned in unison to find three silver suits of armor lumbering toward them. It appeared as though Tommy's day had gone from bad to worse, for as they made a run for the opened doorway, another silver suit trundled out from their would-be refuge. Dogs to the right and shiny metal monsters in front and to their left, they found their backs against the railing overlooking the grand marble foyer thirty feet below.

"Quick!" Tommy barked, "Give me your belt!"

He grabbed it, attached it to his own and to the railing and ordered, "Now get on my back!"

Even though they had only known one another for a couple of days, Cassandra understood his tone, and knew not to argue. She climbed on like an organ grinder's monkey as Tommy scrambled over the railing. As the dogs exploded in yaps and howls, and the armored men reached out for them, Tommy lowered himself down the railing until he and Cassandra were left dangling a few feet below the onslaught. But smarter than the average pack of mutts, the snarling horde bolted back down the staircase, taking up residency directly under the dangling children, where they sputtered and spat their ferocious dance of starvation.

They hung there like a side of beef waiting to be butchered until one shiny metal hand reached through the railing and took hold of the leather belt and began to pull them upward. Slowly and methodically, they were hoisted up, closer and closer, to the clamor above.

"What do we do?" Cassandra screamed.

At that moment, one huge steely hand lurched forward grabbing hold of Tommy's shoulder. He grunted and writhed to loosen the monster's grip but it was no use. The hand dug into him and lifted him to his feet. He closed his eyes and waited for the end.

"Jesus Christ!" Ed shouted.

Dazed, Tommy opened his eyes to find his father shaking him firmly by the shoulder.

"Tommy!"

Tommy darted his head about, surprised and confused to find himself safely on the dock next to the lake. He finally made eye contact with his father who went on, "I've been calling you for ten minutes! What's the matter with you? The car's all packed. Let's get going?"

His father stormed off of the dock and up the grassy incline to the gravel driveway. Tommy followed, still perplexed but hustling just the same. He had unwittingly pissed off his father and unless he made every effort to rectify the situation, he feared it would be an especially long ride home. He hopped into the waiting pickup truck and the three sped down the lane, leaving a plume of gray dust to linger behind. It wouldn't be until they reached the George Washington Bridge that Tommy would realize, that in the flurry of drama back on the dock, he had left behind his book.

ELEVEN

The following Thursday, the shit hit the fan. Released only two days earlier, *The Keeper of the Key,* had nearly sold out in every bookstore in New York, Boston, Washington, D.C., Philadelphia, Chicago and Los Angeles. Gwen's cell phone had been ringing non-stop since Wednesday with requests for interviews and book signings, updates from the printing house and calls from a very worried Rich. Should he buy a new suit? Should he quit his job? Does he need a Blackberry? Does he really have to get on a plane? Additionally, Volos had added his two cents on a regular basis, each time chipping away at Gwen's confidence like a jackhammer to a slab of marble.

She handled it all like a knife juggler. Although she had no business or experience managing an author, her motivation to please Volos was such that the actual task at hand was a cake walk.

This morning, she stood quietly by in the hallway of NBC studios. Poised for any contingency, she held her clipboard tight to her chest as she peered across the room and following Rich's every move.

Stoically, he sat in a plush yellow chair, one of two facing each other, on a carpeted platform. Behind him, through a wall of tinted plate glass, gathered a mass of tourists, not there for him, but for Anne Curry. They waved, jumped and held high their homemade signs and banners, their chants and raves muted by the bulletproof glass.

A man wearing headphones and juggling a clipboard, a mug of coffee and a copy of Rich's book, shouted out to the room, "We're back in ninety!"

Astutely, Gwen took her cue from the newly at-ease on-air personalities, and headed over to Rich. "Are you okay?" she asked.

He nodded but said nothing, continuing only to pick at his fingernails.

"Where's your copy?"

"It's right here," said the voice from behind her, as the stage manager brought it to Rich.

He placed the book on his lap and continued to fiddle with his cuticles while his eyes darted around the studio.

"Stop that," Gwen ordered, shooing and separating his hands.

Just then the stage manager bellowed, "Thirty seconds!" Then turned to Rich and commanded, "Don't be nervous."

Rich forced a smile, nodded and continued the assault on his fingers. His posture stiffened as Anne

Curry approached. Smiling, she greeted, "You look nervous."

"A little," he admitted.

"This is really new to him," Gwen added.

Anne sat across from him and leaned in, taking his hands in hers. "It's just gonna be you and I having a conversation. That's all." She smiled as warmly in person as she had come across on the air.

"Yup," Gwen added, "Don't pay any attention to the cameras."

Anne smiled as she stood, "It'll be over before you know it." She crossed the stage and took her seat at her news desk.

He had heard the words before, *it'll be over before you know it.* In fact, he could suddenly recall specific instances when such assurances had been dispensed; at fifteen, as he waited in a dentist's chair to have all four wisdom teeth extracted, at twenty-two, when he entered the operating room for the removal of a cyst under his arm, and at camp, he couldn't remember how long ago, when the counselors assured him that being thrown in the deep end of the pool really was the best way to learn how to swim.

"Settle everyone!" the stage manager belted out.

Straightening Rich's hair, Gwen counseled, "I'll be right over here, not ten feet away."

She turned, but before she could take a step, Rich grabbed her arm, stopping her in her tracks. "Gwen," he whispered, "Thank you."

She smiled, walked away and tucked herself into a corner and watched.

The crew went into action, busily tending to their tasks while focusing on the stage manager, waiting for his call. He waved to the fill-in morning host. "Natalie! Camera two! In five, four, three," everything went quiet as he finished the count with only his fingers.

Two red lights went on, one on the top of camera two and one over the main door to the studio.

Natalie King's face lit up. She cocked her head and made love to the camera, "Move over, Lord of the Rings, when we come back, we'll sit down with New York's newest literary phenom, Richard Rossi. Anne Curry has that story. But first, your local news."

As the red lights went out, everyone's posture relaxed. "Two minutes everyone!"

Like a condemned man in his final moments, Rich remained glued to his seat. He turned his head to Gwen as if to offer his last words but was interrupted. "Ready?" Anne mused, "Take a deep breath." Posing like a yoga instructor, she inhaled, encouraging him to follow.

He did.

"Now out through your mouth."

He followed.

"Great," she said. "Now here's how this will go. I will just ask you some questions about what inspired you, how long you've been writing, things like that. No probing questions. I promise." She smiled and sat back in her chair, adjusting her body mic.

"Settle everyone!" Came from the stage manager.

Anne reached over to Rich. "Now don't forget to smile, and remember, don't look at the camera. Just look at me."

"In five, four, three."

Once again the red lights went on and Natalie King greeted America. "And now, Anne Curry."

"Thank you, Nat," Anne launched. "You've all heard of the most successful fiction series in history, The Harry Potter sorties, well now it's time for a new generation of children's adventure tales. Dale Haverford has the details. Dale."

A monitor near the center of the room echoed what millions of Americans were watching. "Good morning!" Haverford announced. "Anne, we've put together video from over a dozen cities, cities like Denver, Miami, Chicago, and what we've concluded is that America is crazy! Crazy for Richard Rossi."

The video cut from Haverford to an edited montage of film footage. Overhead, shots of crowds storming various buildings, street-level scenes of pandemonium and random shots of Rich ducking in and out of a limousine, Gwen clearing a path in both directions.

Haverford spoke over the footage, "That's right! He's a veritable nobody that came out of nowhere. He's Richard Rossi."

The video cut to one of Rich's new headshots, the one where he was ordered to, *relax and pucker,* while the audio remained broadcasting the shrieks and grunts of thousands of rioters. For a moment, he finally understood that this was all for him. The screaming, the pushing and shoving, all because of him. He had not only succeeded in publishing a novel, but had become famous in the process. Then just as promptly as his heart swelled with pride, he became awash with dread. Again, only this time more soberly, he thought to himself, this is all because of me. Distracted by his own musing, he missed most of the report.

"Back to you, Anne," Haverford offered.

Anne Curry spoke to the camera. "Thanks, Dale. I'm here with Richard Rossi. Good morning. It's great to see you."

"Good morning," Rich smiled, avoiding the camera lens.

"Can I call you Richard?"

He nodded, "Certainly."

"Richard," she went on, "You've seen the video, you've heard the reports. What do you make of the enthusiasm for your book?"

"Gosh Anne," Rich confessed, "I couldn't tell you. I mean, I know I'm supposed to sit here and tell you that it's the best book ever written and that everyone should buy it, but honestly, beyond that, I don't have a clue how to sell books. I owe that all to my publisher and my," he paused, turned to Gwen and smiled, "my agent."

Gwen smiled back and shooed him away.

Anne read from an index card. "According to Barnes and Noble dot com and Amazon dot com, your book has broken all first week release records. Does that surprise you?"

"It does in a way," he started, "but my publisher was so enthusiastic about the concept of the story that I could see he was going to do his best with it."

"And what about the concept?" Anne asked. "I've read it, but can you explain to the audience what makes your book so different from so many other stories in the genre?"

"Well, I think it's a lot edgier. It doesn't speak down to children. And the ending is pretty... off the wall."

"Well," Anne teased, "we won't give it away."

Finally feeling a little more comfortable, Rich joked, "Well unless there are some crazy fast readers out there, I don't think anyone has made it to the end yet. So I gotta keep it under my hat."

"Is there a sequel in the works?" Anne probed.

Toying with her and the rest of America, Rich squinted his eyes and smirked, "Maybe so."

"Oooh, that sounds promising. We'll have to keep an eye out for you. Richard Rossi, thank you so much for being with us this morning."

"Thank you Anne."

Anne turned to the camera and continued, "Richard Rossi's debut novel, The Keeper of the Key, is available now. Back to you, Natalie."

Natalie took over while Anne crept out of her chair, pulling Rich along with her. They tiptoed with Gwen to the back hall where Anne whispered, "It was great meeting you both. Good luck on the book, although I doubt you're going to need it."

Gwen and Rich shook hands with Anne Curry then headed down the hall to the exit stairway. They descended half of a flight and landed back in the underground parking garage where the black Lincoln Navigator limo had dropped them off earlier. The driver tamped out his cigarette and opened the door for them.

"Thank you, Bill," Rich said as he helped Gwen into the back.

"My pleasure," Bill answered, slamming the door and rounding the SUV. Once inside, Bill checked his itinerary. "It looks like," he scanned the clipboard, "we're heading back to Astoria, picking up your bags, Mr. Rossi, then heading to La Guardia."

"That sounds about right," Gwen added.

Rich squirmed in his seat then reached for the mini-bar.

"You better get used to it," Gwen scolded. "If you've got to have a cocktail every time you fly, you're going to be a hopeless alcoholic by the end of the month."

By the time they reached the departure terminal, Rich was better prepared for his first flight. Bill retrieved the bags from the back of the SUV and handed them off to the curb-side check-in. Rich lit a cigarette and joined the ostracized, bonding straight away with strangers puffing away at the designated smoking area.

"Will that be all, Ms. Wright?" Bill asked.

"I think we're in good shape. Thank you."

"Okay. Well, you have safe travels and I'll see you back here in a few days." Bill slammed the door shut, rounded the tank-like SUV and drove off.

She watched for a moment as the shiny black monster zoomed away, then turned her attention to Rich, a blur in a cloud of smoke, leaning against a cement pillar. Checking her wristwatch as she approached him, she said, "We have exactly eighteen minutes to get through security and to our gate, which, I should mention, is all the way on the other side of the terminal."

She plucked the cigarette from his mouth and flicked it into the street like a sailor. "Let's go," she commanded, pointing out the way.

As they trekked their way through the cavernous airport, to the gate, Rich couldn't resist making hushed wisecracks about bombs and high-jackings. Gwen was mortified, sure they would be stopped and questioned. Certain that at any moment armed guards would whisk them away to a dingy back office, strip search them, outfit them in orange jumpsuits and haul them off to Guantanamo Bay, never to be heard from again.

But Rich had an infectious wit, especially when he was drunk, and by the time they reached the gate,

Gwen found herself biting her lip, trying not to encourage him by her amusement. And knowing full well that he was getting to her, he focused his energy, ramping up the torment, until he finally realized he was stepping onto the plane.

As the passengers trailed in, he took note of his surroundings, counting the seats between himself and the exits. He had heard somewhere that eighty percent of plane crashes are survivable, that most victims are found to have smoke residue in their lungs, meaning that they had survived the impact, but perished in the ensuing fire. He took another look and assessed the actual passengers amid him and the doors. Clawing his way over the two old women, the four Boy Scouts and the single mother with her infant would be no problem. However, as he formulated a plan to surmount the two six foot tall linebackers that sat directly behind, a flight attendant foiled him by asking, "Seat belts buckled?"

He quickly sobered when one of the staff pulled the door shut, entombing them all with one final thud. He sat up, straining against the seat belt, peering out the window and fighting for breath.

"Are you alright?" Gwen chuckled.

He shook his head as she reached overhead and turned knob, letting in a stream of fresh air. "How's that?" she asked.

He nodded, and as the engines revved and the plane began to move, he clutched the armrests and shook his head once more.

Gwen giggled, then placed her hand on his. "It's going to be fine. I promise you. Just sit back and try to enjoy the experience."

The plane bumped along the tarmac and turned toward the runway. He could see from his window the planes in the distance lining up to land. Without turning from the window, he said to Gwen, "You know, the worst air disaster in aviation history happened on the ground."

"Oh really?" she replied casually as she leafed through the magazine pouch in front of her.

"Yup. Remember the Canary Islands?"

Finally, the plane came to a halt, paused for a moment, then turned, taking its place at the end of the runway.

"I think it was in the early eighties," he continued.

Just then, the engines revved louder than he had heard before, and seconds later he was being forced backward into his seat. The gravity held him there as his knuckles turned white and Gwen grabbed his hand. As the tire scuffed cement raced past them, he imagined that he was now travelling faster than he ever had. He managed to turn slightly to Gwen and asked, "How do these people remain so calm during this?" his voice bouncing in tandem with the plane.

She gave his hand a squeeze but said nothing.

"I mean," he went on, "aren't they the least bit impressed that something bigger than most houses is screaming through space this fast?"

She leaned over to him, "Most of these people have done this a time or two before. But trust me, no one really every gets used to this part of the trip." She leaned farther over still and peered out the window. "It is quite amazing though, isn't it?"

Before he could answer, an all new feeling stirred his senses. The bottom of the world seemed to drop out from under him as the plane became airborne. Now suddenly reclined as the ship rocketed it's way skyward, he turned to the window and became instantly mesmerized by the sights below. The airport, no longer in sight, gave way to a model neighborhood complete with houses, parking lots and highways. Before he could blink, the neighborhoods expanded into suburbs and the suburbs into pastures, until they glided over a large body of water. Probably Long Island Sound, he thought. The plane banked and began its journey West to Los Angeles, and he became a little rattled as the Earth disappeared from sight, but quickly settled in as they leveled off to a comfortable altitude above the clouds. Almost immediately thereafter, a ding could be heard from above and the Captain made his announcement. "Ladies and Gentlemen, this is Captain Rogers. We want to welcome you aboard Continental's flight 397 for Los Angeles. Our cruising altitude will be about thirty-three thousand feet and we should be arriving in sunny L.A. at about two o'clock local time. So just relax and enjoy the flight. Our flight attendants will be around shortly with some beverages."

"Beverages?" Rich lit up. "What kind of beverages?"

Gwen smiled and closed her magazine. "Anything you want."

"Well, nobody told me there would be beverages. This changes everything."

They had a few good laughs and several beers as they shared the stories of their lives. Gwen learned that Rich's parents had both been killed in an auto accident in 1998, that his sister had fought and beaten breast cancer, that his Nephew was the closest thing he would ever have to a child of his own and that he had been celibate for more than six years. Likewise, Rich discovered that Gwen had been a stay at home mom, learned more than anyone should about Batten's Disease, that her husband had left her for a woman in her twenties, and that before going to work for Mr. Volos, she had never in her life received a paycheck.

"I'll bet he's hard to work for," Rich sympathized.

Gwen was silent, sipping her beer to keep from speaking.

Rich went on, "I mean, he's so opinionated and impatient. How long have you been with him?"

She thought for a second. "A little over two years now."

"Wow," Rich said, raising his bottle to her, "There's a special place in Heaven for you, putting up with him for two years."

She gulped hard, nearly choking on his sentiment, then changed the subject.

By the time the plane had landed, Rich had become a fan of air travel. It was fascinating to him how one could move about the planet so readily, and at the same time a little embarrassing that he had been so out of the loop. His fear conquered, he now looked forward to the many more flights Gwen had scheduled. Denver, Chicago, Milwaukee, Houston, Seattle, Miami, in that order, were on deck, and like a child with a newly discovered toy, Rich's mind obsessed with the anticipation of each new trip.

After retrieving their luggage, they made their way through the terminal, searching for the taxi stand and the limo that awaited. Finally, they spotted the driver holding a small dry erase board, upon which was scrawled, "Rossi". Gwen made it to him first and said, "This is Mr. Rossi."

They hadn't heard the murmurs from the group of Girl Scouts nearby until they moved toward the limo, but soon though, a screech came forth, "It's him!" And with that, Rich found himself at the center of a small riot. Screams surrounded him as he was pummeled and pressed.

"We're all reading your book, Mr. Rossi!" one girl gushed through her braces.

"Oh!" he smiled and nodded. "That's great!"

"Myra here is blind, so we take turns reading it to her! Aren't you Myra?" another cried.

"Yeah! I'm blind!" Myra cheered.

"Oh. Okay." Rich stammered. "How do you like the book?"

They all spoke at once, jumping and shouting. "I'm half way through!" one yelled.

"Me too!" shrieked another.

"Well, listen girls. I have to get going. But keep reading!" he waved as he backed out through the sliding glass doors that to the sidewalk and the limo.

As they sped away, Gwen primped her hair, turned to Rich and said, "Its official, you're famous."

And famous was expensive. After a full nine hours of book signings, three radio interview tapings and a meeting with an executive at Warner Brothers, Rich and Gwen were on the brink of exhaustion. Battle weary, they spoke not a word as they made their way from the limo, through the hotel lobby and up the fourteen floors to their adjoining rooms. As they swiped their key cards, both barely managed a unison, "See you in the morning."

Bright and early the next day, after waking from a near coma and having his first coffee and cigarette on the balcony, Rich called to check in with his sister in Manhattan. He readied himself to boast of his first flight, the mob of fans and the view from his suite, but his thunder was stolen when Rachel answered.

"Thank God you're okay!" she shouted. "When did you get in? How was your flight? It wasn't that bad was it? Here, Tommy wants to talk to you."

There was a tussle and then Tommy spoke from three thousand miles away. "Hi, Uncle Rich! I saw you on TV! Have you met any famous people yet?"

Suddenly homesick, Rich felt his eyes begin to sting a little. "Nobody famous yet. How'd you like the book?"

"Please don't be mad," Tommy began.

Rich was silent, waiting for the ultimate critique.

Tommy went on, "I forgot it at my Dad's cabin. Mom wanted to go buy me a new one, but I'm gonna wait until Dad brings it over."

"How could I be mad at you?" Rich consoled, "You're my favorite nephew."

"Uncle Rich, I'm your only nephew."

"Oh yeah," Rich chuckled.

"So, how does it end?" Tommy pried.

"No way, Jose'. I'm not giving away the ending!" Rich exaggerated with a howl. "You're gonna have to wait it out until next weekend. Man, it sucks to be you. Now put your mom back on the phone, and if you tell her I said it sucks to be you, I'll deny it."

Rachel's voice interrupted him from the other end of the line. "Rich, you're paying for his future psychiatry."

They talked and laughed and enjoyed each other's company for nearly forty-five minutes. Rich couldn't remember when his sister had last spoken to him with such high esteem. Finally, it seemed as though he had accomplished something that she regarded as a triumph, that warranted praise and bought him a place at the grownup's table.

TWELVE

Meanwhile, from coast to coast, *The Keeper of the Key* was in the lap of nearly one hundred thousand people. Children and adults alike devoured every word. In Memphis, a single mother read aloud to her daughters a chapter each night at bedtime. In Nashua, an elementary school librarian scanned it for content before allowing it a place on the shelves. In Detroit, Baltimore, Milwaukee, Cincinnati and Austin, fathers wrapped them as birthday gifts. In Syracuse, twin brothers fought over who got to read it each morning.

In Tampa, undaunted by the passing hurricane, twelve year old Rebecca Babcock sat by candlelight enthralled, her face awash with streams of light emanating from the book, walking in the medieval shoes of her heroine, Cassandra.

It was a frightening journey. Treachery reared its ugly head at every turn. It had been two days since her friend, Billy had been carried away by the talons of the giant winged caterpillar, and the mission had come to a halt until she could rescue him. She had hiked for miles, fording icy cold streams and chopping her way through one dense patch of forest after another.

Finally, in the waning light of dusk, she could make out the cave in the cliff that jutted up from the pasture before her in the distance. But the timing had been all wrong. She decided to make camp for the night and wage rescue at first light. She retreated to the wood's edge and found a fallen tree near a tiny brook. Gathering dead leaves around her, she would take refuge and hunker down next to the damp and musty bark, knowing that several days of tumult since climbing under the shed in the junkyard would lend itself to a deep and peaceful sleep.

In the early morning hours, just before dawn, the treetops rustled softly overhead in a gentle breeze, the grassy meadow following suit. Thunder growled off in the distance, but her slumber had not been disrupted. As the storm grew nearer, tiny droplets of rain sprinkled down upon her, and the gentle trickle of the nearby stream slowly grew into a torrent of mountain storm runoff. Only when the level of the flash flood reached her feet did Cassandra stir. But she dismissed the sensation, relegating it to her dreams, and turned away snoring.

Rebecca's mother bolted down the stairs from the bedrooms screaming with panic. "Becky!" she cried over and over as she scanned the living room. But her daughter was nowhere in sight.

As the hurricane's trailing edge swept past, it had spawned tornados throughout the region, and her neighborhood was now under an official warning. Frantically, she plucked her infant son from his playpen and swaddled him in the cover of her fleece windbreaker. The sweat of anguish poured down her face as she raced through the kitchen and out the back door. "Becky!" she screamed again, but to no avail.

Sirens pulsated in the distance as the approaching clouds on the horizon began to organize. Unfamiliar lawn ornaments and patio furniture flew through the air from neighboring yards as if gravity itself had abandoned the Earth. Her voice, nearly raw with fear, cried out for her daughter as she sprinted around to the front of the house, splashing ankle deep in the newly formed creek that once was her lawn. Dodging limbs and debris, she finally made it to the front yard where she found her Honda Civic bouncing on its shock absorbers in protest to the wind. The street before her was now invisible, completely transformed into a raging culvert. As hail began to rain down upon her, she shielded her son and made a dash for the safety of the front stoop. She squinted, scanning the yard one last time, when finally the fabric of her daughter's pink dress, bundled in a wad, caught her eye just next to the split log bench near the mailbox. It was moments away from being carried off in the flash flood. She blinked and refocused and saw that the wad of material was indeed her daughter.

"Becky" she screamed, running to her. "Oh my God! Becky!"

Unresponsive, Becky lay curled up clutching her book, the torrent lapping up above the curb and over her legs. Her mother reached down and grabbed her shoulder. "Becky!" she insisted, but was ignored.

"Becky! Goddam it! What's wrong?"

Rebecca's eyes remained transfixed on the pages before her. The world around her in its fury did not exist. The hail, the horizontal rain, the inundation swallowing her, nothing would dissuade her from the hypnotic words she read. Her lips seemed to quake as she mouthed the sentences to herself.

Her mother latched on to the novel and pried it out of Rebecca's grasp, tossing it into the raging waters on the street. She then took hold of her daughter's collar and, with one swift herculean tug, hoisted her to her feet.

Cassandra too awoke and found herself cold and wet, staggering into the arms of the Hag, Neltha.

THIRTEEN

Fourteen year old Kathryn Wood of Burbank, California, twelve year old Sylvester Marsh of Greensburg, Tennessee, Mason Rogers and Miles Young of Little Rock, Arkansas, and Jon Eastwood and Yvonne Miller of Salt Lake City, were only a few of the countless children that were spellbound by *The Keeper of the Key*. Their youthful hands would seize the hardback cover and absorb the story as though the paragraphs gave life itself. Their fingers would caress the ink, the binding, the spine of the book like a priest regards the body of Christ. All over the nation, any child that happened upon the book would become so seduced by the words that they would forgo meals, withdraw from friends and sacrifice the scorn of family simply to get a dose of the drug that even a few pages supplied. And they relished the drug, slowly and methodically drinking in every syllable of the sweet nectar, as though their very existence depended on it.

Jason Reed was a typical twelve year old boy. Even with his bright blue eyes and wispy blond hair he didn't stand out in any particular way. Even in the small town of Battle Creek, Nebraska, population 1,139, where his mother kept house and his father raised hogs, he was easily overlooked. He attended the town's only elementary school, had just one real friend, and passed the time by sneaking away in the evenings after supper, to climb the town water tower and dream about what lay beyond the featureless, drab horizon. On a clear day he could see all the way to Norfolk, the next town over.

Today was no different than the day before. He awoke, washed his face, dressed for school then walked the half mile into town for class. He spoke very little to other kids, keeping to himself, knowing even at this young age that study was the only way out of the malaise that was Battle Creek. And his seventh grade teacher, Miss Fletcher was happy to pile on the extra work.

When she assigned her pupils that Friday to complete a book report due the following Wednesday, the entire class, save for one child, Jason, groaned in despair. Their weekend shot to hell, they at least found solace in the fact that they were allowed to choose their own topic and story.

As the class broke for lunch, they were instructed to visit the school library before returning to class. The smallest boy in the room, Jason was routinely shoved to the side and thus the last one to leave for dismissal. Today he waited at his desk for the crowd to thin out before heading to the classroom door.

As he passed Miss Fletcher's desk, she stopped him, "Jason, do you mind if I give you a special assignment?"

His eyes lit up as he turned to face her. Getting little attention at home during everyday life, he consumed her interest in him and reveled in her use of the word, special. "Yes, Miss Fletcher?" he said going to her desk.

She opened a drawer and retrieved a brand new copy of *The Keeper of the Key*. Handing it over to him she said, "Not only do I want you to do your book report on this book," his eyes widened, as she continued, "since I know you're the fastest reader in class and you'll probably be done with this by Sunday, I want you to read it to the class after recesses next week. Can you do that?"

He opened the book and fanned through the pages, measuring the heft, the honor of his new task. "Yes Ma'am," he beamed.

"Good," she said, standing and reaching for her purse. "Now go get some lunch, and instead of going to the library after lunch, you can come back here and clean the black board for me. Is that okay?"

He felt himself grow a little taller just then as he puffed himself up and thanked her, then ran out the door.

That very night, after he had finished helping his mother dry the dinner dishes, Jason took to the book and began to read. He tucked himself into his usual spot, an overstuffed recliner in his bedroom, and drank in the story until his eyes stung with exhaustion, and he finally fell asleep. He spent much of the next day captivated by the same enchanting glow of the letters before him, breaking only when given an ultimatum by his mother to, "eat or die".

His folks had seen him this way before, enthralled by a good book. In fact, they took it as a sign that the good habits they had taught him had sunken in. More times than they cared to count, his mother and father had preached to him to get his homework done. You don't want to farm pigs for a living, do you? So the spell that he seemed to be under came as no surprise.

But by Sunday morning, things had to change, at least temporarily. By eleven AM, when he had yet to come downstairs for breakfast, his mother made the climb up to his bedroom and opened the door. "Jay, you gotta put that away for now and help me get this place ready."

Jason looked up from his reading and stared blankly at his mother. But he didn't see her. Instead, he saw through Billy's eyes, Princess Romaine, tattered and torn. Exhausted and barely able to breathe, she reached for him and managed, "Billy, you've got to help us now! Hurry!"

The rumble of hurried footsteps drew nearer from the hallway behind her. "They're coming! They'll kill me if they find out I'm setting you free!"

Billy jumped to his feet, grabbed his shield and ran to her.

"Put that book down," Jason's mother ordered.

Jason came to, frozen for a moment as he scanned the room and wondered how he came to be standing in front of his mother.

"I said, put that book down!" his mother repeated. "Everyone will be here in less than two hours!"

Still confused, he barely uttered, "Huh?"

"Come on, Jason," she went on. "Your father's mowing the lawn, then he has to run to Diebert's for the groceries. I need you to go give Charley a bath and then brush him out. And when you're done with that, you need to pick up your room."

He frowned for a moment as she snatched the book from his grasp and slammed it onto the dresser. "Now go!" she ordered.

He stomped down the stairs, whistling for the dog, turning only once to share a dirty look with his mother.

By six o'clock, the cookout in the Reed's backyard was winding down. Aunt Florence and Uncle Grover debated with Aunt Jill and Uncle Alex over the merits of clean coal technology. Cousins Michael and Dave battled out their millionth game of horseshoes. The twins were fast asleep in their playpen. Grandma and Grandpa Owens played team Canasta against Tony and Fran, and Aunt Gretchen was helping herself to her third plateful of macaroni salad.

The shadows in the yard grew longer with each passing minute and so did Jason's face. Clearly unimpressed with the conversations, the food and the company, he sat alone on the cement steps that lead up to the back door. Head in his hands, elbows on his knees, he daydreamed, longing for the opportunity to slip away unnoticed to finish his book.

As his mother approached him from the yard carrying an empty casserole pan, she stopped and mussed his hair. "You're over this aren't you?" she offered.

Barely looking up, he nodded in resignation.

"You want to go finish your book, don't you?"

He could see where this was going and instantly knew that the next few seconds needed to be handled very delicately. He was on the verge of being left off the hook and if memory served him, looking up with only his eyes and not his entire head, would seal the deal. So like a scorned puppy, he met her sympathetic gaze using just the slightest bit of raised eyebrow. "It's okay," he baited.

If experience had taught him anything it was that, at this point, the next person who speaks loses. So with as much discipline as he could muster he sat in silence, leaving his mother to dangle on her own conscience.

"Well, why don't you go say goodnight to everyone and tell them you have to go do your homework," his mother offered as she climbed the steps.

He hopped to his feet and opened the screen door for her, then made his rounds to his extended family, bidding them all farewell. Seconds later he was in his bedroom retrieving his book, bolting down the stairs three at a time and dashing out the front door. He sprinted across the front lawn, crossed the road and tore through the wheat field. After a minute or two, he was out of breath and slowed his pace to a brisk walk the rest of the way to his personal hideout.

As he squeezed between the eight foot tall, padlocked chain link gates, he could feel himself begin to relax. There was something about this place that made him more content than any other place in the world. Maybe it was the solitude. Maybe it was the privacy, or the simple beauty of the trees and bushes that surround the fence. Perhaps it was the panoramic view from the catwalk on top. He never analyzed it, but because of his time here over the months, he became aware of the concept of refuge. Things even smelled better here. Maybe it was the way the tower and the cluster of trees and shrubs at its base shielded the ground from the rays of the sun. He didn't care. All he knew was that this was an oasis in the middle of a flat and barren life.

Alone in the cool, moist afternoon sanctuary, he stood for a moment, silent, eyes closed, and inhaled deeply. As he released the breath of the outside world, a family of gray partridges, recognizing him, crept out from their home under the Chokeberry bushes and resumed scratching about the ground. He smile down at them and wondered if he would ever feel this at ease with the likes of Aunt Gretchen or Cousin Dave. He knew, however that he mustn't dwell on such ridiculous things. If he did, it would only mean another night of feeling stupid, lame and different. And tonight, there was no way he would allow himself to go anywhere ugly.

So with his book stuffed inside the waist of his blue jeans, and the partridges cheering him on, he began his ascent. The pale green metal of the ladder was cool and welcoming, and within a matter of seconds he was popping out from the treetop canopy into the warmth of the late afternoon sun. He climbed on until he reached the catwalk and then planted himself in his usual spot. With his back against the warm metal water tank, he surveyed the countryside beneath and beyond him. Off to his left he spied his house and watched as the visitors all hugged one another then packed themselves into their cars and drove away.

He opened the book to the page where he had left off then closed it and gazed into the sunset, calculating that he had just enough time to finish before nightfall. When he opened the book once more, the stream of golden light beamed forth from the pages like a thousand suns, and he was again under the spell. His eyes, feverishly scanning the lines, reflected the intensity of the glow from within the book.

The pages turned more quickly than ever. Of course they always do toward the end of a great saga.

But today the words, and the time itself, elapsed so rapidly that he seemed to be absorbing the story rather than reading it. Beads of sweat broke out upon his brow as the strain of such osmosis ravaged his innocent soul. His body began to quake with exhilaration as the suspense of the final two pages came to light.

As firmly a hold as he had on the hourglass, Cassandra was still able to snatch it from his grasp. He closed his eyes for a moment and recalled the words that Neltha had spoken, "Let go of time and you shall fly." He repeated it to himself over and over as he watched Cassandra hold the hourglass out to the monster by the boulder. For a split second he thought it was all over, that she was giving up and handing over everything to the giant toad. Their backs forced to the cliff's edge, they had no way out. But just as the toad looked up, Cassandra turned the hourglass upside down, and the monster began helplessly moving backward, plucking a grub from his mouth and shoving it back into the ground. They watched for a few seconds before Cassandra turned the hourglass upright once again.

The toad screamed for her to hand it over, but she upended it once more, sending him a few seconds backward in time.

Cassandra turned to him and said, "We've got to erase everything we've done here."

Battle weary and wise, he nodded and replied, "Then let go of time. And fly?"

He smiled at his friend, took her hand and the two of them inched backward until they reached the very edge of the Earth. He took the hourglass from Cassandra and lowered it to the ground, again turning it slowly upside down before setting it on the ground. He watched for a moment as everything, birds, clouds, people and even sounds reversed themselves and ran in the opposite direction of time.

Somewhere in his soul he knew that it was all a dream, that he and Cassandra would do the right thing in this world and come out unscathed in the next. After all, if there's a talking toad, a thousand year old witch and time travel, how real could it be? He knew that his friend felt the same way. So, with almost no trepidation they turned to face the sky before them and the gorge below. The eerie sound of time undoing itself behind them blended with the raging waterfall below.

"Don't look down," he told his friend, just before they both did. They held on to one another, and to the hope that reality would scoop them up somewhere between the edge of the cliff and the jagged boulders on the canyon floor.

Cassandra turned to him one last time and said, "Let go of time and you shall fly?"

They nodded together, tightened their grip and closed their eyes, leaning ever so slightly into the cool and comforting breeze wafting up from below.

Jason Reed's broken little body was found the next morning by a township maintenance worker at the foot of the water tower, a gray partridge cooing at his feet. Completely intact, *The Keeper of the Key* lay undiscovered in the thicket of a Chokeberry bush.

FOURTEEN

That same Monday morning, nearly 1,500 miles away in Miami, Gwen awoke to the sound of urgent pounding on her hotel room door. As she gathered herself and stumbled to the door, she glanced at the alarm clock on the night stand, 7:15 AM. As she wiped the sleep from her eyes, she groaned, "Who's there?"

"It's me," came Rich's impatient voice through the heavy steel door. "Come on!"

She tied the white terrycloth robe shut and unbolted the door. "What's going on?"

As he pushed his way in, Rich reminded her, "It's our only day off. We have nothing until that WPOW thing at 3 PM."

"Exactly," she grumbled, grabbing the coffee pot.

"You said we'd hang out on the beach today!"

Apparently Gwen had not only forgotten the promise, but had also forgotten who she was dealing with. Ten years her junior, Rich still possessed the enthusiasm she had long ago stored away in moth balls. It had been fifteen years since she had spent any time on a beach. In fact, the last time she could recall interacting with sand in any capacity was with Casey in their rooftop sandbox nearly thirteen years earlier.

By now, however, Gwen had come to appreciate Rich's zest for life, even if it had reared its head on the only morning of the week she could sleep in. Traveling with him these past few weeks, his contagious personality had begun to rub off on her. Each plane trip was an adventure to him. He had marveled at details that seasoned travelers had long taken for granted, the miniature bottles of Southern Comfort, the piping hot towels. With childlike exuberance he pointed out the architecture, raved over local cuisine and thrilled in the regional dialects.

"I remember," she relented, tearing open a foil pack of coffee.

"So? What are we gonna do first?" he begged, plopping down on the edge of her bed, bouncing with anticipation.

She tossed him a scowl and said, "I'm gonna have my coffee. Then I'll hop in the shower." She unwrapped a Styrofoam cup and went on. "I want to call home before Casey goes to school. Then we can go get some breakfast." She paused long enough to straighten her bangs in the mirror above the mini bar and, glancing at Rich's freshly shaven face, asked, "How long have you been up?"

He sprang up from the bed and went to the window, pulling back the heavy beige curtains. As the morning light streamed in, piercing Gwen right between the eyes, he chirped, "Since five."

"Well, how about this," Gwen said, moving him closer to the door. "You go to your room and find out what the weather's gonna be like. Maybe you should call home too. See if Tommy got his book back yet."

He nodded in thoughtful agreement as she continued, "When I'm done here, I'll come over and get you. How's that sound?"

Standing in the hallway Rich opened his mouth to speak, but before he could make a sound, Gwen shut the door and returned to the coffee pot.

Rich spent the next forty-five minutes in his room pacing, checking in with the morning news on the television and smoking cigarettes through the three inch wide opening of his hotel room window. Puffing and fanning, he cursed Gwen for reserving him a non-smoking room. He checked himself in the bathroom mirror, clipped his toenails on the edge of the bathtub and finally, in an effort to quell his boredom, planted himself in front of the television and surfed through Miami's local channels.

Mindlessly clicking away, he longed for something, anything to catch his eye. Click, "... more than 300 points down..." click, "...members of the administration to meet behind closed doors..." click, "...body of the twelve year old girl was found..." click, "...other news, police have not released the name of a twelve year old girl who fell from a bedroom window from the seventeenth floor of the Windmill Tower apartments..."

With complete disinterest he hit the power button, silencing the news, then reached for his cell phone and dialed his sister. When it went directly to voice mail, he checked the clock on the end table and imagined they were on the way to school. Before he could finish leaving a message, call waiting beeped in and, checking the caller ID, he answered, "Hey, I was just leaving you a message."

The garbled sound of pandemonium echoed from the other end of the line as Rachel shrieked, "Oh my God! Rich!"

He could barely make out her words over the hysteria in her voice.

"What's wrong? What's going on?" he begged.

Sirens and panicked shouting in the background mingled with her words as she yelled, "Tommy! Get over here!"

"What's going on Rachel?"

"Hold on! Let me go inside!"

Tommy's cries and the rumbling tumult of fright reverberated through the phone until she retreated to the relative calm of her lobby.

"What's going on?" Rich insisted.

"Tommy, stay right here!" Rachel commanded. "Rich?"

"Rachel? What the fuck is happening?"

"Oh my God!" she began to weep.

"Rachel, calm down and tell me what's happened."

She sobbed into the phone, "It's the neighbor boy! You remember! Mark is his name!"

Rich heard Tommy in the background shout to his mother, "Marty!"

"Marty," Rachel corrected herself. "He killed himself!"

"Is that the kid with the really dirty bike?" Rich quizzed.

"Yes! He's," she gasped on the words, "he's dead! On the sidewalk! Right now!"

"Oh my God," Rich consoled.

"His poor mother. She's outside with him right now!" she added. She saw it happen!"

"Holy shit! That's horrible!" Rich added.

Just then, Rich heard a knock on his door. He listened to Rachel as he unlocked the door and let in Gwen.

"Tommy is freaking out," Rachel whispered into the phone. "Hold on."

As Rich waited, he relayed the gist of the story to Gwen, who quietly lowered herself onto the chair next to the table. Her face clouded over with fear as she listened to Rich's end of the conversation.

When Rachel came back to the phone, she continued, "I sent him back upstairs. I feel like I'm in a dream!"

"Okay," Rich said calmly, "tell me exactly what happened."

As she began to speak, Rich interrupted, "Do you mind if I put you on speaker? Gwen is here and that way I don't have to worry about getting it wrong."

"That's fine," she waited.

"Okay, go ahead."

"Am I on? Can you hear me?"

"Yes," Rich and Gwen replied in unison.

"Hi Gwen. How are you?" Rachel began.

"I'm fine, sweetheart. What happened?" Gwen said, leaning into the phone.

"So, Tommy and I are heading out of the building on the way to walk him to school. Then, like two seconds after we step out of the lobby, I hear a scream from across the street! I look over and see this lady pointing up at our building! By the time I could turn to see what she was pointing at," she paused for a moment, catching her breath and swallowing tears. "Before I could turn around I heard the most," her voice cracked as she began to sob.

Rich and Gwen hung on her every word. "It's okay," Gwen comforted. "Take your time."

Rachel took slow, deliberate breaths, steeling herself as she went on. "I can't even describe the sound," she waited and then continued, "but that poor boy had just hit the ground. There was blood everywhere! On the wall, on the cars parked outside. It even splattered on me and Tommy!"

Her labored breathing changed to full blown sobs. "Oh my God! Tommy got covered! I gotta go!"

"Wait!" Rich barked. "Don't hang up!"

"I have to go check on Tommy. This is exactly the kind of thing that'll push him into playing with matches again."

"Did they say what happened?" Gwen asked.

As she related the details, Rachel's voice steadied. "Well, I was just in shock! All I could think to do was to keep Tommy from seeing everything! A crowd gathered around and the cops were here in like ten seconds! They start clearing everyone away and then the boy's mother comes screaming through the lobby and just goes crazy."

As she went on, she fought to keep her emotions in check. "That poor woman. She kept screaming something in Spanish. Someone said that he jumped!"

Rachel's story struck Gwen deep in the center of her heart. The agony in her voice spoke to every mother's utmost fear, the inability to protect her child. Only recently had she begun to heal from her own helplessness with her daughter's sickness. She had wept and prayed, screamed and fought, and went so far as to visualize actually eating Casey's disease.

Gwen couldn't listen to any more. She stood, straightening her blouse, and headed for the door, apologizing as she made her getaway. Once the door closed behind her, she paused in the hallway, rummaging through her purse for her room key as a tsunami of thoughts washed over her. How would that poor woman ever survive losing her son? How would Tommy ever be the same after witnessing such a horror?

Once inside the sanctity of her room, Gwen retrieved her cell phone from her purse and dialed her mother's number. As she listened to the ring, she contemplated what to say and then quickly realized that she didn't need an excuse for checking up on her daughter. She simply wanted to hear Casey's voice, to soothe the newly reopened wound with the love of her child.

Her solace had to wait though, as the recorded sound of her mother's voice said to leave a message. So she did. "Hi guys! Mom, tell Casey I love her! Casey, I love you! I hope you're minding your Gamma! I should be back home in a week or so! Call me back when you can!"

An hour or so later, just as they were finishing breakfast at the rooftop café, Gwen received the return call she had been waiting for. "Hi Mom," she said.

Rich excused himself and headed for the restroom.

"How's Casey?" she asked, folding her linen napkin and placing it on the table.

Her mother spoke from the other end of the line in New York, "She was really down a couple of days ago, but she's okay now."

"Down?" Gwen quizzed. "Down about what?"

"Well, I think we narrowed it down to her just missing her mom," she said. "She finally let the cat out of the bag when she said, 'That book they're trying to hawk better be good!' Can you believe her? What a pistol. She reminds me of you."

With measured relief, Gwen allowed herself to smile. Until this morning she hadn't realized just how homesick she had been. "Well, when she gets home from school, tell her I love her and that I'll be home soon."

"Oh she's fine now. But she got really peeved once we started talking about it. So, and you can thank me later, we went out and picked up a copy of your friend's book. I told her, see for yourself. Read it and see if you think it's worth your mom's time and trouble."

Although Casey's eyesight had not been entirely restored and she was a painfully slow reader, Gwen imagined her critiquing the book. Undoubtedly she would be making highlights and footnotes, and would expect to have a personal meeting with the author himself. She would dissect each paragraph and in no uncertain terms, question, confront and cajole Mr. Richard Rossi until her issues with the story had been slaked.

"Thanks Mom. That was good thinking," Gwen added.

"I think it'll keep her occupied until you get home. Listen honey, your father's calling me. We're on our way to that mall in Paramus. I'll have Casey call you tonight, okay?"

"Okay, Mom," Gwen smiled, "I love you. You guys be careful."

As she flipped the cell phone shut, Rich returned. "Everything okay?"

She beamed the rest of the morning.

Although she found it exasperating and difficult to relax, Gwen spent the remainder of the morning and early afternoon lounging on the beach. Too pale for the Miami sun, she spent most of her time repositioning herself under the giant beach umbrella slathered in SPF 75, looking on as Rich waded, bobbed and dug for seashells in the foamy Atlantic surf.

Later, after the WPOW radio interview and an impromptu book signing at the downtown Barnes and Nobel, they returned to the hotel. Bent on drinking by the pool for the remains of the evening, they parted for their rooms to change clothes and would meet back downstairs at the bar.

Rich returned first and ordered for them both. Having scanned the lounge and found it completely devoid of even the most basic video game, he turned his attention to the television screen that hung over the bar and ogled the busty blond anchorwoman.

She took her cue from Co-anchor, Ted Phillips, "Back to you Wendy."

An important looking graphic, complete with yellow police tape over an animated chalk outline of a body, popped up behind her left shoulder as she spoke. "Tragedy struck last night in the Brickell area when twelve year old, Susan Closky was found dead on the street in front of her home at the Windmill Towers Apartments. Early reports stated that she had fallen from the dining room window of her family's seventeenth floor apartment, but investigators now say that it was an apparent suicide. Tom Carter is on the scene."

A live video feed filled the screen as the well-lacquered reporter spoke, "Wendy, I'm on the scene at Police Headquarters where we've just learned exclusively that the death of twelve year old Susan Closky, earlier reported to have been a tragic accident, was indeed ruled a suicide. Earlier today I spoke with residents of the Windmill Towers Apartments."

A taped interview replaced Tom Carter, and a woman spoke into the camera. "She was such a good little girl," the elderly Latina woman cried. "Everyone is devastated."

A grief-stricken couple hugged a group of youngsters and sobbed in discord, "Our baby! I don't understand!"

A microphone butted in as an off camera voice asked, "Can you tell us what happened?"

The girl's father held tightly to his wife and sobbed, "I don't know what she was thinking! One minute she was reading her book, and the next..." he disintegrated and immediately became the nucleus of the distraught crowd as they bolstered him with hugs.

After various shots of the window on the seventeenth floor and a makeshift memorial on the sidewalk, Tom Carter reappeared live. "As you can see, Wendy the entire community has been affected by this tragedy."

Back in the studio, Wendy Phelps asked, "Tom, are there any indications as to why this young girl did this? I mean, had she shown any signs of depression, or..."

Just then, Gwen joined Rich at the bar, "What's on?" she asked, reaching for her vodka and cranberry.

"It's odd," Rich answered, keeping his eyes on the television. "A little girl somewhere around here killed herself."

Gwen shook her head as she sipped and glanced up at the screen. "Wow. A little girl?"

"Well, a twelve year old," he said, turning and taking his drink.

Gwen shrugged it off until Rich continued, "It's just like the kid in my sister's building."

They turned to one another, puzzled and Gwen said, "How odd."

"Yeah," Rich added. "What a weird coincidence." He grabbed his napkin and motioned with his head, "Let's go to the pool."

They parked themselves on a pair of reclining lounge chairs and quietly watched as parents and children frolicked in the cool, clear water. After granting each other time to unwind from the last several days of hectic travel, they both began to speak at the same time, chuckled it off, then Rich began, "This has been a real trip."

Gwen turned in his direction, "I know. But I'm looking forward to getting home."

"Your daughter's gotta be going crazy without you all this time."

"She was," Gwen sipped then went on, "but my mother bought her your book. Now apparently she's in hog heaven."

Rich smiled and said, "I can't believe you didn't get her a freebie!"

"I know. I'm a horrible mother, but it didn't even occur to me." She reclined further and continued, "I'm just really focused on getting through this project."

Rich reclined and turned to her, leaning on his elbow. "So what's next for you after this?"

She sighed and tried not to boast. "I'm done."

"What do you mean, done?"

"Done. Retired. Joining the ranks of the unemployed."

"Seriously? How can you retire? You're too young," he quizzed.

Just then, a waiter approached. "Can I bring you another round?" he said, bowing into their shady alcove.

"Two more of these?" Rich raised his glass and rattled the ice cubes as the waiter flew into action. Turning his attention back to Gwen, "If you can afford to retire, what in God's name are you working for in the first place?"

Gwen sucked up the last drops of her cocktail and changed the subject. "Look at that little one over there." She nodded toward the pool. "He swims like a gold medalist."

Rich's eyes narrowed, examining Gwen, and came to realize that she had a secret. "Oh no," he sat up, "don't try to change the subject."

"What?" she turned to him, very poorly feigning innocence.

He turned on his recliner and put his feet on the concrete. "Every time the conversation starts to get a little personal, you get all evasive. What's up with that?"

She made a lame attempt at laughing him off, turning away and stirring her ice. "Could I really be so transparent," she thought?

She had never been even a remotely decent liar. Any attempt had always landed her in a puddle of blushing embarrassment. From the days of her youth, all anyone had to do was make eye contact with her and she would sing like a canary. Only recently had she begun to simply avoid conversations that might warrant a lie. Even still, she found the act of avoidance just as daunting, requiring more effort than she could spare.

But she had to come up with something, anything that would satisfy Rich's natural need to know other people's business.

Just as she began to speak, the waiter returned with two new cocktails. "Your room number?" he asked.

"918," Gwen replied.

"So?" Rich continued to pry, "Am I in the company of a wealthy divorcee?"

She giggled like a school girl as she sipped from her drink.

"Am I missing the boat here?" Rich teased. "Should I be hitting on you? Give up this whole running around hawking my book thing and work on swindling you out of your treasure?"

They laughed together, a little louder than they should have, but the alcohol had begun to kick in and neither really cared. For the first time since the trip from New York to Los Angeles, they felt comfortable just being. At this hour, it was not an interview or an autograph session that brought them together. It was the basic need to simply communicate with another human being, one on one, and to bask in that company.

An hour or so later, as the shadow of the hotel grew longer, blanketing the pool, something caught Gwen's eye. She reached over and tapped Rich on the arm and said, "Look over there," motioning with her head. "She's reading your book."

Thirty or so feet away, a girl of about sixteen sat curled up in a lounge chair engrossed in *The Keep of the Key*. They both noticed, but neither of them would admit to the other that the girl's face seemed to glow from a light within the pages of the book. An uncomfortable silence washed over them as they both reconciled the illusion to themselves.

By about nine o'clock, long after the girl across the way had been dragged away by her father and the tiki torches had been lit, Gwen and Rich were hammered. Their conversation had bounced from

Rich's mother having a secret abortion in the seventies, to Gwen's college experience with a lesbian named Gus, short for Gussie. It went unspoken, but they became friends in those few hours by the pool.

Later that night, as Rich lay in his bed watching the nighttime news, being reminded of the horrible coincidence, Gwen sat in her bathrobe at the desk in her room, waiting for her mother to answer her phone.

Finally, a voice crackled from the other end, "Hello?"

"Hi Mom," Gwen greeted. "How's everything there?"

"Oh, Gwen, hi! Things here are wonderful. How about you? Are you ready to come home yet?"

"I'm hoping about this time next week," Gwen answered. "Is Casey around?"

"Oh," she chuckled, "no. I have the whole house to myself tonight. Your father took her to see a show."

"On a school night?" Gwen protested.

"That's just it! School's closed tomorrow and Wednesday. Some kind of in service day thingy," her mother reveled.

"Oh."

"Yea, so they're up late tonight, and tomorrow we have a picnic planned."

"Oh?"

"Yup," her mother touted.

"Wow," Gwen half-scoffed, "sounds like you have everything taken care of."

"Now don't get like that, Gwenny. She still misses you terribly. Although, you wouldn't know it."

"What do you mean?" Gwen asked.

"Well, ever since we gave her your friend's book, you'd think we don't even exist!"

Gwen chuckled. "So I'm guessing she likes the book?"

"Likes it?" Mom screeched. "She's had her face buried in it every waking hour! In fact, yesterday, she tried to pull a fast one on me."

"Really?"

"Yes Sir. She pretended to be sick. First it was a horrible stomach ache, then it was an atrocious, her word, not mine, sore throat, then a head ache, all in the course of about five minutes. Well, I didn't just fall off the turnip truck. I remember when you kids used to try to bamboozle me. Turns out, she just wanted to stay home and read that book!"

"Well, don't let her take it to school," Gwen warned.

"Oh no. I already learned that lesson."

"How so?"

Her mother went on, "I let her take it last Monday and got a call that very afternoon. She was reading it during all of her classes!"

They shared a good laugh, thrilled that Casey was once more exhibiting the traits of a normal child.

"But seriously," Mother added, "it's not healthy for her to be cooped up all the time with her nose in that book. So your dad's trying to distract her.

Tomorrow ought to be good too, if the weather holds out. It's supposed to rain at some point. If it does we'll just go Wednesday."

"Well," Gwen concluded, "Have fun, and tell her I'll call tomorrow."

"Okay, sweetheart. I'll talk to you then. Now get some sleep and sell lots of books tomorrow. Oh, and by the way," she almost forgot, "your father read it and thinks it's creepy. Who ends a children's book like that?"

Gwen laughed and said, "Well, if Dad thinks it's creepy then we must be doing something right."

"Alright. I'll talk to you later. Love you."

"Love you too, Mom."

Gwen slept well that night, knowing that her daughter was in good hands. The alcohol and the peace of mind conspired to set her adrift quicker than usual. As she slipped into unconsciousness, she dreamt of the sunny days to come, herself picnicking in the park with Casey.

FIFTEEN

Early the next morning as she packed her suitcase, Gwen caught the tail end of the Today show in time to hear Al Roker proclaim that the entire Northeast would be a washout. Computer models had changed overnight and what was to be a perfectly glorious day for her daughter's picnic had transformed into a soggy, colder than normal mess. Making a mental note to call Casey, she hoisted a bag over her shoulder, and did a final scan of the area before leaving to gather Rich from his room.

As it turned out, they met in the hallway. Rich scampered past her to the elevators. "Come on!" he said with alarm. "Something's going on in the lobby!"

She followed dutifully, "What? What's going on?"

"I don't know!" he snapped, pressing the down arrow on the wall. "I just heard two of the housekeepers speaking in Spanish. Cayo´ and muchacha and calle. I think it means something about a girl in the street."

"A girl in the street?" Gwen puzzled.

Just then the elevator doors parted and they boarded. When it landed on level "L", the doors opened to reveal the lobby in a state of chaos. Guests were herded off to one side, forced to enter and exit through a delivery entrance. Employees moved deftly through the expanse juggling paperwork, overnight bags and luggage carts, and a pair of Miami Dade Police officers were half way through cordoning off the main entrance with bright yellow crime scene tape.

They were silent as they followed the crowd to the side exit, eavesdropping and compiling the fragments of whispered conversations. "I heard she was only fifteen!" one person said.

"Where were her parents?" said another.

As they made their way through the exit, Rich craned his neck one final time to see a familiar man speaking to an officer. "That's that guy!" he whispered to Gwen.

"What?"

By now they were being funneled, shoved into a cinderblock hallway by the mass exodus behind them. "That guy!" he repeated, turning back to her.

"Who?" Gwen said, stumbling over her own suitcase.

Finally, making it to the light of day in the side parking lot, Rich pulled Gwen aside to the relative calm near a Juniper bush. "The father! Of that girl at the pool! The one who was reading my book!"

"What about him?"

"He was talking to the cops in there!"

"Jeeze," she offered, checking her wrist watch, "I wonder what that's all about?"

"I don't know," he said, planting his suitcase in the flowerbed, "but I'm gonna find out."

As he turned to leave, Gwen barked, "Our plane for D.C. leaves in less than two hours!"

"Just stay put!" he yelled as he disappeared around the corner of the hotel.

Gwen followed, torn between stopping Rich and protecting the luggage. He passed a fire truck, a police van and two ambulances as he made his way to the back of the mob that had gathered. As politely as he could, he weaved his way through the crowd, apologizing as he went, until Gwen lost sight of him. She returned to the bags, strapping one over each shoulder and balancing the others in her grasp and headed to the edge of the parking lot in search of a taxi.

A few minutes later, as she stood with the cab driver, Gwen saw Rich emerge from the crowd. His face, in fact his entire body was heavy with grief as he lumbered toward her. Forlorn, hands in his pockets, he was oblivious to the bustle about the parking lot and nearly walked into a car that was circling, looking for a spot. As he grew nearer, Gwen could tell that he had been crying.

"What happened?" she quizzed.

Lowering his gaze and averting eye contact, he shook his head and climbed into the back seat of the taxi. He was silent, staring out the window as Gwen got in and pulled the door shut.

As the taxi sped off onto the highway, Gwen repeated herself, "What happened?"

Without taking his eyes away from the passing scenery, Rich recounted what he had seen. "Once I had gotten to the front of the crowd, I could see they had a blue curtain type thing blocking everything. Every now and then when someone would step in or out of the curtain, you could see inside just enough to see blood all over the cement."

Gwen grimaced as he went on, "There was a lady next to me that had just gotten finished talking to the police so I asked her what happened. She said she saw everything, that the girl just kind of fell out of the sky. Those were her words. Another woman there said she saw the girl jump."

"Oh my God," Gwen consoled.

The driver, listening from the front, shook his head in despair and said in a thick Cuban accent, "This is getting ridiculous."

"How do you mean?" Gwen asked cautiously.

The driver looked at her in the rearview mirror and went on. "Yesterday this happened to two boys and the day before another girl. What's going on around here?"

Rich continued, "Remember I said I saw that guy? The father of the girl that was reading my book?"

"Yeah," she said, "he came to the pool to get her."

"He's the guy. It was his daughter." Rich finally turned to Gwen. "The girl that was reading my book."

Mystified, Gwen was silent, her eyes scanning thin air, as her mind groped for an explanation.

"Gwen," Rich paused and then added, "My book, it was on the ground with her."

"What?"

"I saw them carry it out of the curtain. It was in a big clear plastic bag. It was covered in blood." Rich then fell silent, and stayed that way nearly the entire flight to Washington, D.C.

SIXTEEN

As they crossed over the Arlington Memorial Bridge and entered Washington, their driver lowered the tinted glass that separated him from his passengers. "Excuse me, Ms. Wright. I just got off the phone with Four Seasons security. It seems it was leaked to the press that Mr. Rossi would be staying there and now a rather large crowd has gathered on the street in front of the hotel."

"Hmm," Gwen bit her bottom lip as she quickly volleyed with the ideas in her head.

The driver went on, "There's a couple options you have. We can make arrangements to place you in another hotel. Or, we can have a decoy vehicle used near the front entrance while we use the service entrance. Or, we can exit the vehicle and walk the final block to the hotel, as to not attract undue attention."

"I knew I should've bought that fake mustache back in Milwaukee," Rich chimed.

The immediate decision facing her briefly disintegrated, relieved that Rich had finally regained a bit of his humor. She had begun to rely on his wit and upbeat temperament to pull her through her bouts of homesickness, and had sorely missed it over the past few hours.

With renewed enthusiasm for her vow to enjoy this experience, Gwen sat up and poked her head through the opening that led to the front seat. "Can't we just plow them all down?"

She turned back, checking for Rich's reaction.

"Yes. I'm laughing," he said and pointed to his chest, "in here."

"Believe me, Ma'am," the driver quipped, "nothing would give me more pleasure."

"What do you normally do?" Rich asked.

"It depends, Sir. If I'm delivering a politician or business exec, we usually go through the back. But it's usually all prearranged. If it's a celebrity, we usually just go right up to the front door. They like the photo ops."

"Well," Gwen surmised, "if a crowd is there because of the press, then the press should be there too." She turned back to Rich. "Let's just go through the front. You'll sign some autographs, get your picture in the paper. It can't hurt."

Rich shrugged in agreement. The order was given and they proceeded up the Rock Creek Parkway.

Traffic went from heavy, to gridlock as they forged their way up Pennsylvania Avenue. The cause soon became apparent as they inched their way closer to the hoard of people that had overflowed onto the street in front of the hotel.   Rich and Gwen sat upright and peered over the driver's shoulder. "Will there still be security if we go in the front?" Gwen asked.

"Oh, absolutely," the driver assured. "It usually looks a lot worse than it really is. They'll have people keeping things in line. The worst part of it to me is all the noise."

"God, I feel like a rock star," Rich croaked and then nervously cleared his throat.

As they merged into the valet lane, the thunderous roar of screaming teenagers rumbled through the tinted glass. Flashes from paparazzi cameras riddled the limo as it came to a stop just in front of the lobby entrance.

While Rich sat dumbfounded in awe, Gwen, feeling slightly intimidated, muttered, "This is bigger than I had imagined."

The driver gave instructions. "Don't worry. Here's how it'll go. I will get out and open the door for you. Ms. Wright, I will escort you out of the vehicle first, and then close the door. You will head straight up between those barriers and get inside as quickly as you can. Stay in the center of the walkway. Mr. Rossi, I'll open the door again after Ms. Wright has securely entered the building. You will follow the same path as Ms. Wright. It's your prerogative if you want to stop and sign autographs or let them take your picture, but when I take your left arm and pull you toward the door, you need to stop what you're doing and come along. I'll be standing directly behind and to your left the entire time. Are there any questions?"

Like plebes readying for battle, Rich and Gwen nodded in unison, silently memorizing the instructions.

"Here we go," the driver ordered and hopped out of the car.

A second later the back door was flung open and Gwen stepped out and into the deafening throng. Keeping her head down, and steering herself up the center of the walkway, she made it to the revolving door without incident.

On cue, the driver again opened the limo door. As Rich stepped out his senses were bombarded with screams, howls, flashbulbs and marriage proposals. Hands reached out holding pens and copies of his book as he reluctantly moved up the walkway, prodded along by the limo driver. He smiled as he moved along, embarrassed by the attention. Before very many steps though, he raised his head and stopped. With that simple gesture, the crowd exploded into cheers. He moved to one side of the walkway and took a pen and a book from a young girl. As he leaned in to ask the girl her name, he was immediately pulled back by the driver. She shouted to him, but her words were lost in the cacophony surrounding them. Hurriedly, he scribbled his name inside the front cover and handed it back to her.

As Gwen and other onlookers watched from the safety of the lobby, her cell phone rang. The caller ID indicated that Volos was on the other end of the line.

"Hello?" she said, stiffening up and stepping away from the window.

"Ms. Wright? How are things going ?" he growled, daring her to give the wrong answer.

"Oh, Mr. Volos, things are going fine. We should be wrapping up our tour in a few days," she answered.

"Good. You'll be happy to know that things on my end are working according to plan as well. I've been following your progress and have to say that I think you are doing a wonderful job. He's been either in print or on air in nearly every major market in the country. Fine job, Ms. Wright. You're in the home stretch now."

For a moment, she was speechless. Praise, in fact a compliment in any form was a rare commodity from Volos. For the first time since he had promised to let her out of her contract, she was beginning to see a light at the end of her tunnel.

But her morsel of reprieve was short lived as Volos spoke again. "But we're not finished yet," he warned, "so don't fuck it up."

With that, the line went silent. She flipped her phone shut and sank into the arms of a nearby chair.

The following morning, Rich and Gwen discussed the day's itinerary over breakfast. As the waitress refilled their coffees and removed their dishes, Gwen opened up her day planner and perused her notes. "11 AM," she began, "you'll be accepting a debut author's achievement award at the Press Club." She unfolded a sheet of paper and passed it to Rich. "Here's the acceptance speech you'll be reading."

Rich scanned the lines as Gwen went on. "At 2:30..."

"Wait," Rich interrupted. "Why do I have to read this? Can't I just say a nice thank you and a few words off the cuff?"

Gwen dropped her pen onto the table, crossed her arms and sat back in her chair. "Really?" she mocked.

"Well," he paused, "why not?"

"Really?" she repeated.

He was silent, taken aback by a menacing, sarcastic tone in her voice that he hadn't heard before.

Scolding him, she went on. "Off the cuff? Is that how you think all this has happened these last few weeks?"

Stunned by this unprovoked visit to the woodshed, Rich kept quiet, fearing the unknown.

She leaned in, placing her elbows on the table. "Do you think for one minute that any of this has happened by accident? Off the cuff?"

He opened his mouth to speak but was handily muted by her. "Everything!" she continued, "Every goddam minute! Every step! Every trip! Every reservation! Every interview and publicity stunt has been scripted and choreographed down to the last goddam blink of your eyes!" She retrieved her pen, sipped her coffee and added, "So, no. You will not be saying or doing anything, off the cuff. Not this close to the end."

Rich was completely nonplussed. In the weeks since they had begun travelling together, he had only seen the pleasant, mothering, nurturing side of her. Sure, she seemed a little uptight now and then, but he understood that she had a lot on her plate. Logistically, he thought, this whole junket had to be a scheduling nightmare, yet she had never complained. Not once. The interviews, the people and places she had to have known, nothing would have been possible without her. On top of that, he pondered, it can't have been easy putting up with all of his immaturity and impulsiveness. Had he thanked her enough? Had he taken her for granted? Had he once ever stopped to buy her a little trinket from one of their stops?

Feeling foolish and guilty, he kept silent. But his nature wouldn't let him stay that way for long. He couldn't allow the day to pass with even the slightest hint of animosity. So as they were leaving the dining room he spoke, "Gwen," he paused. "Gwen, I'm sorry."

They stopped in the middle of the lobby. Gwen stared at the tile floor as Rich went on, "I think I've taken for granted how hard you've worked on this."

She raised her head to speak, but this time was shushed.

Rich continued, "No, now you listen."

They took a seat across from each in a pair of orange velvet wingback chairs other under a television screen. "Here's the thing. I know I'm crazy and impulsive and sometimes even reckless in my life. I've always been that way." He leaned in and took her hand. "I've just always been about keeping things light. I mean, the world can be an ugly, unfamiliar, lonely place, and I guess I just do what I gotta do to keep sane and happy."

His eyes began to well with tears, "I never meant to be flip about your work and I promise you, I do know and appreciate everything you've done. There would be no *Keeper of the Key* without you."

"I guess..." she started.

"Not done yet," he smiled.

As did she.

"Just know that I respect you for everything you've done for me. Mr. Volos should be very proud. He's gonna miss you when you retire. Although I still think you're too young and talented to retire."

"Is that it?" she asked.

He nodded.

"See, Rich," she offered, "He's got me by the short ones right now. And if I don't come through for him, I'm screwed."

"You never told me how you came to work for him in the first place. It was right after your husband split, right?"

There was silence, then Rich added, "Never mind. It's none of my business.

"One of these days, you and I will have a good long conversation about Mr. Volos," she promised.

As they stood and hugged, a single word from the television hanging above their heads caught their attention, "...suicide."

They turned their attention to the screen and listened as Sandy Manning reported, "...among children sixteen and under. The National Institute of Health in Bethesda, Maryland, in cooperation with the CDC in Atlanta, have confirmed an apparent spate of suicides throughout the nation. According to early findings, the statistics have crossed every socio-economic divide. While the suicide rate among children between the ages of ten and nineteen was 1,983 total deaths last year, health officials have learned that the number has doubled to nearly four thousand in just the last four weeks alone.

"In other news, the National Zoo is welcoming..."

Rich and Gwen turned to one another and shared a puzzled gaze. Rich broke the silence. "That cab driver in Miami was right. Something really is going on."

Gwen returned to her chair. "I'm gonna call home."

"Good idea. Me too," Rich dug his cell phone from his pocket and headed for the revolving door and onto the street where he could smoke.

A true multi-tasker, he had his cigarette lit and the number dialed before even hitting the street. As he waited and puffed, he noted how calm and desolate the front of the building was compared to yesterday.

Finally, Rachel answered, "Hi! How is everything?"

"Hi Sis. Everything's good. I just wanted to check in. How's Tommy?"

"Oh he's fine. He's off school today. I promised I'd take him to Liberty Science Center. I've been following you all over the place on the internet. You ought to be a millionaire by now, the way they're talking. You sold a lot of books!"

Listening to her ramble sent a warm and reassuring wave through him. For an instant, her voice resembled that of his mother's, and everything once again seemed right. He wanted so to bask in the comfort of her words, to selfishly wrap himself up with what little familial love came his way. But the eerie tide of events crept back in, reminding him of the actual purpose for the call.

"Rachel," he began, "have you been watching the news?"

"Of course," she said in an almost indignant tone.

"Have they said anything there about kids and suicide?"

"Oh, yeah!" she said. "It's all over the news! Kids have been killing themselves! What's up with that?"

"Has anything ever been said about your neighbor? That boy, what was his name?"

"Marty," she replied.

"Did you ever find out what was going on? I mean, was he depressed or something?"

"I never heard anything else," she said. "But he liked your book."

"He read it?"

"Yeah," she offered. "Yesterday afternoon, I was talking to Tommy, just making sure he was okay. And he told me that Marcus' father had bought him your book, and that Marcus wanted to get your autograph."

For a brief moment, Rich wished he hadn't placed the call. More uneasy than ever, his mind flashed back to the scene in front of the hotel in Miami yesterday, and the blood spattered copy of his novel being carried away in a plastic bag marked, evidence. He pondered for an agonizing instant the possible connection between Marcus, the girl from Miami and *The Keeper of the Key*.

"Are you there?" Rachel said, interrupting his torment.

"Yeah. So, where's Tommy?"

"He's getting dressed. Hold on."

While he waited for his nephew to come to the phone, Rich strolled to the sidewalk next to the street. He deliberated, then dismissed the notion of his book being linked to suicides. An idea that ridiculous might end up as a movie of the week, he imagined, but not in real life. Still however, the unprecedented and unusual ending that Volos had incorporated into his book gnawed at him in some remote place in his gut.

"Hi, Uncle Rich!" piped Tommy from the other end of the line.

"Hey, little dude! How you doing?"

"I'm dying, Uncle Rich. I'm just dying!"

Not funny, Rich thought, but instead asked, "Is it that nasty tumor of yours acting up?"

"Ha ha. No!" Tommy snapped. "I'm counting the hours until this Saturday!"

"What's this Saturday?"

"I finally get my book back!"

"What happened?" Rich quizzed.

"So you're so famous now you can't even remember the plight of your only nephew?"

"Refresh me," Rich commanded.

"Remember? I left it at the cabin?"

"Oh, yeah!" Rich recalled. "Weren't you supposed to get it back by now?"

"Yeah, but my dad hasn't been able to get over here. It's been sitting in the back of his truck all this time!"

"You know, I could've just sent you a new one. Or God forbid your mother go get you a new one."

"It wouldn't be the same. I want to finish the one I started. The one you autographed for me."

"Aw," Rich sighed, marveling at the young boy's sentimentality.

"My two friends from school, Roscoe and Vaughn are both reading it. They're both about half way through it. I keep telling them I don't want to hear about it, but they insist on giving me little hints about what's happening. I'm going nuts I tell ya!"

"Well, hang in there, buddy," Rich consoled, "Saturday is only three days away."

Tommy whispered into the phone, "Mom thinks that taking me to the science center will get my mind off of it. But it won't. Roscoe and Vaughn are both home reading your book, while I gotta go look at exhibits about kites and gravity and stuff like that."

"You gotta chill, little dude," Rich said. "Just go have some fun and stop being such a worry wart."

"You know," Tommy went on, "we've had two days off of school. When I go back tomorrow, Roscoe and Vaughn are gonna be spilling their guts! I just know they're gonna ruin it for me!"

"Punch them in the throat if they start," Rich concluded. "Now, put your mom back on the phone. And go have fun! You're thirteen for God's sake!"

Rachel returned to the phone and the two wrapped up their conversation.

Meanwhile, Gwen sat under the television screen in the lobby, consoling her daughter.

"It's a gorgeous day! It'll be good to get out," she said.

"But I only have one more chapter! I literally have twenty-nine more pages to read!" Casey countered.

"Jesus, Casey. Take the goddam book to the park with you! Finish it while they're setting everything out."

"They're not gonna let me bring it!" she moaned.

"Put your grandmother on the phone."

As Gwen awaited her mother's voice, Rich rejoined her in the lobby, sitting and watching the news.

"Mom? Mom, just let her take the effing book," covering the phone and whispering to Rich, "no offense." Then, returning to her mother, "She has one more chapter. Just let her finish it while you guys set up the picnic. I don't know what else to tell you."

"Gwenny," Mother said, "I think it boils down to a lack of discipline. I know you feel guilty punishing her, but she's just a normal child now and..."

"Mom, I don't need to have this goddam conversation now. I'll be home soon and then I'll beat her ass. Is that okay?"

Flustered, her mother ended the conversation with, "Jesus Christ, Gwendolyn, I don't know where you ever got that fowl mouth of yours," then hung up the phone.

She sat for a moment, silent, then sighed to Rich, "What the fuck is the big deal about this goddam book?"

As they stood and headed for the exit, Gwen laughed out loud, "Well, I guess when we said we were gonna cram this book down the throat of every kid in America, we meant it!"

They emerged into the bright morning sunlight, squinting as they absorbed the picture perfect weather. Then, like Dorothy and the scarecrow hoofing it to Oz, they linked arms and strolled the mile or so down Pennsylvania Avenue to the National Press Club.

∞

SEVENTEEN

Back on the Upper East Side of Manhattan, Casey, flanked by her grandparents walked the three blocks from their apartment to the river's edge at Carl Schurz Park. Saddled with a blanket, a basket and a cooler, the three made their way down 85th Street to a shady spot a dozen or so yards from Gracie Mansion.

Casey found that, like always, her mother had been right. It was a gorgeous day. There was really no other single word to use but, gorgeous. From the fragrance of the mountains of Petunias that lined the pathways, to the lighter than normal traffic, she couldn't remember a day more, gorgeous.

What had started out as a contentious morning, complete with the great book debate among her grandparents, and an old fashioned cussing out by her mother, suddenly began to show the promise of a memorable afternoon. Casey actually caught herself humming as they cleared a place on the grass and spread out the blanket. Still though, she was chomping at the bit for ten minutes alone with her book. As she set about smoothing out the blanket on a level patch of grass, she spied out of the corner of her eye an empty bench next to the railing above the river.

Her grandparents were not fools. They knew that in a young girl's mind every moment spent away from her passion was like an eternity. That there would be no rest, and she would find no contentment until she had completed her book. So, impressed by Casey's self control and sacrifice for the sake of the family picnic, her grandmother proposed, "Casey, honey, why don't you go and finish your last chapter while Pop Pop and I get lunch set up." Then turning to her husband, "Besides, Edgar, you need to run to the corner and get some diet soda."

Casey didn't need to be told twice. Before her grandfather could check his wallet for some cash, she was gone, clutching her book and skipping onto the glaring white cement sidewalk.

"Stay where I can see you!" her grandmother shouted.

Without turning, Casey waved in acknowledgement, then took her spot on the bench that faced the East River, the Roosevelt Island Lighthouse and Astoria Queens just beyond. She sat for a while, drinking in the view, savoring the moment. It had been a long time since she had been outside, alone. It made no difference to her that her grandmother was only fifty yards away. To Casey, she might as well be fifty miles away. This was freedom at its best. The river mist, the hum of the traffic on the highway beneath the park, a bench all to herself and *The Keeper of the Key* tucked safely under her right thigh, she considered that perhaps this utopia was a reward for putting forth the effort it took to love her grandparents.

As she opened the book, the world around her ceased to exist. The tour boats on the river, the joggers that passed behind her, the gaggle of mothers with their strollers, all vanished from her conscience. Finally, she was able to escape into the world from which she had been so rudely interrupted.

Alma leaned back on her elbows watching Casey, waiting for her husband to return. And while the shouting, honking horns and sirens, typical sounds of the city, all persisted, they could not keep her from finding peace upon the sun dappled blanket. She closed her eyes for a moment and let the late spring breeze tickle her arms, legs and face, and quietly praised herself for making today a success.

Soon though, the shouting, the honking and the sirens prevailed and she opened her eyes to find random park goers racing from the river's promenade, past her toward East End Avenue. She sat up and instinctively glanced in the direction of Casey's bench. Finding her granddaughter safe and unfazed, she stood and watched as more and more people scrambled up the incline and disappeared onto the street. The approaching sirens became louder until an army of emergency vehicles had descended upon the corner of East End Avenue and 87th Street.

Just then, a figure moving in the opposite direction of the crowd emerged from over the incline. It was Edgar, and he was carrying a white plastic bag, stretched to capacity by a two liter bottle of Diet Cola.

Alma headed toward him and shouted, "What's going on?"

He said nothing, shaking his head in despair.

As he grew nearer, she repeated herself, "Edgar! What's happened?"

When he made his way to the blanket, Alma could see that he was in tears. "Honey?"

He shook his head once more, wiped his eyes and took a seat atop the cooler. "Another kid," he whimpered.

"What?" she insisted.

He unscrewed the bottle and poured some soda into a cup. "Another kid jumped."

"Oh my God," she muttered, sinking to her knees next to her husband.

"It happened right there on the corner," he added, pointing toward the street behind them.

Together, they raised their heads to check on Casey and found her standing stoically at the railing, her face still buried in the pages of her book.

"We ought to get her home," Edgar said, taking to his feet and moving toward Casey.

"No!" Alma cried, following and grabbing his arm. "Leave her have some normalcy! Look at her!"

they both stopped. "She's completely okay. Let's just let her be."

They returned to the blanket and sat, brooding silently over another teen suicide.

As Alma set about unpacking the picnic basket, Edgar unfolded his lawn chair and his newspaper and leafed through the pages. "Look. Right here," he said from behind the paper. Reading an article, he went on, "Suicide rate reaches epidemic proportions."

Alma listened as she set out the paper plates, napkins and plastic forks.

He folded back the pages and continued reading. "Health officials reported today that the national spike in teen suicides has reached unprecedented levels. Where the national yearly average of teen suicides normally remains 9.1 per 100,000, or approximately 1900, a startling new report shows that last month alone saw over 5,000 suicides by children between the ages of ten and nineteen.

"Robert Meade of the Center for Disease Control and Prevention in Atlanta said today that, 'barring any outrageous miscalculation in the formulary, this outbreak of adolescent suicide is a damned scary thing.'

"He went on to say that it is important to pay attention to the common warning signs of teen suicide. They are, changes in eating and sleeping patterns, an obsession with death, dramatic changes in personality or appearance, poems, drawings or essays dealing with death, severe drop on school performance and giving away belongings. He goes on to say that four out of five teens that have attempted suicide have given clear warnings. For more information," Edgar's tone changed, "yada, yada, yada."

He folded the paper and went on, "Well, we certainly don't have anything to worry about with Casey. Her grades are great. She's always very happy..."

Alma interrupted him, "And she's never given anything away."

They shared a healthy laugh, almost inappropriate for what was going on one hundred yards away back on East End Avenue. Realizing, they stifled themselves.

"Well, everything's ready here. Run and go get Casey, will you?" Alma asked.

Edgar stood and peered into the distance toward the water. Noticing an empty bench, he pointed and asked, "Wasn't she right there?"

"Dam it. She probably went up the block to see what all the commotion was. I'll go up and look for her. You go see if maybe she's on a different bench."

They split up, Alma heading up the incline toward the throng of onlookers on East End Avenue and Edgar down toward the desolate footpath at the river's edge.

What they didn't realize was that, as Edgar was reading and Alma was arranging the place settings, and they were both discussing how well-adjusted their granddaughter was, Casey had departed this world.

Already hypnotized past the point of no return, walking in the shoes and seeing through the eyes of Cassandra, confident in the teachings of the hag, Neltha, she had climbed the railing and leapt into the East River. Her imaginary friend, Billy held her hand the entire five story plunge, over the edge, past the stream of traffic on the FDR and into the muddy filth.

Twenty minutes into their search for Casey, Edgar and Alma met and separated half a dozen times. They would retrace one another's steps, calling out to her as they went, then meet back at the blanket. They approached strangers for clues, and even resorted to checking beneath bushes. But as forty-five minutes grew into an hour, concern turned to panic, then to dread. At one point, hoping that Casey may have returned home, Alma stood vigil at the blanket while Edgar ran as best he could back to the apartment.

By the time an hour had elapsed into three, Edgar and Alma helplessly notified law enforcement of their granddaughter's disappearance. And by six that evening they were sitting together on their sofa, wringing their hands and being interviewed by police.

"And no one on the boardwalk reported anything?" quizzed Officer Handler.

They shook their heads in unison as Alma added, "Everyone had either gone up over the hill to see the commotion, or was staring in that general direction."

"And you say she was sitting alone the whole time?"

"Yes. Except the last time I looked down at her, she was standing at the railing."

"What was she doing? I mean, was she just standing there? Or was she talking with anyone? Staring into the water? What?"

"Reading," Alma said. "Just standing there, reading." She turned to Edgar, "We've got to call Gwen."

"And who is Gwen," asked Officer Handler.

"Our daughter," Edgar said. "Casey's mom."

"That's your call, folks, but in the vast majority of these cases, it turns out that the child has just wandered off. They usually come home before nightfall." Handler closed his note pad and reached into his breast pocket, retrieving a business card. "You folks call me if you think of anything else."

"That's it?" Edgar mused.

"Well," Handler added, "we'll be passing along copies of the photo you gave me. At this point we just start looking for her."

Edgar stood and saw Handler to the door.

As he left, he added, "There'll be an officer up shortly to wire your phone for any incoming calls you might receive."

Alma stood and moved toward them, "You think she could have been," she choked, cautious to used the right word, then continued, "taken?"

"Ma'am," Handler consoled, "We just want to cover all our bases. I'll be in touch with any updates.

You folks just try not to worry too much. The department takes these cases very seriously."

"Thank you, Officer," Edgar said as he closed the front door.

When nothing had transpired by eight o'clock, Alma and Edgar resolved to make the call to Gwen. With more fear, trepidation and courage than they had ever known, they sat together at the kitchen table, holding hands and staring at the phone. Then, Alma dialed.

EIGHTEEN

The first thing Casey noticed when she regained consciousness was an incredible fluidity to the way her body moved. It had been many years since she had experienced even a single moment that did not include stiffness in her joints or tenderness in her muscles. Her fight with Batten's had left her in a constant state of discomfort. Mild though it might have been, its absence at this moment was still quite striking. Like a newly oiled tin man, she stood for a moment, stretching her arms, twisting her spine, bending and squatting, all the while marveling at her renewed mobility.

While she knew she was awake and alive, her vision seemed to fail her, for pitch darkness surrounded her. She could tell that her sense of touch remained intact because she could feel herself standing. Beyond that, she found herself relying primarily on the smells and the sounds that abounded. She took a step forward in an effort to distance herself from a damp, rotting odor, and groped her way toward the distant sound of machinery. Completely blind, she reached out hoping to touch something, anything that might orient her to this unfamiliar territory.

Years seemed to pass until finally her right hand came in contact with something. A wall, she guessed. And although it was jagged and razor sharp, she used it as her guide, slicing her fingers and hands as she fumbled her way along. Each step she took brought another stinging tear into her flesh until she could feel the blood trickling down her arms. The floor, once smooth and cool, became progressively rocky, and as it buckled beneath her she realized that she was indeed barefoot.

As the monotonous thudding, grinding and scraping sound of a factory in full swing grew nearer, the prickly sharp walls on either side of her narrowed into a corridor. Pushing forward, she bumped her head on the craggy ceiling, slicing a nasty gash at her hairline. In her mind's eye she imagined herself growing, filling up the passageway with her ever thickening body. Actually, the opening was tapering to a barely passable gap. Yet for reasons she could not understand, she was compelled to soldier forward, tripping, climbing and crawling over and through the flesh-eating pumice. Mangled and soaking in her own sweat and blood, she pushed on toward the machine. Somehow she knew that it held the answer as to her whereabouts, but also hoped that it meant she was not alone. Soon, the opening was no larger than a tire swing, yet she pressed on.

Finally, when she could go no further and the mechanical grinding was almost in reach, a burning hot blast of wind pierced a crack in the rocks before her. As her face and shoulders scorched, she could finally begin to perceive a hint of light beyond the narrow tunnel. As she squinted and tried to focus, she saw the outline of a person, a man, only feet away. With the sting of sweat burning her eyes, she peered with all her might and was finally able to make out the man's face.

As if knowing she could see him, he welcomed her. "Hello, Casey," he growled.

Somewhat astonished, she replied, "Mr. Volos?"

"Ah, you do remember me." He reached out to her and at that very moment, the spiky donut hole dilated, shredding her clothes as it opened.

She stumbled to her feet and fell forward onto a markedly smoother surface. "What are you doing here?" She asked.

"I live here," he answered then asked, "What are you doing here?"

She thought for a moment, examining her surroundings, her bloody arms and her tattered clothes. "I'm not sure," she puzzled. "Where am I?"

Volos chuckled and took her hand. "Come with me, Child," he ordered as he led the way.

They walked for what seemed like days, passing aisle after aisle of humongous industrial machinery. The sound was deafening. Each gigantic cog, rocker arm, press and belt, sang their own horrific tune, creating a miserable, discordant symphony. As they passed, she marveled at the workings. The stainless steel, chomping and pounding, glistened from stem to stern with a sticky goo, some byproduct of the operation, she thought.

Turning her head to the right as they marched forward, she noticed a wall that, like a surrealist's painting, seemed to go on to infinity. And along the wall, doors labeled, Staff Only were spaced about every ten feet or so, until they too disappeared into the distance.

As her feet began to throb, Volos, as if on cue, reached for a doorknob and escorted Casey inside. He closed the door behind them, muffling the noise from the clamoring factory, and motioned for her to sit.

"Wait here," he said, then disappeared behind another door.

Now convinced she was dreaming, Casey sat quietly on a metal chair in what appeared to be a waiting room. Outfitted with only a few chairs and a coffee table, there were windows on the walls that separated her from a multitude of identical rooms. As she stretched to see above the window frame, she saw a boy waiting next door. Beyond him, through another large pane of glass, sat a girl. Beyond her, yet another girl. She turned and crossed to the window on the opposite wall and found the same thing, children sitting alone in rooms that stretched as far as the eye could see. Puzzled as she was, she was comforted by their presence and returned to her seat.

She waited. And waited, until months seemed to pass. And as the tepid simmer of boredom started to boil into a seething caldron of frustration and anxiety, a loud clank reverberated throughout and the back door of the room swung open. A woman's voice that came from nowhere in particular announced, "Step forward."

As she approached the opened door, she glanced from side to side and noticed the children in the other rooms following suit. They too were watching each other, waiting for someone to exit first. Finally, as if compelled by a concert master, they all took a giant step through the door and were left standing in a dark and cavernous room. A boy about ten feet down, cried out, but before she could turn her head to see from where the protest came, the boy evaporated into a cloud of powder and smoke, leaving only a pair of charred blue jeans in a dusty heap. Casey and the others knew then and there to keep their mouths shut and to comply.

Before each child lay stamped on the floor an arrow that seemed to glow and pulsate in the darkness. Their instincts compelled them to march forward, following the arrows that seemed to converge until the children came to stop in a single line.

The disembodied female voice announced, "Turn left."

Without so much as a murmur, every child, nearly a thousand in number, turned.

"Go forward," the voice commanded.

And they did. Like recruits in basic training, they marched forward, following the child in front of them. As they snaked their way through the darkness, they passed a sign, lit by the same pulsating glow as the arrows in the floor. It heralded, "Children should be seen and not heard," in an ancient, fading text.

What felt like miles later, they came to another road sign, this one in yellow print on a blue background. It said, "Youth is a wonderful thing. What a crime to waste it on children. George Bernard Shaw." Still another quipped, "A child is a curly, dimpled lunatic. Ralph Waldo Emerson."

One by one the procession moved forward until they eventually came to an entryway, above which a final billboard displayed, "He alone, who owns the youth, gains the future. Adolf Hitler."

Now in the complete pitch of darkness, the children reached for one another, grasping a blouse, a belt, or a sleeve of the one in front of them. Confident that she was now immersed in an unbelievable hallucination, Casey had no particular fear. Likewise, the other children marveled more than dreaded their state. As she continued on though, Casey began to hear the faint sound of screaming echoing throughout. And as trepidation teased and flirted, testing her wonder, a willing sport of follow the leader turned quickly into a compulsory march into certain doom.

As the shrieks of terror grew louder, surging from somewhere before her, the once orderly single file of obedient children became a crush of panic and desperation. Without so much as a glint of light, she could only imagine what lie ahead, and the closer she got to the source of the horror, the more deafening the cries became.

In concert, panic struck the children as they neared their unseen destiny. Now prodded instead of willingly moving forward, she caught wind of an odor that had lingered in her memory. With the melee of terror getting closer and closer, she recognized the smell from her childhood, when her family lived in a one bedroom apartment above a butcher shop on East 105th Street. Regularly, the sweet and dank smell of freshly sawn beef, pork and poultry would waft upward through the apartment's ventilation system.

Suddenly a bolt of dread ran up her spine, but before she could turn to fight her way back through the onslaught, the ground fell out from under her. She clawed at the shirt of someone next to her, only to tear away a handful of cloth that she carried downward with her. As she descended, her screams, once unique and wholly her own, melded with those of the dozens of children that tumbled along with her, creating a concerto of misery and fright.

Finally, she landed on a cushion of squirming bodies that had fallen before her, and was soon pummeled from above by those that came afterward. They scrambled and writhed in a twisted mass of flesh, all the while being funneled downward. As the bodies continued to fall, their weight and volume crushed down from above, muffling the shrieks of the children who had yet to land. And the sound of screaming was now replaced by a mechanical, churning hum. Now, nearly suffocating from the weight, and moving still downward, she felt the sting of metal as it tore through her flesh. It clawed and diced its way, pulling her in to the workings of a giant shredder, mixing and pureeing her body parts with those of the other fallen.

Yet she was not dead. While somehow disconnected from her body, her soul watched in agony as her remains, now a mangled pile of ground meat, moved unceremoniously up a conveyor belt and disappeared into a smoking metal hopper. Her essence traveled along, all the while hovering beside the vestiges of her physical self. She floated in disbelief, watching as her former self landed on a stainless steel platform where it was compressed and sent along. With every pass from one conveyance to another, pounded, extruded, and molded, her soul quaked with excruciating pain.

Finally, after nearly a thousand days of torturous suffering, her soul and her body parted company. Her remnants issued forth from a final conveyor belt and splattered into a shiny, bloody ditch, drifting away with countless other wads of shredded sinew. Like a ball of household dust, her soul, on the other hand, was sucked into an overhead tube, transported to another room and promptly collected in a tiny, vacuum sealed tube.

From inside her glass cocoon, she watched helplessly as she was categorized, sorted and labeled.

With giant hands, faceless workers shuffled untold numbers of glass tubes from one side of a sterile white table to another. Carefully, they counted and stacked the vials, placing them in perfect order, to be inventoried and finally displayed. There, her purified soul would wait, to be called on when needed.

Ω

NINETEEN

Rich and Gwen had had a long day. After accepting his award from the National Press Club and mingling with writers far more notable and talented than himself, Rich followed Gwen's cues to wrap up lunch and move on. The next stop had been a reading of excerpts for a fieldtrip group of elementary school children at the Library of Congress. There, suffering from a combination of street vendor hotdogs and the miserable heat of the summer afternoon, a boy of six handily vomited all over Rich's brand new Bruno Magli shoes. After that, an interview taping for a local Washington, DC, Fox affiliate, then another book signing, this one at the famed Kramerbooks and Afterwards. Happily, though, after a quick dinner, they made it back to the hotel by 6:30. An hour and a half later, Rich was fast asleep, and down the hall in her own room, Gwen was just stepping out of the shower when the call came from her parents.

"Hi, Mom," she said after checking the caller ID.

"Honey," Alma began, and then paused.

Instantaneously, Gwen knew by the tone of her mother's voice that there was a problem.

"What's wrong, Mom?"

Alma immediately began to sob and then passed the phone to Edgar.

"Honey?" he whimpered. "There's a problem."

Gwen took a seat on the edge of her bed.
"What's wrong? What's going on? Is Casey okay?"

"Gwen," he continued, "we think she might have run away."

"What?" she yelped. "Run away?"

Her mother howling in the background, Gwen listened as her father recounted the events of the past several hours. She was dumbstruck as he detailed the steps that were retraced, the panic they had endured and the reassurances they had been given by the police.

Her mind began to swim with scenarios that only a mother could conceive. She searched her memory and tried to recall whether they had ever had the 'don't talk to strangers' talk, and now cursed herself for not allowing Casey to have a cell phone. She imagined Casey's father, and the possibility that he had taken her without her knowledge or consent. No, he was a lot of things, she thought, but not a kidnapper, and dreaded having to call him for help. "You've always been a lousy mother," he would say.

"Because of you she got picked up by some rapist! She's probably half way to Texas by now!"

She agonized, trying to remember her conversation with Casey this morning. It hadn't gone well, as she recalled. While she had caved regarding the book, she was terse, and had snapped at her several times. With this memory, Gwen found a tiny sliver of consolation and clung to the hope that Casey had run away, and after teaching everyone a good lesson, would return in a few hours none the worse for wear. But as she peered out of her hotel room window, knowing darkness was only forty-five minutes away, her hope quickly faded.

"Dad. Dad, stop," she demanded. "Let me get off of here and get my things together so I can get home."

"Gwen," he started but was interrupted.

"Dad, write it down so you don't forget it. But right now I'm hanging up so I can get going. I love you." With that, she flipped shut her cell phone and picked up her room phone, dialing Rich.

She began to speak before he could get the phone to his ear. "Rich, I need you to come to my room right away."

He paused for a second, gathering his thoughts then gurgled, "Gwen, I like you and everything, but..."

She broke in, "Don't be an asshole. Just get over here. Something's come up."

"What's going on?"

"I'll tell you when you get here," she snapped, hanging up the phone.

She went about stuffing her dirty clothes into her suitcase, then ran to the bathroom to pack her toiletries.

She came back to the telephone and dialed the concierge. After a few moments, she said, "Yes, this is Gwendolyn Wright in room 718. I'm going to need a car." She paused and then continued, "No, a rental that I can take one way."

Just then Rich knocked. "Hold on," she said into the phone.

She ran to the door and let him in, then returned to the phone. "Sorry. How soon can I have one delivered?"

Puzzled, Rich sat on the edge of her bed and tried to read her expressions.

"Okay," she said, "I'll be down in twenty minutes." She hung up the phone and resumed packing.

"What's going on?" Rich asked.

As she moved about the room, gathering her belongings, she said, "I've got to get home."

"Why? What happened?" he asked, his gaze following her around the room.

She retrieved her day planner from her bag and tossed it to him. "Open it up to tomorrow."

He did.

"There's an address for the Spy Museum. It should say what time you're to be there. The guy's name is right underneath the time. Fred somebody. Then look down the page at 4:30, I think. You have..."

He broke in, slamming the planner shut and tossing it upon the bed as he rose. "What's going on?"

"Seriously, Rich you'll have to do tomorrow and perhaps the rest of the tour without me." She snapped the suitcase shut and flung it onto the bed with her pocket book and overnight bag.

He crossed him arms like a cranky nine year old and huffed, "I'm not doing anything until I know what the fuck is going on! Why do you have to go home? What happened?"

She stopped in her tracks, pushed her wet hair back away from her brow and sighed. "We think Casey might have run away."

"Run away?" he repeated in disbelief.

With nothing more to pack, Gwen returned to busying herself by folding her towel and smoothing the bedspread.

Rich went on, "What happened?"

She ignored him until he grabbed her by the shoulders and demanded, "Why do you think she ran away?"

"I gotta go," she snapped, grabbing her luggage and pushing past him.

As she reached the door, Rich panicked and seized her purse from atop her stack of belongings. He bolted past her and headed down the corridor toward his room, tucking the purse under his arm like a running back, shouting back to her, "Then I'm going too!"

"I need that!" she yelled.

"You'll get it back as soon as I'm done packing! I'll see you downstairs in ten minutes!" With that, he disappeared into his room, the door slamming shut behind him.

Resigning to his insistence, she moved to the elevator and pressed the down button. By the time she had checked them both out and met with the concierge, Rich, bed headed and untied sneakers, had packed and joined her in the lobby. Thirty minutes later they were motoring up New York Avenue. The GPS programmed, and the 7-11 coffee snug inside the cup holders, they settled in for the four hour trip.

Half way between Washington and Baltimore, Gwen's cell phone rang. She pulled to the shoulder of the parkway, threw the car into park and rummaged through her purse. "Hello?"

It was her father on the other end of the line, about to deliver the worst news a mother can get. He had promised himself that he would be strong but when he heard his daughter's voice, his tone eroded into a barely recognizable string of sobs. The exact words that he uttered were unimportant. But the message was clear, Casey was dead.

Gwen dropped the phone, stared straight ahead and clung to the steering wheel, holding on for dear life, sure she would not survive another moment. Her head drooped to one side as her circulatory system betrayed her, sending her blood to her feet. Her hands released their grasp on the wheel and fell into her lap as her loss of consciousness became complete.

Stunned, Rich reached to her and screamed, "Gwen!" But she did not respond. "Gwen!"

He fumbled about the floor just next to the gas pedal and retrieved the cell phone. "Hello?" he begged. But the line had gone dead.

Turning to her, he wedged his knees into the console, crushing the Styrofoam cups full of coffee and pulled her by the collar until she slumped forward. "Gwen!" he howled, shaking her with all his might.

Finally coming to, she stared blankly into his eyes. "Casey!" she wailed.

Easing her back into her seat, he straightened her collar as she began to sob inconsolably. "Gwen! What's going on?" he demanded.

Barely catching her breath she wept, "Casey! Casey is gone! My baby!"

"What did they say?" Rich said, holding her hands in his.

"They found her!" she whimpered as she pulled away from him and reached for the gear shift.

Rich quickly forced her hands away from the controls and grabbed the car keys, turning the engine off. "No," he commanded. "I'm driving."

He pulled the keys from the ignition, opened his door and crossed around to the driver's side of the car. Opening her door, he reached in, unbuckled her seatbelt and heaved her out of the car, walking her around to the passenger side as she sobbed. He bundled her into her seat and buckled her in, then returned to the driver's seat. As the traffic whizzed by, rocking the car as it passed, Rich sat for a moment and collected himself.

While Gwen muttered to herself through her tears, Rich once again took her cell phone, this time redialing the last incoming number. After a few rings, Alma answered, "Honey?"

"Mrs. Cross?" Rich asked.

The woman on the other end of the line sniffled and said, "Yes?"

"This is Richard Rossi. I've been traveling with Gwen for all these weeks."

Alma began to cry and said, "Is she okay?"

"No ma'am. Please, tell me what I can do," Rich begged.

"Ask if she's on the way home," Edgar bawled from the background.

"Is she coming home?" Alma sniffled into the phone.

"Yes, Ma'am. I'm bringing her home now. We're about," checking the GPS on the dashboard, "three and a half hours away."

"Please, Mr. Rossi, please make sure she's okay."

"I will. I promise." He started the car and put it in drive. As he eased his way into the stream of traffic, he asked, "Are you able to tell me what happened?"

With one eye on the road and the other on Gwen, he listened as Alma described the prior few hours. How Edgar had been waiting outside at the front of the building, anticipating Casey to round the corner. She herself had been sitting by the telephone, waiting for it to ring. She told of how hard she had prayed that Casey, or her father, or even a kidnapper demanding a ransom would call, anything that meant Casey was still okay. She recalled how, as she paced from the telephone in the kitchen to the living room window and back again, she never imagined how such a glorious day could end so terribly, and how her hopes and prayers were destroyed when she saw the police car pull up in front of the house just a while ago. How she nearly passed out when the officers reported that Casey's body had been found, washed up on Governor's Island, still clutching her copy of *The Keeper of the Key*. And the most horrible truth, that a surveillance camera at the Roosevelt Island lighthouse had captured video of Casey leaping over the railing.

As he drove on, Rich agonized over the fact that the suicides were getting closer to home. His mind returned once again to the girl in Miami and his bloody book. He couldn't escape the gnawing possibility that somehow, *The Keeper of the Key,* and how Volos had insisted on the twisted new ending were not a coincidence.

Gwen gazed out the window watching the scenery pass by, picking her fingernails, mumbling to herself until Rich flipped shut the cell phone. "This can't be possible," she whimpered. "There's no way. She's just pulling a prank." She looked at Rich and pleaded, "She's always pulling those goddam pranks."

Turning back to the scenery, she repeated, "It's just a prank."

"Gwen," Rich began, but was interrupted.

"I don't want to hear it!" she argued. "Whatever they said, I don't want to hear it! It's just a prank!"

Rich knew this was going to be a long trip, but keeping his eyes on the road, he tried again. "Gwen," he paused and then went on, "it's not a prank."

"What did she tell you?" Gwen snapped, but in the same breath said, "Never mind. I don't want to hear it."

Realizing he was now saddled with the formidable task of relaying the grizzly details to a grieving mother, Rich felt his stomach coil into a knot. He reminded himself how just an hour earlier he had been sound asleep in the downy comfort of his Sleep Number bed, dreaming of a fishing trip he had taken with his father nearly thirty years earlier. And how, once again, the fickle wheel of fortune had taken an ordinary evening and reduced it to a twisted minute that would change everything.

He took a breath, ready to begin again, but stopped and decided to exit the parkway. With an abrupt turn of the steering wheel, they found themselves on a dark suburban road leading to a shopping plaza. Gwen, hardly noticing the change in navigation, made no protest. Within a mile or two they had come to a traffic light, just beyond which was the object of Rich's desire, a liquor store. He pulled into the parking lot, threw it into park, grabbed the keys and headed inside. Within a minute, he had returned with a sleeve of plastic cups and a chilled bottle of vanilla flavored vodka. He tore everything open and promptly poured Gwen a glassful. And she accepted it without question, sipping immediately. A few minutes later they were back on the Baltimore Washington Parkway, speeding northbound.

Fifteen miles later, Gwen had finished her drink and reached into the back seat to retrieve the bottle. "You know," she said, breaking the silence, "Casey always pulls pranks."

Rich smiled and nodded and, keeping his eyes on the road, said nothing. Over the past several weeks of traveling with Gwen he had learned that her introverted personality compelled her to think before she spoke. It had taken years for him to learn to pay attention to such traits, but he was now thankful that he did. So he waited, letting her drink her way to comfort, before engaging her.

Pouring from the bottle, she went on. "When she was about nine, this was before she got sick, we had this pet parakeet." As she twisted the top back onto the bottle, she paused and then went on, What the hell was that bird's name? Oh yeah, Clint."

Rich smiled once again but said nothing.

As she returned the bottle to the floor in the back, she continued, "Can you imagine? A bird named Clint." She chuckled and added, "Anyway, Clint would fly all over the house. In fact, you could leave the windows wide open and it would get loose and fly all around the block and still come home. Can you believe that?"

"Wow," Rich answered.

"Anyway, one night, her father and I were having a few people over. I'm getting everything ready and I get the ice bucket out and find Clint inside! Casey. I'm telling you this is all a prank of hers."

Rich remained silent, hoping all the while that she would fall asleep and stay that way until they reached Manhattan. But it wasn't to be.

"Seriously, though, what did my mother tell you?" Gwen prodded.

Rich sighed and turned on the radio.

She promptly reached over and turned it off. More forcefully now, she pressed, "Really, Rich. What did she say?"

"Well," Rich said, steeling himself, "she said that they found her body."

"See!" Gwen yelped, "That's what they told me! How could they find her body? I'm telling you it's all a joke! What else did she tell you?" She took another gulp of her drink.

With both hands planted firmly on the steering wheel, he began. "Your mom said that ever since this teen suicide thing, the police have been really diligent about anything having to do with kids. So they started looking for a," he paused, swallowed and then went on, "started looking for a body. Her body."

Gwen took another gulp, tightened her jaw and said, "And?"

"They told your folks that they got a hold of a video."

Gwen choked on her vodka, "A video? Of what?"

By now Rich was fighting the overwhelming urge to throw up. But he braced himself and went on. "There's security cameras all along the shore of Roosevelt Island, and supposedly someone there saw her...jump."

"Jump!" Gwen shouted, nearly flying out of her seat. "Jump where? You mean into the river?"

Rich nodded.

All was silent until finally, Gwen spoke up. "They think she did it on purpose?"

He nodded again, secretly begging her to stop asking questions. And for a while, until they were just on the other side of Baltimore, it was quiet. They were both in deep thought, Rich, calculating the odds of his book playing a part, and Gwen trying to wrap her mind around the likelihood that her daughter might actually have killed herself.

By this time Gwen was drunk. But while physically uncoordinated, her mind remained sharp as steel. She mulled over what to do next, then asked, "How do they know it's her? I mean, the body they found. How do they know it's her?"

"I don't know," Rich gave in.

"Did my mom and dad identify her?"

"I'm not sure. I don't think so. From what I gathered, they just found out a few minutes before they called." He paused, a glimmer of hope seeping in. "Do you suppose it really might not be her?"

Gwen returned her gaze to the passing traffic and said, "I don't know, but that's all I got right now."

He couldn't bear the thought of dashing her hopes, but there was more to say. His inner editor struggled to find the right words, but all he could do was say, "There's more."

Gwen snapped back to attention and turned his way.

Rich added, "I'm not saying that it was Casey that they found," he swallowed hard and went on, "but whoever it was, was holding on to a copy of my book."

The words hung inside the car like napalm. Rich, not daring even a glance in her direction, stared forward onto the highway and waited for Gwen to comment.

But she didn't. Now on her third tumbler of vanilla vodka, Gwen sat stoically peeling away the skin on her cuticles. She took this opportunity to quietly reflect on the course of events over the past several days and weeks; The suicide epidemic that seemed to exclusively affect kids, and how it had followed them all over the country. How upon closer inspection, many of the kids had enjoyed Rich's book just before their deaths. How Volos was steadfastly adamant about ending the book with the heroes' suicides. She knew that Volos had something up his sleeve when he tricked Rich into signing on with him, but only now did she begin to suspect what the big secret was.

Now, with the very real likelihood that Casey was gone, and with nearly a quart of vodka coursing through her veins, Gwen's thoughts compelled her to consider that the suicides might be more than just a horrible coincidence.

Likewise, Rich was fixated on many of the same thoughts. As he mulled over the events that had led to his book's success, the changes that Volos had made, the lightening speed of the printing, the seamless ease with which the advertising had been launched, he longed to quiz Gwen about her relationship with Volos, how they met and where he's from.

But he remained quiet, fearing he would insult Gwen's hard work and attention to detail. How could he look a gift horse in the mouth and imply that Volos was up to no good. And what, other than a nibbling in his gut, did he have as evidence? Yes, Volos had wanted, no, insisted on the change to have the main characters commit suicide in the end of the book, but beyond that everything just seemed like an incredible series of chance occurrences.

As he stared blankly onto the highway, he formulated a way to broach the subject of Volos. Finally, as they were crossing the Delaware Memorial Bridge into New Jersey, Rich broke the silence with, "Jesus, I hate these bridges. They're just so high." Realizing how lame that just sounded, he added, "I don't mind bridges in general, but these really high ones give me the creeps."

Gwen must've been ready to explode because as soon as he finished his sentence, she pounced on the subject. "I don't like heights much either," she paused and went on, "I've been thinking of heights."

"Oh?" Rich urged.

"Yeah," she said, frowning and staring out the passenger side window. "If Casey jumped into the East River, it would have only been about five stories from the railing to the water."

"Yeah?" Rich egged.

She turned to him as if he held the key to all wisdom, "Wouldn't someone survive that kind of fall? I mean, into the water?"

There was a clinical air in her tone. One that bespoke of logic and reason, not emotion. Rich shrugged his shoulders and tried to maintain the same detached quality, answering, "Five stories is pretty high up."

"You know," she began, "tonight, before I took my shower, I was reading the Washington Post. They were saying that almost all of the kids that killed themselves did it by jumping. By jumping. Isn't that odd?"

Rich finally found his way in and said, "You know, Gwen, there' something I can't get out of my head."

She turned in her seat and waited. "Yeah?"

"Ever since yesterday morning, in Miami, when I saw my book in that evidence bag, I keep thinking. That girl carried my book to her death."

A tingle of dread zipped up Gwen's spine, but she said nothing.

Rich went on, "And whoever it is that they found on Governor's Island, she was holding my book too." He grabbed a cigarette from the pack in his shirt pocket.

"Give me one of those," Gwen ordered.

"I didn't know you smoked," Rich said as he reached for another cigarette.

"I don't."

"Well, you don't want to start now!" he cautioned.

"If not now, when?" she retorted with a smirk of resignation. As Rich drove on, Gwen lit both cigarettes.

"Here's the thing," Rich carried on, "I think my book is somehow linked to all these kids committing suicide."

Gwen seemed to stare right through him as she said, "How in the world could that be?"

"I just think," he confessed, "that Volos is kind of shady."

"Rich, can I tell you a story?"

"Sure," Rich said nonchalantly.

She reclined her bucket seat a single click, but enough to settle in and began. "I told you how Casey was sick and everything, right?"

"Yeah."

"Well," she hesitated, "I never told you how she got better." She flicked her cigarette butt out the window and reached into Rich's shirt pocket and pulled out the pack.

"I don't think I ever really expressed to you how sick she really was. I mean, by the time she was fourteen, she had been bedridden for almost two years. Oh sure, once a week the nurse would come and we would get her out of bed for the day, but Rich, for two years she couldn't even feed herself. She couldn't even go to the bathroom.

"And I already told you how her father left. What a dick," she slurred. "I was alone! I took care of his father before he died! That was bad enough! But to watch your own child slowly slip away right before your eyes," she stopped and lit another cigarette.

"Anyway, I was out of money. I mean broke. Casey was blind and couldn't even speak." She paused for a second and then confessed, "There were times when I thought of ending her life. And then my own." She whimpered a bit but forged on. "You know, if it was her that they found in the river," she stopped dead.

After a few seconds, Rich looked her way. "Go ahead, I'm listening."

"If it is Casey that they found tonight, that would still be better than the life she had two years ago."

Silence filled the air for a few moments before Gwen went on. She let out a cleansing sigh and said, "Casey had gone through so much. When she first got sick, I can't tell you how many different tests she had to endure. It was so hard to watch her be in pain. Every time they would stick her with a needle or strap her to a table, it just rips your heart out." She poked Rich on the shoulder, "Wait 'til you have kids of your own. You'll know what I'm talking about.

"Anyway, after they finally figured out what it was, and that there was no cure and barely any treatment, I went crazy! I mean, let's see, she was eleven then. And from that point on, I can't tell you how many different things I tried. She was on all sorts of experimental treatments. We tried Human Growth Hormone, something called luko-something or other, they tried some of the HIV medicines. I took her to acupuncture, hypnotists, I even took her to Italy where they were trying some sort of body heating therapy! But nothing worked.

"Then one Saturday morning, Saturdays my mother would come over and hang out while I would go grocery shopping and pay bills, that kind of thing. Anyway, I'll never forget the date. It was the fifth of August. I was at the Laundromat doing some throw rugs, and I overheard these two gay guys talking about one of their friends who had AIDS. They were saying how none of his meds were working anymore and how the guy had been to a faith healer."

She took another long drag off her cigarette and continued, "Anyway, if you'd have asked me five years ago about faith healers I would have laughed in your face. But going through a terminal illness really makes you change your perspective on a lot of things. So I'm eavesdropping and I hear them saying how this guy has made a miraculous recovery.

"I know it sounds stupid. I even look back on it sometimes and it reminds me of some kind of commercial for aspirin or something. I said to them, I couldn't help but overhear, blah, blah, blah, and they were so nice. We talked and talked about Casey and they got my number and said they'd see if their friend would call me. And that was it. I left the Laundromat really hopeful."

She poured herself another cup of vodka. " It's funny how resilient hope is. After years of trying everything under the sun and being disappointed every time, you still let yourself get your hopes up. I just always thought that was an interesting trait of human nature.

"Anyway, a week goes by and I had almost given up hearing from the guy. Then the following Friday, my phone rings and it's him. He couldn't have been nicer, but the whole thing seemed like some kind of a drug deal or something. He was very secretive, very careful what he said. You could tell by the tone of his voice that something shady was going on. But I didn't care. I was willing to try anything. One thing led to another and he gets me in touch with Mr. Volos."

Rich frowned and turned to her. "That's how you met Volos?"

"Yeah," she answered. "Anyway..."

"Wait a second," he injected. "Volos was Casey's faith healer?"

193

"Well," she conceded, "yeah."

Rich glanced into the rearview mirror then quickly turned the wheel to the right steering the car to the shoulder of the road. He threw it into park and turned to her. "Volos is a faith healer?"

Stunned and a little dizzy from the quick juke of the car, Gwen remained silent.

"What the fuck is a faith healer doing publishing my book?" he demanded.

She caught her balance and barked, "Well what do you care? You got the goddam thing published! You're a wealthy man now!"

"That's not the point!" he shouted, then softened, "Gwen, what exactly are his qualifications as a publisher?"

"I don't know!" she shouted, unlatching her seatbelt and bolting out of the car.

"Wait!" Rich opened his door and went after her, a truck horn wailing as it passed inches away. "Goddamit! Gwen!" he shouted as he chased her down an embankment. "Gwen stop!"

When he finally caught up to her, he grabbed and turned her. "Come get back in the car! Look, it's starting to rain!"

As the traffic whizzed by, Gwen shouted, "All I know is Mr. Volos gets the job done!"

"That's right," Rich agreed, guiding her back up to the open car. "Let's just get back inside before it starts to pour."

They stumbled together back up the embankment where he tucked her back into the car and slammed the door shut then returned to the driver's side. They sat for a moment in silence as the raindrops gathered on the windshield.

Finally, Rich broke the tension and lit them both a cigarette. "So," he commenced, "you were saying that you got in touch with Volos. What was that like?"

She sighed and began, "Well, I called his office and a lady answered. It was Veronica. You know Veronica."

"Yeah."

"Well, she worked for him at the time. Anyway," she went on, "I made an appointment and went to his office and he said he needed to meet Casey. So the next night, he came to the house."

She stopped abruptly and clicked her seatbelt shut. Rich took the cue and latched his as well, then eased back into the New Jersey Turnpike traffic.

"So, what did he do? I mean to help Casey," Rich probed.

"Well, we all just sat there for a while and got acquainted, had some tea. Then, he got up and went to Casey's bedside. He looked so weak and frail. I don't know how old he is but, let's just say I was afraid he would fall and break a hip or something."

They chuckled together and Gwen continued, "So he goes to her and sits on her bed with her and takes her hands. He was so gentle with her. It was like he was born to be a nurse or caregiver of some kind.

Anyway, he caressed her forehead and neck and arms. It was like he was just feeling her energy or something. And Casey was so calm. Usually she was really combative around new people but it was like they were old friends or something.

"Then he left. That was it. I mean he didn't even say anything. I mean, he said goodbye, but didn't say one single word about Casey, just that I was to meet him at his office the next afternoon.

"So the next day I went to his office. I thought I was going to see him, but I only saw Veronica. She had," Gwen paused, her internal censor sputtering back to life.

"So?" Rich pressed. "She had what?"

Having gone past the point of no return, Gwen took a deep breath and recommitted to telling her story. "She had a contract for me. Like the one he had for you. Only mine said that I would agree to work for him for two years, or until I proved my loyalty, whichever came first." She grimaced and said, "Sounds like a new car warranty."

"And managing me is proving your loyalty to him?" he asked.

"I guess so, to him it is" she admitted, "because he said that after this book thing is over, I would be released from my agreement."

"So you signed the contract," Rich surmised.

"Yes. And I'm glad I did. Do you know that Casey started to show an improvement within a week? Within a month, she had her vision back. Then her speech. I was elated. After the years of suffering, she was recovering! I mean, I still can't believe it sometimes! It was like a miracle! By her fifteenth birthday she was walking again!"

Rich squinted and tried to cobble together a way that Gwen's story might be connected to his, but all he could come up with was that Volos sounded like a jack of all trades. And a damned good one. He was more convinced than ever that he should stop trying to analyze what was beginning to seem like coincidences, and start being grateful for Volos' abilities. Still, he felt that Gwen was holding something back and try as he might, he couldn't escape his nagging intuition that Volos was somehow a bad person.

Gwen went on, "So, I started working for him the day after I signed the contract. I always thought it was kind of odd that he needed me to sign a paper to work for him. He didn't know, but I would have worked for him for free after what he did for Casey.

"Anyway, Casey was getting better and better, so I didn't look a gift horse in the mouth. He was paying me well and everything seemed hunky dory. But," she hesitated, "I've seen some weird shit while I've worked for him."

"Like what?"

She became silent, contemplating, then instinctively checked over her shoulder before resuming. "It's like he's got eyes in the back of his head. You've heard that expression right?"

"Of course."

"Well," she went on, "It's like he knows everything before everyone else. One night, I had left the office and got all the way to the subway before I realized I had forgotten my bag with my fare card in it. So I went all the way back to the office and used my key to get in. As soon as I got inside, I heard this really strange noise coming from inside his office. I had thought that he had left for the day, so, thinking that someone had broken into his office, I went to his door and listened and I could hear his voice, but I couldn't make out what he was saying. Actually it sounded like a foreign language or something. So I cracked the door open really slowly. And just as I got it opened about a half an inch, one of the hinges squeaked. I only got a split second of a look, but I swear on a stack of Bibles he was floating. But as soon as the squeak happened, I ducked away, grabbed my bag and ran. To this day, I don't know if he knows I saw anything or not."

"Are you sure?" Rich frowned. "You really saw him floating?"

" I know. It seems unbelievable." She shook her head and added, "I don't know. It's just so unbelievable, sometimes I doubt what I really saw. But I wasn't going to make an issue of it. Casey was all that mattered."

Rich remained silent for a while and then finally spoke. "Still, I can't get something out of my head. How does a so-called faith healer get so good at selling books?"

Gwen shook her head and said, "I don't know. I mean, maybe I should ask more questions, but I just feel so indebted to him. I mean, if he knew we were even having this conversation, he would take it as a sign of disloyalty. And I don't want that. What if he undoes all the good he did for Casey? Besides, so what if he is a little shady? So are half the people doing business all over the world."

After a few miles of complete silence, Rich turned to find Gwen sleeping comfortably, her head bobbing in time with the ruts and bumps in the highway. Relieved, he settled in for the remaining hour long drive. Alone with his thoughts he felt foolish for fretting so over Mr. Volos. Like any good businessman, he probably just knows how to get things done. After all, isn't that why we ally ourselves with savvy people?

He struggled to keep his eyes open, cracking the window and chain smoking along the way, until just outside of the city, Gwen's cell phone rang, startling her awake.

She fumbled about the console and grabbed it, flipping it open, "Hello?"

It was her mother on the other end of the line. She spoke unimpeded for several minutes without Gwen getting in a single word. Finally, Gwen said, "Okay," then flipped the phone shut and remained silent.

Gaining a second wind, Rich asked, "Is everything okay?"

Gwen nodded without a sound and lit another cigarette. She opened her window and leaned into the muggy night air. She closed her eyes and turned back inside and said, "Do you mind if we make a stop before heading uptown?"

"Of course not. What's going on? Where are we going?"

She took a deep breath and said, "520 First Avenue."

"In the city?" he asked.

"Yeah."

"What's at 520 First Avenue," he pressed.

Her hands began to shake as she said, "The Medical Examiner's office. They want me to identify the girl they think is Casey."

Ψ

TWENTY

At about the same time Rich was collecting Gwen from the embankment on the New Jersey Turnpike, Volos and Veronica were relaxing in his office, sipping on chilled Absinthe. They had done so on a fairly regular basis since April of 1792 when their acquaintance blossomed into a partnership. It was over a dusty bottle of Absinthe that they had arranged for the employment of Giovanni Bugatti as official executioner for Pope Pius VI. And in 1801, while plotting the assassination of Paul I, Emperor of Russia. In fact, whether planning or celebrating, Absinthe was almost always part of the process, and tonight was no different.

The room was dark, illuminated only by the lamp on the desk and a few bookshelf display lights. They sat across from one another, Volos in his throne-like desk chair and Veronica in her usual leather wingback. As they nipped at their spirits, they reminisced, flirted and delighted in each other's company.

As Gwen and Rich eased back onto the turnpike in South Jersey, back in lower Manhattan Volos continued his story, "To this day, I'll never know where Mary Todd got that acting ability."

They laughed hardily, both nearly choking on their drinks.

Veronica took a good long drag from her cigar and chortled, "And you! With your, Sic semper tyrannis!"

Nearly doubled over in laughter, Volos was scarcely able to say, "Booth! What a mess he was. I told you at the time, there's no way he could do it without the dramatics!"

They snorted and cackled that way for most of the night, sipping their Absinthe and regaling themselves with memories of old acquaintances; Maximilien Robespierre and the delightful Darjeeling tea he had served, Belgium's Leopold II and his Force Publique, and their most beloved, the innocent and naïve, Pol Pot, whom they had met during his college days in Paris.

Volos arose from his chair, his bones cracking in protest, and headed toward the liquor cabinet. "Another for you, my dear?" he asked as he reached for Veronica's empty glass.

"That would be lovely," she said, passing the glass to him. "So, Seth, things working out the way you had planned?"

Pouring the drinks, he answered, "A little too well, I'm afraid."

As she joined him at the liquor cabinet she asked, "How so?"

"Well," Volos began as he returned to his seat, "it's this whole CDC thing."

"CDC?"

"Yes. You know, the Center for Disease Control," he grumbled.

Taking her seat, she consoled, "Oh that's nothing, darling."

"I just don't like all the attention."

"Well," she chuckled, "this isn't like the old days. Back then we could do whatever we wanted, and the rumor and speculation would be neatly turned into facts by the history books. Now, you've got news channels that run twenty-four hours a day, seven days a week."

Volos leaned back in his chair. "I just can't have any of this coming back on me."

Veronica took to the edge of her chair and leaned in. "Darling, how in the world could it possibly come back to you? Anyone who so much as alluded to the idea that those suicides are because of you would be locked up in a mental institution."

She reached out to him across the mammoth desk, took his wrinkled, ashen hand and continued, "In a few weeks all of the hype will have blown over, Rossi's fifteen minutes will have expired and you'll have all the fresh young souls you could ever want."

Sitting back in her chair, she added, "And after all is said and done, I'm sure you'll be handsomely rewarded."

Volos nodded, but said nothing.

Sensing he was not convinced, Veronica went on, "When was the last time you produced for him so much innocence in so little time?"

Volos peered up at her from over his eyeglasses and grinned. "You know," he said sheepishly, "it was an amazing idea. Wasn't it?"

Veronica jumped up from her seat and sprinted around the desk as they both broke into laughter. He turned and welcomed her as she planted herself upon his lap. "You see?" she chirped. "When he read me that story, the first person I thought about was you!"

She leapt up from his lap and nearly pirouetted around the room, her long black hair streaming behind. "You could see it in his face! Hear it in his voice!" She stopped and leaned against the desk. "People like him disgust me. They want their fame and their fortune so badly they'll do anything for it!"

Volos beamed like a proud father as Veronica danced about the room. "He was indeed ripe for the picking," he snorted.

"Yes!" she stopped. Then, marching slowly toward him like the condemned to the gallows, she added, "And you, the way you put your special touch on the story. It's genius! In a million years I would never have dreamt of something so simplistically perfect."

"I just thought..."

"I know what you thought," she interrupted, as she sauntered to one of the gigantic display cases that hung on the wall. She opened a pair of stained glass doors to reveal shelves stacked with dozens of wooden containers about the size of cigar boxes. She reached in and removed a box and peered into its glass front at the miniature clear tubes inside. Tiny puffs of pink, green, blue and gray vapor swirled inside each tube. "What better way to get the purest souls?"

She paused, mesmerized by the hundred or so captives in her hand. " They've all reached the age of accountability, yet they're still so chaste, so untainted."

She returned the box back to its spot in the cupboard then moved on to another cabinet, opening its doors and moving on to yet another, then another marveling at the collection before her. Intoxicated now with unearthly appreciation, she turned back to face Volos. As she meandered toward him, she hiked up her skintight dress, exposing more thigh than any good girl should, then knelt before him and unzipped his old man trousers.

TWENTY ONE

By 1:30 AM, Rich and Gwen were sitting in
their rental car parked in the loading zone in front of
the Medical Examiner's building. While they were
inside, the rain had picked up, until now at its peak,
when they sat motionless, the windows steaming from
the high humidity. Gwen's dark red hair clung matted
over her forehead as the rain trickled down each
strand and mingled with her tears. She held a
crumpled pink tissue under her nose and sniffled
quietly.

Rich had never felt so ill at ease. Speechless
from the sight of Casey's grey, bloated body, his
thoughts darted from one subject to another, partly to
avoid conversation and partly to find something to say.
Turning his attention from the graffiti on the side of a
blue dumpster, to an old woman waiting in the rain for
her poodle to squat, then to a window four stories up
whose curtain rod had fallen half way off, he groped for

anything that might slap him back into reality. For certainly, he thought, this must all be a bad dream.

Gwen too was confused and disoriented. Had she really just watched as a stranger unveiled her daughter's corpse? How could this be? What's next? As she spiraled deeper and deeper into a cavernous pit of emptiness, her sense of loss and loneliness suffocated her soul.

Whimpering into her tissue, she suddenly clutched her chest and began to gasp for air. Her tiny frame heaving like a doomed asthmatic, she fumbled for the door latch and freed herself, crumbling to her knees in a puddle.

Rich bolted from his side of the car and kneeled down onto the glistening wet sidewalk next to her. He said nothing, only holding her tightly while she sobbed. As the storm pelted them from above, passersby scurried along dodging puddles barely taking notice.

Both of them now soaked to the bone, Gwen finally said something audible. "I don't want to go home."

Rich repositioned himself and sat squarely on the ground, his underwear soaking up the rain on the sidewalk. He took her head in his hands and said, "Then, let's go somewhere else."

She looked up at him, more grateful than ever for not being alone. He stared her back in the face, smiled and nodded. "Where do you want to go?"

She managed a smile and said, "Any place dry."

With that, they hoisted one another up, steadied themselves, then stretched. Their clothing, now plastered to their soaking skin, stretched and dripped from the weight of the water.

"Let's go to my house," Rich offered as he tucked Gwen back into the passenger seat.

Minutes later they were crossing the 59th Street Bridge and heading into Astoria. Gwen had caught her breath and had shifted her focus from the gaping maw her life had suddenly become, to the overwhelming impulse to tear off her now freezing wet blouse.

As they shivered along, up 31st Street, Rich chattered, "I've never had to park here before. I wouldn't have the slightest idea where to look."

But after ten minutes of circling the neighboring blocks, they found a spot, gathered their luggage and sprinted through the rain the two blocks to Rich's building. Another half hour later, they were cozy and dry, waiting for the coffee to finish brewing.

Gwen sat curled up on the futon and read from her date book. "You really need to head back to Washington in the morning. If you take the train early enough you can be there in time for the 1:30 at the Spy Museum. You can get the tickets right at Penn Station."

Rich emerged from the kitchen with two cups of steaming coffee. "I think I should stay here and help you with all the running you'll have to do tomorrow." He took a seat next to her.

Taking a mug of coffee, she said, "My father will come with me. I'll be fine."

Rich sighed with disapproval, "I don't feel right leaving you here. I don't feel right going without you."

She smiled and patted his hand, "You're a big boy."

"But what if I can't find the guy?"

"You'll be fine," she affirmed, "How long have we been at this? You know what to do."

They bantered for another fifteen minutes or so until finally, it was settled. Rich would leave the apartment at 7:30 and catch the 8:48 Amtrak Acela. He would fulfill the next three day's worth of commitments and head back home after his Sunday morning interviews.

By 2:30 AM they had retired for the night, Gwen in Rich's bed and Rich on the futon.

Gwen didn't sleep well, and Rich could tell from her pacing in the next room. She leaned onto the windowsill and poked her head out into the muggy city air. Her mind raced with the details of surviving, not only life without Casey, but the next few minutes. And the ones after that. Every second that she outlived her daughter seemed like a year. Every guilt ridden breath she took seemed to tear her heart deeper and deeper.

Her thoughts strayed from choosing a proper outfit for Casey to be buried in, to the image of returning home to find the imprint of her daughter's head in her pillow, her empty shoes in the hallway. Would she now finally get rid of the wheelchair that

209

had been parked in the corner of her living room for the past two years? Should she bother doing a load of Casey's laundry? Can she keep her hands still long enough to get a decent manicure for the funeral? What will life be like to never again have peace?

She peered about the alley beyond the fire escape and, briefly calculating that the fall would not kill her, turned her thoughts to other ways of ending her own life. As she sat on the edge of the bed and stared blankly at the bare stucco walls of Rich's bedroom, she took a mental inventory of her medicine cabinet. A half a box of Pamprin, A bottle of Extra Strength Tylenol and some hair gel, none of which would be serviceable to her.

Feeling more foolish than ever before, she climbed into the bed, pulled the sheet over her head and cried herself to sleep.

Having never slept in his living room, Rich lay awake on his futon dissecting the unfamiliar shadows cast upon his ceiling and walls. The family photographs clustered on a wall now resembled an ancient pirate's map. The ceiling fan, a preposterous spider with a pearl necklace. The bookcase, a dark and formidable Sponge Bob.

As her muffled sobs became fewer and softer, he imagined that Gwen had finally drifted off. At last, he allowed himself the luxury of a peaceful thought, Horseshoe Bay in Bermuda, and the Atlantic mist spraying up from the bow of the cruise liner that carried him there. The memory of the gentle pitch and yaw of the vessel slicing through the waves always put him to sleep.

As he drifted off, a sudden bang awoke him. Keeping still and listening with intent, he could hear Veronica in her apartment next door. As she moved throughout her apartment, Rich could hear as she tossed her keys onto her dining room table and kicked off her shoes. And with that, his mind raced back to Volos.

Before too many more seconds slipped by, he found himself once again pondering his own culpability for the troubles of late. Had he given in to Volos too easily? Had he been blinded by the promise of fame? Or had Volos simply done a hell of a job? If only he hadn't seen his book being carried away in an evidence bag, he thought as he glided into unconsciousness.

"Keep your eyes open," a voice murmured.

In one swift motion , Rich's eyes snapped to attention and he sat bolt upright. He scanned the room for the source of the intrusion, but found nothing. Crediting his imagination for the disturbance, he laid back down and wondered where he had heard those words before.

TWENTY TWO

The next day, taxiing to his hotel from the Spy
Museum, Rich thumbed through Gwen's day planner,
checking the schedule and making a mental timeline.
Finding only a few commitments planned over the next
few days, he decided to order room service, take a good
long nap, then head out to a few nearby watering
holes. As he shut the calendar, he checked his watch
and, figuring school was out, decided to call home. He
opened his cell and dialed his sister.

"Hello?" Tommy answered.

""Hey sport! How's it going?" Rich blared into
the phone, startling the cab driver.

"Hi Uncle Rich! You were on the news!"

"Oh yeah?"

It didn't come as any surprise. Over the last
several weeks he had grown accustomed to seeing his
face and hearing his name in public. Gwen had seen to
that. She had arranged everything so meticulously.

With their arrival in each new city, either his face or his book was plastered on every billboard, bus stop and taxi roof.

"Yeah!" Tommy shouted.

"Cool. Hey, did your friends finish the book? Did they ruin the ending for you?"

"Nah. They didn't even come to school today."

"Oh, well that works out fine!" Rich bantered. "Now you only have to avoid them for one more day. Then your dad's bringing your copy on Saturday! See, now all is right with the Universe."

Just then, Rich heard a rumble from the other end of the line as the phone changed hands.

"Rich?" Rachel hailed.

"Hey Sis, what's happening?"

Rich waited for a response as his sister scolded Tommy, "Just go now!"

"Rachel?"

"I'm here," she said.

"What's going on?"

"I'm trying to get him to pack," she sighed.

"Where are you guys going?"

"He's going," she snapped, "I'm staying."

"Ah," Rich mocked, "Finally sending him away to military school?"

"No, and that's not funny!"

He suddenly recognized a tone in her voice he had only heard once before, as she struggled to explain to him that his parents were dead. It was the tambour of a woman wringing her hands and losing control.

"What's going on?" he asked.

"Wait a minute," she said, and then yelled to Tommy in the next room, "Close the door!"

After he heard the door slam through the cell, he pressed, "Rachel, what's going on?"

"I don't want him to hear me," she whispered into the phone. "They're closing the schools tomorrow."

"Okay. And?" he posed.

"Just listen. This whole kids killing themselves thing is getting really scary," she said. "Those two boys that didn't come to school? Those two boys that were reading your book?"

The blood drained from Rich's face as he sat silently in the backseat of the taxi. He knew what was coming.

"Those two boys killed themselves!" she yelped under her breath. "And that's not the half of it! At least a dozen other kids did the same thing just over night!"

Rich remained quiet, his brain filling once again with doubt, swirling with misgivings about Volos, suicides and bloody books as evidence. Finally, he asked, "Is Tommy alright?"

"He's fine. He doesn't know anything. He just thinks his friends stayed home sick. But I did find a throw away lighter in his back pack."

"And they're closing the schools?" Rich repeated.

"Yes! I'm telling you, it's like the city is on lockdown or something. They're asking parents to keep their kids home! I guess they don't want the liability!"

Rachel went on, "And don't think I didn't see the news this morning."

He wracked his brain, but came up with nothing. Finally he asked, "Was there something special on the news?"

"You're publisher lady. Her daughter."

"I know," Rich consoled, "can you imagine? It was on the news?"

"Yes!"

"Did Tommy see it?"

"He only caught the last part," she explained. "The part where they said Gwen's name and showed your picture."

"Yikes."

"So I just got off the phone with Ed," she continued, "and he's going to take Tommy for the weekend. I just want him to get out of here away from all the bad news."

"Good idea," Rich concurred. "Is he okay though? I mean," he struggled for the right words, "psychologically?"

"What do you mean?" she quizzed.

"I mean, he's still the same well adjusted Tommy, right?"

"Look Rich, I know what you're thinking. I've been thinking the same thing. He seems to be fine, but then again, they're saying that most of these kids that killed themselves didn't show any signs of depression or anything like that." She caught herself raising her voice then took it down a notch. "That's why I'm sending him to be with his dad. There's no way I'm leaving him alone. It was Ed's weekend anyway. So he'll just have him an extra day. I think they're going to Niagara Falls. He's gonna let me know. If I didn't have this merger thing at work tomorrow I would just stay home with him."

"No need to explain," Rich comforted, "Stuck here in DC is the last place I want to be."

"And you're done on Sunday?" she asked.

"Yes, thank God."

"Then come over here around six. Tommy will be home by then. We'll order Chinese take out."

As they said their goodbyes, Rich's taxi stopped in front of his hotel. Hopping out and paying the driver, Rich wondered, as he made his way through the lobby, if he would actually get his nap.

Meanwhile, back in New York, Gwen had spent the day arranging her daughter's funeral. As a mother, it's something she never thought she would have to do. Planning the burial of a child was as unnatural for a mother as breastfeeding a rock. She hadn't a clue what to do, and relied heavily on her father for guidance. After all, a man of his age should have experience with such tasks.

When all was said and done though, it boiled down to contacting a funeral director and picking out some clothes. In fact, her day was done before 2 PM. The remainder of her time was spent standing at the river's edge in the park where Casey had spent the last few minutes of her life. She relaxed on the bench and meandered throughout the park until nearly nightfall when, finally concerned for her own safety, she pulled herself away from the guard railing and caught a taxi home.

Around ten PM that night, her telephone rang. She picked it up to find Volos on the other end.

"Ms. Wright, I heard the news today and I'm so sorry for your loss. Is there anything I can do?"

She sank into her woolen chair by the front window and exhaled a sigh of resignation. "Thank you," she mustered, "but I think I have everything taken care of."

"Casey was a sweet girl," Volos offered. "The world will be far less bright with her gone."

"I appreciate that, Mr. Volos, I really do. I keep thinking of the extra time we had together because of you. I'll be forever in your debt."

"Well," Volos went on, "you don't have to think about that right now. Besides, your commitment to me is practically at an end anyway. You've done a fine job, Ms. Wright."

She paused for a moment, thinking her next comments might be inappropriate, but went for it just the same. "Mr. Volos, I have to ask, what exactly, besides doing some scheduling and traveling, have I done that's so great?"

Silence filled the line. Even though he was an emissary for the Devil, his diplomacy and poise remained intact. Finally, he offered, "Ms. Wright, your enthusiasm and your grace have touched every aspect of this project. It may be a while before you comprehend the full impact of your contribution, but understand here and now that the end result would have been impossible without you. And therefore, without Casey."

"Thank you, Mr. Volos. And I want you to know that Mr. Rossi is still in Washington finishing up. He'll be finished on Sunday afternoon and returning home at that point. Is there anything I need to do to wrap things up on our end?"

It was her moment of truth. For weeks she had harbored a seed of doubt, wondering if Volos would keep his promise by letting her go. While she knew he was a man of his word, she couldn't escape the fact that he was also underhanded and tricky, and might pounce on any detail or loose end that would keep her indebted to him. She waited for what seemed an eternity for his reply.

Finally he said, "I'm leaving for Paris tonight for a few days, but I've left a folder on your desk. It contains everything you need and instructions for wrapping things up." He paused for a moment and added, "Are you absolutely sure there's nothing I can do before I leave?"

It was not the definitive answer she was looking for, still she kept the faith that she had crossed all the tees and dotted all the I's.

"No Sir. But, may I call you on your cell if something comes up?"

"Indeed, yes," he offered. "Be safe, Ms. Wright."

And with that, the line went silent.

About that same time, in Washington, Rich was on his fourth glass of Southern Comfort in as many bars. No sooner would he nestle onto the calm of an empty barstool, then be recognized by a fellow patron. And by now, the news of Casey's death had gone national. The daughter of the manager of the hottest new author was now a personality by mere association. So it was only natural that she have her fifteen minutes of fame and of course any profit seeking news producer would include a duly cropped, hi-def photo of Richard Rossi in the story.

No longer just a face that only a kid would recognize, he would slouch and keep his head down, finish his drink and then move on.

At this moment though, he sat at a bar nursing what he figured should be his final drink of the night, when an obviously intoxicated man bellied up to the bar next to him. "Coors Draught!" he bellowed to the middle-aged woman behind the bar.

As he unwrapped the wrinkled wad of ones from his shirt pocket, his body swayed, turning toward Rich. Squinting at Rich, then back to his cash, then back to Rich, he seemed to put two and two together and slurred, "Hey! You're that guy!"

Immediately, the heads turned and all eyes were on Rich. He feigned a quick scratch of his forehead in an effort to shield himself from the prying eyes around him.

The drunk went on, "I saw you on TV!" He waved his meaty hand in the air and cried out to the room, "It's that guy from TV!"

Rich nodded and forced a smile. Finishing his drink he arose from his stool to leave but the drunk grabbed him by the arm.

"My kid's reading your book!" he barked, then turned to the room and repeated himself. "My kid's reading his book!"

"That's fine," Rich answered and shrugged away from the drunk's grasp.

"Hey! Can I get your autograph?" The drunk spat, turning to the bar and grabbing a stack of napkins. "Hey Honey!" he yelled to the bartender. "Can I get a pen?"

She brought a pen from a cup next to the cash register and handed it to the drunk and said to Rich, "My grandson read your book."

"Oh, that's nice," Rich managed. "Did he enjoy it?"

Her face clouded over as she answered, "We don't know. He seemed to, but," she was interrupted.

A man playing pool behind him chimed in, "I bought that book three weeks ago! I was gonna give it to my daughter for her birthday, but I've been hearing some weird things about it."

The drunk shoved the napkin and pen into Rich's hand, but his attention was on the pool player. "What kind of weird things?" Rich pried.

The drunk interrupted, "Make it to Sam."

"They're saying that kids are acting funny when they read your book," Pool player said.

"I heard that too!" a man in a suit heralded from across the bar.

"Like what" said the bartender.

"Like the kids are under some kind of spell when the read it." Suit's drinking partner said.

Rich sat, stunned by the barrage of comments until he was nudged by the drunk.

"Are you gonna sign it?" the drunk insisted. "Make it out to Sam."

"A trance?" smirked the bartender. "That's the stupidest thing I've ever heard."

Pool player leaned on the table and countered, "Rosie, you yourself said your grandson was acting real funny just before he, you know."

The bartender turned her attention to two new patrons as Rich signed the napkin. With an almost unbearable sensation of the ground falling out from under him, Rich then turned to the pool player and in a hushed tone asked, "What happened to her grandson?"

Rich knew what the answer would be, and regretted asking the question as soon as the syllables tripped off his lips.

Pool player leaned in and whispered, "He killed himself." He paused and shook his head in despair. "Fourteen years old. Him and his family were on a cruise and the boy jumped overboard."

Rich closed his eyes, dizzy with nausea.

Pool player went on, "For days they thought he fell over. It wasn't until they got a hold of security tapes that they saw he really did it intentionally."

He turned to resume his game, then turned back and whispered to Rich, "You wanna know the most fucked up part?"

Fully expecting to faint at any moment, Rich braced himself.

Pool player went on, "That boy was holding on to that damned book of yours like it was a life jacket or something."

He aimed and sank the nine ball and continued, "My wife says I'm being superstitious, but I'm playing it safe and keeping it locked in my trunk until the jury comes back on this one."

As his Southern Comfort began to gurgle its way up his esophagus, Rich pushed his way past the drunk and through the front door into the legendary DC humidity. He stopped for a moment and leaned over a cement planter box, ready to throw up, but could only manage a few dry heaves. Collecting himself, he straightened his polo shirt, took a deep, purifying breath and made for his hotel.

The ground flew swiftly beneath him as his strides grew longer and longer. His breathing became heavier and more labored as he marched up Massachusetts Avenue and finally into the hotel lobby.

Once in his room, he stripped and sat naked on the edge of the bed directly in front of the air conditioner. His head was spinning from a combination of the strenuous walk, the Southern Comfort and the renewed sense of dread brought on by the pub regulars. He laid back onto the bedspread, brushed his hair from his forehead and stared up at the ceiling. As the cool, dry air flowed over his body and he began to drift into slumber, the disembodied voice that had visited him the night before once again interrupted his descent into sleep. "Just keep your eyes open," it said, coming from nowhere and everywhere all at once.

His eyes popped open as he sat up, grabbed the edge of the bed and planted his feet on the floor. This time, however it all seemed more familiar, and more urgent. This time he could tell it was the voice of a man, a man giving some kind of direction or warning. As he sat in the chilly darkness of his room, he rubbed his forehead struggling to place the voice and the words. Finally, exhausted from worry he laid back down and pulled the bedspread over his shivering naked body.

TWENTY THREE

Gwen opened the door to her brownstone the next morning to find a dozen or so reporters and cameramen waiting for her at the foot of the steps. She glanced around for a second, wondering what all the hubbub was about, until she realized they were there to see her.

All at once they began shouting her name and barking out their questions. It was a swarm of faces, microphones and flashes, and a cacophony of declarations, queries and conjecture.

She steeled herself and began the agonizing descent down the stone stairway. Smiling and nodding as she went, she soon found herself dead center of the melee.

The questions were hurled about as the microphones were shoved in her face. "How do you feel about losing your daughter?" yelled one.

"Are you still working with Richard Rossi?" cried another.

"Is it true your daughter killed herself?"

"Sources say your daughter was on drugs!"

She pressed her way through the mob, kicking and elbowing when she had to. Her blood boiled as the attack persisted.

"Does suicide run in your family?"

"Some are saying that Rossi's book is causing suicides! Was your daughter a victim of that?"

Realizing now that rumor and innuendo had seized upon the media, she stopped dead, determined to set the record straight. Hoping to quell the hysteria, she spoke in a low, deliberate tone. "I'll answer all of your questions, one at a time," she conceded.

A hush made its way through the crowd as one by one reporters silenced one another.

A woman from Channel One spoke up first and was interrupted by a man from MSNBC. A third reporter refereed and quickly assumed the role of moderator. "One at a time!" he admonished.

Suddenly what was once a quagmire of pandemonium settled into a press conference with the order of a United Nations convention.

The woman from Channel One spoke first. "Ms. Wright, can you tell us how you found out about your daughter's death?"

The microphones converged in front of her face.

"Yes," she muttered. I was in Washington wrapping up Mr. Rossi's book tour and I got a call from my parents where Casey was staying."

MSNBC spoke next. "So you are still working with Richard Rossi?"

"Officially, yes, but the book tour is ending this weekend," she answered, "but my daughter's death had nothing to do with the end of the book tour. It had been scheduled to end this week for a long time."

A woman with The BBC asked, "How does it feel to lose your daughter?"

Gwen looked up at the woman and asked, "Do you have kids?"

Slightly embarrassed, the reporter nodded her head.

"Then I guess there really are stupid questions. Next?"

A man from the back of the crowd shouted, "Was it really suicide?"

She hesitated then shouted back in kind, "Yes!"

Someone behind her said, "Some are saying that Rossi's book, *The Keeper of the Key* is related to the suicides of the past months."

She turned to the direction of the comment and said, "It's a ridiculous notion that a children's fantasy could influence kids to kill themselves. I can say from personal experience that the spike in suicides has been a tragedy for many families, and as much as I would like to have answers about my own daughter's reasons behind what she did, and as much as I would like to find something or someone to blame, it's a gigantic leap to think that a book would have anything to do with it." She paused and then continued, "Have any of you read the book? There is nothing within those pages that advocates or even implies that kids should kill themselves. I admit, it does have a shocking ending, but the epilogue clearly states..."

The same man interrupted, "They're saying it's more mystical than that, that the kids seem hypnotized, like they're in a trance or something."

Dismissing him, she turned back to face the crowd and asked, "Are there any more legitimate questions?"

With that, the flood gates seemed to explode. The photographers snapped, the cameras flashed and the reporters reverted once again into a pack of hounds vying for a scrap of meat. As the questions and comments burst forth, Gwen again felt the crush of the mob and fought her way through to the freedom of the vacant sidewalk. She strode confidently away from the clash, as they begrudgingly disassembled and retreated to their respective news vans.

It wasn't until her taxi dropped her off in front of her office that her heart resumed its normal rhythm. As she rode the elevator up to the twenty fourth floor, she rummaged through her purse to retrieve her keys. When the elevator doors parted, she crossed the hall and unlocked the office door, hoping to get in and out as quickly as possible.

Once inside, she found the folder that Volos had left for her on the top of her desk and tucked it neatly into her bag. Then, set to end her tenure with Volos, she checked the storage closet for a box that might hold the personal belongings she intended to reclaim. Finding nothing, she returned from the closet, glanced around the office and then reached for Volos' office door. Oddly though, it was locked. He had never before locked his office. In fact, he had always made it a point to leave it unlocked and available to her incase he needed her to enter in his absence.

For a split second, an icy chill spirited up the back of her neck and she immediately turned to the wall mirror Volos had had installed months earlier. Suddenly she felt as though she were being watched, as though Big Brother, or some other all-knowing entity was spying, judging, undressing her. Only one other time, when Rich had signed his contract, did she experience this sensation. This time however, she paid closer attention to her instincts and moved a little closer to the mirror. Reluctantly, she ran her fingers over the ornate gold leaf framing. As she caressed the reflection, tapping on the glass, she detected an unusually hollow tone. She took a step back and grasped the frame. Attempting to hoist it from its perch, she realized that it was fastened to the wall by more than a mere picture hook. In fact, upon closer inspection, it seemed to be somehow built in to the wall itself.

Just as she had resolved to give up and move away, an odd glint of light permeated from a flaw behind the quicksilver layer that made up the reflection. Moving in closer, she cupped her hands around her eyes, blocking out the light from the reception area, and pressed as closely as her nose would allow. To her astonishment, behind the mirror she could see the outline of a file cabinet. She blinked, repositioned herself and peered once again into the mirror. This time, upon a shelf, she recognized a pair of candlesticks she had given to Mr. Volos as a gift.

Intrigued, she moved swiftly to the window where she closed the venetian blinds, then to the light switch on the wall next to the door. With the room now darker than she had ever seen it, she returned to the mirror and peered past the reflection into an area she had not seen before.

Suddenly it dawned on her that her instincts were correct and that Volos must have been watching her whenever she was at her desk. She pushed herself away from the mirror and darted back to her desk. Although she hadn't a need for one in the past, surely, she figured, there must be a key to his office. She rifled first through her top drawer, then moved on to the side drawers, all the while knowing full well that she had never before seen an errant key lying about the office. Still she searched in earnest, checking under a potted plant, turning back a throw rug in the closet and going so far as to peer above a few ceiling tiles. Finally, after having broken into a sweat and convincing herself that the point was mute, she gave up, dusted herself off and resolved to leave what personal belongings she could not carry.

Later that afternoon, she leafed through the folder Volos had left for her. Carefully following the enclosed list of instructions, she gathered her notes and all other information regarding Rich's novel and tucked them neatly into a FedEx international shipping envelope. She affixed the label, preprinted and addressed to London, and dropped it into a box on the corner of her block. With this final act, she was free of the burden of managing *The Keeper of the Key*.

Strolling back home, she felt a tinge of pity for the person who would shoulder the European book tour.

TWENTY FOUR

Around that same time, Rich was wrapping up his two hour book signing at the Union Station Barnes and Noble. The store manager attributed a relatively small turnout to the typical Friday exodus from DC to the shores of Maryland and Delaware.

So, with a few extra minutes to kill before the arrival of his car, he opted to browse the music section. Although not necessarily a music aficionado, he found the audio-video department the least boring area inside the store. As he meandered down each aisle, he stopped occasionally and thumbed through the CDs, hoping for something to jump out at him. Unimpressed, he wandered over to the DVD section and began perusing some of the titles. Leafing through the documentary section, he mindlessly passed one DVD after another until suddenly, his hands and eyes worked together and did a double take. There before him, amongst the many forgettable movies, the title, *Keep Your Eyes Open*, leapt forth like a smack on the forehead. He picked up the package and studied it carefully. And while it turned out to be nothing more than a 2002 film about extreme sports, the title itself intrigued him enough that he began to examine the back cover.

Just as he squinted to read the fine print, a booming voice heralded from just behind his left shoulder, "Mr. Rossi."

Rich practically jumped out of his skin.

"I'm sorry," the tall black man in the uniform offered. "I just wanted to let you know that your car is outside and ready whenever you are.

Rich smiled and returned the movie to its obscurity. "I'm ready," he said.

They both exited the complex, the driver leading Rich to the awaiting black Towne Car. As they sped away toward the Barnes and Nobel in Falls Church, Virginia, Rich found himself brooding over the words, keep your eyes open. He gazed out through the tinted windows at the Lincoln Memorial as they approached the Arlington Memorial Bridge, and tried to rid himself of the torment of those words.

He reminded himself of a day back in the mid seventies when he had joined his father on a business trip to Washington, specifically their visit to the Lincoln Memorial. Back then you could circle the entire memorial in your car, stop and take in the Reflecting Pool and the steps where Martin Luther King had delivered his famous oratory. He recalled how his father had impressed upon him the core values of such men as King and Lincoln, and how he had stood in awe upon witnessing with his own twelve year old eyes, the statue of Lincoln. The stoic, but grandfatherly face of the giant as he sat upon his enormous marble throne. And the words inscribed in the wall behind him. He reflected on what he had learned in school about the man, his honesty, his integrity and his legendary height.

As they rounded the curve onto the bridge, suddenly, like a bolt from the blue, the memory of another very tall man from his past erupted forth. Not a notable figure, not a particularly wise man, but the man who had uttered the words, keep your eyes open. With complete clarity, the image of a seven foot tall, flaming queen from New York's East Village assailed his mind's eye.

Vividly, he summoned up the night several months earlier when in a drunken haze he read aloud *The Keeper of the Key* in its entirety to an assemblage of diehard partiers. They had hung on his every word and would call themselves Rich's original fan club. Among the audience, a seven foot tall, flaming queen from New York's East Village, Dennis. The same Dennis he would later run into in a bar, who would give him his business card and say, "Take my phone number in case you get into trouble or need anything," and "keep your eyes open."

That night, around nine, as Gwen sat in a tan early american chair next to her daughter's casket at the Beasley Funeral Home, her cell phone rang. It was a welcome respite from the parade of mourners that insisted upon telling her that Casey had never looked better. She excused herself from the guests and headed to the front porch, taking a seat in the corner.

On the other end of the line, Rich carefully quizzed, "Is everything okay?"

"Boy is it good to hear your voice," she sighed. "I'm at the funeral home now."

"Oh, I'm sorry. You're busy."

"Don't you dare hang up," she warned, and begged all at once. "I had to get out of there."

"Are you all right?"

"It didn't occur to me how many of her classmates would show up," she said, twisting a petal from a geranium blossom. "My ex was here. The media's in and out. It's actually a good thing you're not here."

"Are you holding up okay?" he asked.

"I'm fine. I broke a lot of dishes last night. Tore up the house really good. I got a lot out of my system," she admitted. "I just need something to get my mind off of things for a while."

"Hmm," he teased, "I have something that might get your mind off of things for a while."

"What?"

"If I call my super and get his okay, will you go to my apartment and get something for me?"

"Like what?"

"There's a guy I need to call," he began. " His card is somewhere on my desk."

"And that can't wait until you get home on Sunday?"

"Well, I guess it can," he relented, "but I really need to talk to him."

"Can it wait until tomorrow morning?"

"Oh, of course!" he gushed. "Whenever it's convenient. Don't go out of your way."

"Rich," she mocked, "no matter where I go or what I do, Astoria is going to be out of the way."

"Typical Manhattanite," he taunted, "you act like you need a passport to enter into one of the other four Burroughs."

Just then, Gwen's mother came out of the funeral home and headed toward her. "I gotta run. I'll call you tomorrow and get the details."

"You're the best," he beamed. "Call me if you need to talk."

The following morning, Gwen found herself standing outside of Rich's apartment while the super, who spoke very little English, sorted through an enormous collection of keys. After five attempts and four, "she's-a-no-goods", the dirty brass doorknob gave way and allowed them entry.

Once inside, Gwen made her way to Rich's desk as she called his cell.

"I stay put," the super managed, halting just inside the doorway.

Rich answered his cell, "Okay, so you're in."

"Yes."

"So, on top of my desk there's a green frog with one of its feet broken off."

Gwen scanned the desk, "Got it," she said, picking up the frog, turning and inspecting it.

Rich went on, "Whatever you do, don't pick up the frog."

"What?" she froze in fear.

"Just kidding," he jabbed. "I knew you were going to pick it up."

"You know," she confessed, "As much as you're a pain in the ass, this is still better than spending another morning with my ex and his new wife, Brandi. With an I."

He chuckled and went on. "I think the card is in the little stack of papers under the frog."

She sat at the desk and began to leaf through the dog-eared pile of business cards, receipts and rolling papers. "What am I looking for?"

"It's just a plain white business card. The guy's name is Dennis something. I don't remember his last name."

She thumbed through each slip of paper, leafing past receipts for Café Athena, a haircut and some dry cleaning, before coming across a business card that read simply, Dennis Goodman, above a telephone number.

"Is it Dennis Goodman?" she asked.

"That's it!" He delighted. "What's the phone number?"

She stopped for a moment to study the name, and then erupted, "This is the guy!"

"What guy?" Rich asked.

"Oh my God!" she continued. "The guy that first called me about meeting Mr. Volos! I didn't know you knew him!"

"Refresh my memory."

"Remember the two gay guys at the Laundromat? The ones I overheard talking about the guy with AIDS? They were going to have him call me? This is the guy that called me!"

Rich remained silent as Gwen went on.

"Dennis! I didn't know you knew Dennis!" she declared.

Another peculiar coincidence hopped on board Rich's already laden shoulders. "Well," he hedged, "I don't really know him, per se. I met him the same night I met Veronica, and then again at a bar once. He gave me his card, and now I just have a couple things to talk to him about."

Glad to help, Gwen rattled off the telephone number just as the super, giving the international signal for, let's move things along, cleared his throat.

"Okay, listen, Rich," she said, moving toward the door, "I'm about to get thrown out of your apartment. Besides, I need to get to the airport. My brother's flying in today."

"Thanks again," he chirped.

As the super was relocking the door, Gwen added, "Call me later and let me know how things are going down there."

Rich lost no time dialing up Dennis. Not realizing that Dennis was happily unemployed, Rich didn't expect him to answer.

But he did, "Hello?"

"Is this Dennis?" Rich asked.

"Yes it is. Who's this"

"Hey, Dennis. This is Rich Rossi, Veronica's next door neighbor?"

After a long pause, Dennis carefully replied, "Oh. How is everything?"

Once again, he began to speak without first formulating his thoughts. He hesitated for a moment and then went on. "Yeah. I just..." he stopped, fumbling for words.

"Are you in some kind of trouble?" Dennis quizzed.

"Well, not really, trouble. But I do have to ask you something," he confessed.

Dennis breathed a heavy sigh, "What's going on?"

"Well," he started, "remember the night at that bar?"

"Yeah?"

"When you gave me your business card, you told me to keep my eyes open. What did you mean by that?"

The line was silent for several moments before Dennis once again let out a sigh. "Look, Rich, you seem like a good guy. I just meant, you know, watch your back. You know, your career and everything."

Rich could tell that Dennis was being evasive and replied accordingly. "No, you said to watch myself around Volos. And before you lie to me, I need to tell you that I just got off the phone with Gwen. She's spoken very highly of you and attributes her daughter's recovery to Volos, who you hooked her up with." He took a deep breath and got back on the subject. "So I know you know a lot about Volos and I think I have a right to know. Why did you tell me to keep my eyes open around him?"

Taken off guard by Rich's detective work, Dennis once again remained silent while he weighed his options. Cautiously, he affirmed, "You're right, I do know a lot about Volos."

"Dennis, some weird shit has been going on. I mean, maybe they're just coincidences, but I just have a bad feeling in my gut." He waited for a reply then added, "So if there's something I need to know or if Volos is up to something screwy, I need to know. Like you said, my career?"

Dennis had dreaded this phone call since the moment he watched his business card slide into Rich's shirt pocket several months earlier. It had not been for him to say, but making the gesture those months ago placed him squarely on the witness stand.

"Look," he began, "Where are you? Because I'd really rather not talk about this over the phone."

"I'm in Washington, DC right now."

"How long are you there for?"

"I'm coming home tomorrow afternoon."

"Shit," Dennis sighed. "I'm leaving for Greece for a month tomorrow morning. What time tomorrow will you be home?"

"Not until about four or five."

"That's too late." Dennis cursed himself for not leaving a day earlier, when he had the opportunity. "Look, you're not going to want to let this wait for another month. Why don't I come to DC today. We can have dinner and talk. Then I'll just come back here tonight."

"Wow!" Rich gushed. "You'd do that for me?"

Dennis thought for a moment then concluded, "It's not just for you. Let me get off of here and I'll call you at this number when I get closer."

"My number showed up on your caller ID?"

"Yeah. I'll see you in a few hours."

By two that afternoon, Dennis and Rich were sitting across from one another at LaMotte, an outdoor café on Connecticut Avenue. As their table umbrella bustled in the breeze of an approaching storm, they sat defiant, but ready to dash inside at the first drops of rain, Rich with a Southern Comfort, Dennis with a Cosmopolitan.

After the initial banter of catching up, train rides and summer storms, Rich finally dove in head first. "So, what do you know about Volos?"

After a swallow and chuckle, Dennis replied, "Okay. Good. We really should get to the point."

"Before you say anything," Rich interrupted, "Can I tell you what's been going on?"

"Sure," Dennis said, sitting back in his white plastic patio chair and lighting a cigarette.

"Well," Rich scooted in. "Let me try to put it in chronological order." He leaned forward, placing his elbows on the table. "First, Veronica hooks me up with him. No big deal. We talk and he decides he wants to publish the book. But he wants to make some changes. I say, okay and sign a contract."

Dennis sighed and bit his bottom lip.

"Now, I thought it was kind of weird at first that the contract had all this Latin shit on it, and I swear it was on parchment paper, but Gwen explained that Volos was just kind of quirky, so I let it go. I didn't really give it any more thought until this week."

He took a sip from his drink and went on, "So, I sign the contract. Now, in the contract it says that I have final approval of any of the changes that get made. It says that I have seventy-two hours to nix anything I don't like. So no big deal. I'm feeling really good about everything. Gwen said that a copy was over-nighted to me, and it was. But here's another weird thing that didn't dawn on me until I started picking everything apart. Two minutes after I leave Volos' office, I get clobbered on the head by a tool belt or some shit like that, that just happened to fall off of a scaffold above the lobby of the building."

Dennis grimaced and blew a puff of cigarette smoke into the wind.

Rich nodded, "Yeah, weird, right? Anyway, and I'm not saying it's anyone's fault or if it's just a really fucked up coincidence but, I wake up in the hospital three days later."

"Holy shit!" Dennis barked. "You were out for three days? You're lucky you weren't killed!"

"I didn't even know what hit me. Seriously, my sister had to tell me what happened."

He lit a cigarette and continued. "So I get home, see the FedEx pack with all the changes he made..."

"Wait," Dennis broke in, "Volos himself made the changes?

"Yeah."

Dennis sat up and leaned in, "Shit. I got to tell you, I read the book, and I wondered why it ended so differently than when you read it to us." He downed his cocktail and waved his empty glass in the air, summoning the waiter. "Why the fuck would you let him end it with the two kids jumping off a fucking cliff, Mate?"

"Let me finish!" he nodded at the waiter, handing him his glass. "So I call him and Gwen tells me it's too late because when they didn't hear from me they thought everything was okay and sent it to the printer! So, I'm like, 'tell him to call me'. So he does and we go round and round and the bottom line is it's too late to argue the changes and I'm under contract, and basically I should just shut up and let things alone."

As the waiter returned with two fresh drinks, Rich continued, "Then he gives me fifty grand. And trust me, that kind of money would give anyone temporary amnesia."

Dennis nodded in agreement.

"Anyway, Gwen and I go on this whole book tour thing and last week I start hearing all this suicide stuff."

Dennis froze, slack jawed, having put two and two together.

"Then," Rich went on, "Last week, in Miami we see this girl reading my book by the pool. The next morning they were scraping her off of the sidewalk in front of the hotel." He leaned in closer and whispered, "She killed herself! And she took my book with her."

"What do you mean?"

"Apparently, she was holding on to the book as she fell, or jumped, or whatever." He took a long drag from his cigarette and went on, "Which, by the way is how they found Gwen's daughter."

"I heard about that," Dennis remarked.

"Yeah. Rather than swim for her life, she holds on to the book and drowns. I mean, she literally had a death grip on my book!" He gulped down his drink and added, "So, I'm thinking, either Volos put some kind of a spell or something on my book, or I'm just being paranoid and it's just a bunch of awful flukes that are happening a little too close to home."

Dennis was silent, piecing his thoughts together, careful to measure his words before speaking.

Finally, after a good thirty seconds of scratching his forehead, he asked, "Is the money good?"

Rich squinted, "What do you mean?"

"I mean, it seems like the book is doing well. Is the money coming in?"

"Well," Rich smiled and admitted, "Yeah. The money's great. I can't complain about that."

Dennis finished his drink. "Then what's the problem?"

Rich thought for a moment and confessed, "There is no problem, I guess."

"So, drop it," he said. Then leaning in, he added, "Directly behind your right shoulder, about fifty feet away, is an enclosed bus stop. On the side of that bus stop is a six foot tall poster of you standing in front of a castle. What the fuck more do you want, Mate?"

Rich began to make a nonchalant turn to check out the advertisement, but stopped and turned back. "I don't know. I just have a bad feeling." He leaned in as close as he could and pointed at Dennis. "And the fact that you came all the way down here tells me that you know there's something to my bad feeling."

Dennis could do nothing but sigh in acknowledgment.

"Besides," Rich inserted, "How does the same man successfully publish books and cure diseases? Is he a doctor? A Shaman? What?"

Dennis once again flagged down the waiter and ordered another round. "Gwen told you about Casey's sickness?"

"Yes," he countered, and without hesitation, added, "And she told me about yours too."

Proud of himself for knocking it out of the park, Rich sat back, crossed his arms and waited for a response.

Dennis barked, "That's no one's business but my own."

"I agree," Rich scooted in, "but that, along with everything else raises a lot of red flags!"

The waiter returned and set the two new drinks down. Dennis smiled and waited for him to leave then turned to Rich and said, "I get it! Red flags!"

"So?" Rich goaded. "What do I need to know?"

Dennis hesitated, lighting a cigarette to buy some time. "What you need to know and what you want to know are two different things."

"Don't fuck with me," Rich scolded.

"Here's the thing," Dennis began, "you can't really know part of the story. You have to know everything for it to make sense." He stopped for a moment, then continued, "And I'm not really sure you want to know everything."

"Ah ha!" Rich cried. "So there is a story!"

Four Cosmopolitans and a longing ear conspired to loosen Dennis's lips more than he had intended. "I was saving this for when I got around to writing a book of my own, but I trust you won't steal it."

Rich moved his chair to his left, getting closer to Dennis. "I'm all ears."

Dennis took a healthy mouthful of Cosmo and started in. "I met Seth about twenty years ago, in a bar right here in DC."

Rich interrupted, "So Volos is gay?"

"It wasn't a gay bar. You know we gays do go to other places besides gay bars."

"Sorry."

"Anyway, it was the very day I was diagnosed with HIV. Oh my God, I was so depressed. I mean, at that point, my parents didn't even know I was gay, let alone terminally ill. And my circle of friends had been reduced by three fourths when I told them I was gay. So, after finding out I was positive, I naturally went out to get drunk. Somewhere where I didn't usually go. I didn't want to be around anyone I knew."

"I can understand that," Rich nodded.

"And that's when I met him. It was no big deal at first, but as I got drunker and drunker, I ended up telling him my news. He seemed really intelligent and I figured, what the hell, I'll probably never see this guy again." He sipped from his Cosmo and went on, "So, before long he's telling me how it doesn't have to be a death sentence, and that he might be able to help. So, naturally I'm interested in what he has to say."

Rich nodded and sipped his Southern Comfort, hanging on every word.

"Anyway, over the next few days we speak here and there and then he asks me if I can go to Paris with him. He says he has an experimental drug that he's been using on monkeys and wants to try it on humans.

It's funny, I've looked back on this a million times and I still can't believe I went through with it. I guess if I wasn't so scared about dying I wouldn't have agreed to it, but I went along."

Suddenly, an errant gust of wind swept over them knocking over empty chairs at adjacent tables.

Unmoved, Dennis went on. "I didn't really think it through, because once we got to Paris, I was totally dependent on him. I had only brought a couple hundred dollars so I was basically stuck until he decided to bring me back home."

"Wow," Rich injected. "That's ballsy."

"Tell me about it. Anyway, after a couple days of him showing me around Paris, feeding me and paying for everything, we go to his office. That's where I met Veronica. They worked together. Still do.

"Anyway, right off the bat I start to feel like I'm getting double teamed by the both of them, like a sales pitch. One minute we're talking about my HIV and my life expectancy, and the next minute, they're telling me how I can live forever. For an eighteen year old kid, that's a lot to digest. So I kind of freaked out and ran off."

Unblinking, Rich asked, "Then what?"

"I lived on the streets of Paris for about two weeks. It's amazing how fast you can go through two hundred bucks. I was dirty and hungry and starting to get a cold, and I got so scared that I was going to die that I went back to Seth's office. And it was like they were waiting for me. Like they knew I'd be back."

"So what did you do?" Rich begged.

"I went along with it. And here I am."

Rich sat quietly, waiting for more, and when it did not come he shouted, "What the fuck!"

Dennis let out a hearty belly laugh, sipped his cocktail and said, "It gets better! I just needed to take a breath."

"I'm gonna kick your ass!" Rich groaned.

By now Dennis was visibly drunk, and as the wind picked up and the first smattering of rain sprinkled them, he suggested, "We should go someplace more private."

Rich eyed him wearily, but said nothing.

"Get over yourself, Mary! I'm over you!" Dennis snorted. "I just don't want to get wet!"

They shared a grunt and a chuckle, grabbed their drinks and headed inside to the bar. As the door closed behind them, the heavens opened and drenched Washington with a long overdue soaking. As more patrons rushed in crowding the entrance, Rich and Dennis moved toward the back of the room to a table in a corner.   After settling in, Rich reopened the discussion. "So, what happened next?"

"So, picture me, Veronica and Seth. We're in a sterile looking room next to his office. Veronica has a clipboard and is taking notes on every move Seth makes. I'm sitting on an exam table and he brings over a box with four syringes in it. They were filled with this nasty looking black shit that looked like tar or something. And the whole time, they're both gushing on and on about how different my life will be. Looking back I must've been out of my mind, but at the time, I was so depressed and scared, so I just let them do it."

Rich was dumbfounded and listened intently.

"Anyway," Dennis continued, "He gives me all four shots, one after another. And while he's doing it, he's telling me how happy and grateful I'm going to be, and that all he asks in return is that I let him monitor me for the rest of my life."

The waiter made a stop at their table and they both nodded in unison.

"How often do you have to check in with him?" Rich asked.

"Only once a year," Dennis slurred. "But it's forever."

"Well," Rich pressed, "what was the stuff he gave you?"

"No idea. But I did go through a lot of changes."

Rich scooted in. More curious than ever, he disregarded his own woes and asked, "What kind of changes?"

Dennis giggled to himself, relishing what he would reveal next and how Rich would react. "Well," he began, "I sleep a lot less."

"Okay. That's kind of a cool thing, right? You can get more done, right"

"Yeah," Dennis teased.

"What else?" Rich begged.

"Well, I'm completely HIV negative."

Rich sat up, "Holy shit! Really? Like, cured?"

Dennis nodded.

Squirming in his chair Rich whispered, "Why the fuck isn't this shit on the market?"

Dennis shrugged and replied, "Side effects?"

"What side effects?"

Dennis peered around the room and cupped his hand over the left side of his face, shielding his mouth. Then, he grinned, exposing his pearly white teeth. Rich leaned in, squinting, and in a split second flash, before Rich's very eyes, Dennis' eye teeth tripled in size to pointed, razor sharp fangs, then just as quickly, retracted.

In one swift motion, Rich flew back tumbling out of his chair and onto the floor. Instinctively, he crawled backward, crablike, stopping only when his back hit the wall behind him. Horrified, he stumbled to his feet and glanced around the room searching for the nearest exit, as patrons backed away.

By now, Dennis had closed his mouth and begun to chuckle. "Will you sit down?"

Panic stricken, Rich bumped into one customer after another, all the while his eyes darting from Dennis to the exit and back again.

Dennis repeated, "Rich, will you please sit down?"

"Dude! Chill!" Came a voice from the crowd.

"Yeah, Bro! Relax!" shouted another.

Dennis stood and staggered to the other side of the table, up righting the chair and guiding a nearly catatonic Rich back to his seat. As Dennis returned to his side of the table, the waiter showed up with their next round. Rich accepted the drink and guzzled it down in one desperate gulp.

He sat for a moment, trembling, trying to catch his breath. His head throbbed with shock and disbelief. Finally, he looked up at Dennis and cried, "What the fuck!"

Doubled over in laughter, Dennis could barely muster, "Side effects," between gasps.

Scooting his chair backward, Rich examined Dennis; his face, his skin, his skinny arms and neck, his shaggy hair, all ordinary. As he searched for signs of abnormality, Rich's head became dizzy with questions. But all he could manage was, "Are you for real?"

Dennis nodded and said, "We should go."

Rich sat up, "Go where?"

"Somewhere more private. I know you got a million questions, and I can't really speak freely in here." He stood and tossed two fifty dollar bills on the table.

"I don't know," Rich stuttered.

"Don't be such a pussy," Dennis scolded. Then, heading for the door, he shouted over the din of the crowd, "If I wanted to suck your blood I would have already done it!"

The crowd parted as Dennis disappeared into the storm. And, more embarrassed than afraid, Rich followed like a lost puppy.

Half way up the block, they reconvened under the shelter of the bus stop. They sat quietly, sobering up and collecting their thoughts, all the while the poster ad of Rich staring down upon them. Soaked from the torrent, Dennis shivered as he retrieved his cigarettes from his breast pocket and offered one to Rich.

Lighting up, Dennis muttered, "I'm really sorry, Mate. I could've been more tactful about how I told you."

Rich looked up from the puddle beneath him, shook his head and said, "I feel like I'm dreaming."

"I promise you, you're not," Dennis said. He paused, taking in the storm that swirled around their tiny shelter. Keeping his eyes forward, he asked, "Are you afraid of me?"

Rich thought for a moment then replied, "Not really afraid. Just kind of freaked out. I mean, what you said before makes sense. If you wanted to hurt me you would have done it by now."

Dennis turned to Rich. "I'm sincerely thankful that you believe that."

Rich nodded and smiled, and they finished their cigarettes in silence, gazing out on to Connecticut Ave. As the minutes ticked by and the storm passed, they watched as little by little the street came alive once more with pedestrians.

Dennis was bursting at the seams, overjoyed at having revealed himself for the first time. Ecstatic that

Rich had not run away, Dennis remained silent, waiting patiently for his friend to grow comfortable.

"So tell me something," Rich posed out of the blue. "So, you're a vampire then?"

Dennis nodded but was careful not to speak.

Rich nodded, formulating his next sentence. "Okay. Okay. So... you... drink blood then?"

Dennis again nodded, this time allowing himself to speak. "And Cosmos."

Rich groaned, then said, "You don't look like a vampire."

"I'll take that as a compliment, I guess."

Rich turned on his seat and asked, "So, do you kill people? I mean," he checked for eavesdroppers, "for their blood?"

Dennis shrugged, "Yes. But only assholes."

"I'm being serious!"

"So am I!" Dennis insisted. "Just walking from your hotel to here, how many assholes did you pass?"

Rich grimaced.

"Seriously!" Dennis continued, "You've got your asshole drivers, your asshole thieves, your generic garden variety ill-mannered assholes! Assholes that are rude to waiters! You know, the people the world would be better off without in the first place."

Rich was flabbergasted. While he slowly shook his head in disbelief, and reminisced about his days of slinging coffee, a tiny critic within him understood. "And Volos did this to you?"

"Yeah," Dennis answered, turning to Rich. "But I'm glad. I'm healthier than I've ever been, and supposedly I'm going to live forever."

Rich nodded, feigning a smile.

"At least that's what Seth tells me," Dennis added. "So far so good, right?"

Rich shook his head, saying, "But how come you're out in the daylight? And isn't it depressing to know you're going to outlive everyone you know?"

"Of course, it's only been twenty years," Dennis said. " Talk to me in two hundred years. Maybe by then I'll hate it. But right now, I feel like a can do anything."

Rich turned back to face the street. He scoured his brain searching for more questions, but disjointed and running amuck, his mind could only manage random observations. "But you never said anything about being out in the daylight. And what about the," he swallowed hard, "your victims' bodies?"

Dennis nodded his head, accepting each of Rich's concerns while preparing his responses.

"Oh, God," Rich went on. "Does Gwen know?" then added, "And what the fuck does that say about Volos?" He stood and began to pace the tiny enclosure. Realizing the apparent magnitude of Volos's influence, Rich stopped, turned to Dennis and cried, "What kind of shit am I involved in?"

Just then, a young mother and her infant strolled into the bus stop and sat next to Dennis.

After exchanging smiles with her, Dennis turned his attention back to Rich, and as if the two were still alone, he carried on, "Gwen does not know."

Rich's eyes darted to the stranger among them and then back to Dennis.

"Seriously," Dennis went casually on, "you've been watching too many Twilight movies. We can go out in the sun, just like everybody else."

The woman squirmed, tightening her grip on her child and turned away from the conversation as Rich's eyes nearly exploded from their sockets.

Still, Dennis went on. "A lot of what people think about us is all myth that's gotten blown way out of proportion."

Rich shook his head vehemently as the woman scooted a few inches away from Dennis.

"For instance," Dennis unabashedly continued, "that whole stake through the heart thing...bullshit." He turned to the woman and apologized for the language, turned back to Rich and went on. "It's all crap. Sleeping in a coffin? Crap. Turning to ashes if we go out in the daylight? Crap. In fact, we do just about everything that everybody else does. We eat the same things, pay the same bills, have husbands and wives and jobs and pets and mortgages."

Rich turned away, unable to face the woman.

Yet Dennis was unrelenting. "The only thing that's different is that we can't die of natural causes. And we need to have blood on a regular basis."

Rich threw his hands into the air, utterly mortified and walked away as the woman bundled up her child and scurried across Connecticut Avenue. Watching as she departed, Rich returned to Dennis.

"What's the matter with you?" He admonished. "Do you want to get us arrested?"

Dennis sniggered, "Arrested? For what? Sit down you pansy."

"You can't just talk out loud about being a..." whispering, "vampire."

"What's she gonna do? Come on, sit down," he insisted.

Shock and defeat wedded as Rich plopped down onto the bench.

"Now," Dennis continued, "where was I? Oh, right. So, that's about it. The only thing different about me is that I need to have blood and won't die...of natural causes anyway."

"Natural causes?" Rich asked.

"Yeah. Like food poisoning, or a brain tumor, or any diseases, that kind of thing. But I take back the bit about the wooden stake through the heart. I guess if someone did that, it'd probably suck. And I'm not going to stand in front of a speeding train or jump from a building. I mean, we die all the time. Sooner or later we get hit by a bus, or fall down a flight of stairs, or have a car accident, or fall down an elevator shaft. And no, we can't fly and we don't turn into bats. Let's see, what else? Oh, it's the same with Seth and Ronnie, even though they're not vampires."

"I think I get the picture," Rich moaned. "But, still, you never said what happens to, you know, the assholes."

"Well," Dennis said in a clinical tone, "We're pretty strong after we...drink, and, for me anyway, there isn't a lot left...you know...after." He turned to Rich and asked, "Are you sure you want to know all of this?"

Rich thought for a moment then nodded and said, "Yeah. I do. I mean, I'm completely shitting myself right now, but it's not every day you get to have this type of conversation." He leaned in and repeated himself, "So, really. What do you do...after."

"Well," Dennis turned to face Rich, "I'm very discreet. I'll usually find...an asshole, and follow them until they're alone. Sometimes I have to watch them for a day or two, but eventually I'll get them on a roadside or near a dumpster. You'd think you'd hear about mangled bodies all the time, but you don't. You mostly hear about people disappearing. That's' usually one of us. But some of us are assholes too and do it wherever and whenever they please. They get sloppy, and that's when you hear it on the news. Bloody body found! No eyewitnesses! Stuff like that. But most of us are discreet and very thorough."

Rich nodded, "I see. So, who else knows about you?"

"Seth and Veronica, of course. And some others like me."

Rich thought for while then asked, "Are there a lot like you?"

"You'd be surprised," Dennis said. "Back in the bar just now, there were at least three or four."

"How can you tell?" Rich pressed.

"I can never tell one hundred percent. It's just a feeling. I can't really describe it."

"So, what can you tell me about Volos?"

"Ronnie, I mean Veronica and I had a conversation," Dennis replied.

"About me?"

"Yes."

"Well?" Rich insisted.

"Well," Dennis faltered.

Rich interrupted, "Look, I know you and Veronica are good friends, but I really need..."

"We're not really that close," Dennis offered. "It's just that we go back a long way and she's the only human, present company accepted, that I can be myself around."

"So, what does she say is going on?"

Realizing he had already said way more than he should have, and that Rich deserved the candor, Dennis dove in head first and relayed everything he knew. "First off, the suicides are indeed related to your book."

Rich's face clouded over as he deflated in resignation. He wrung his hands and stared at the ground as Dennis went on.

"Ronnie told me how it all works. There's a lot of differing opinions about what happens to the soul when you commit suicide. Most religions think it's a sin. But unlike all the other sins, you can't ask for forgiveness from this one. In fact, the person that kills themselves, their soul," he said, making air quotes with his fingers, "hangs out for a while. Like in a waiting room. God sort of, forgets about them. And that leaves the door wide open for Lucifer."

Pale and ashen, Rich looked up at Dennis.

"That's really his name," Dennis injected.

Rich heaved a heavy sigh, dreading, yet longing for more.

Dennis obliged, "Seth works for him. Ronnie works for Seth. Anyway, do you know of that Movie, Never Ending Story? Where the boy reads the book and becomes part of the story? That's what Seth did to your book when he made the changes. So the kids, not all of them, but a lot of them, that read your book, get sucked into it. In their impressionable minds they become the heroes. And we know what the heroes do in the end of your book."

Rich stood and moved into the emerging sunlight. He turned to Dennis and growled, "That is the biggest load of shit I've ever heard in my life!"

Startled, Dennis sat back, crossed his arms and waited for Rich's rebuttal.

"First of all," Rich ranted, "How the fuck is that possible? Second of all, why would he need me?

Couldn't he just write a book on his own? And why would Veronica tell you all of this?"

He plopped down on the bench and pouted, all the while unconvinced by his own denial. "What else did she say?"

"That's about it," Dennis said. "Except that Seth is collecting those souls."

Rich sat quietly and ran his fingers through his wavy black hair.

"And to answer your questions," Dennis added, "Those two have been around for a long time. They know more about Heaven and Hell than anyone alive today. This kind of thing is a sport to them. They thrive on the concoction of the scheme. It's the drama they love. It's how many lives they can destroy in the process. Writing a book of his own wouldn't have satisfied his need for the thrill." He paused and then went on. "That's why I was glad you called. I mean, I had no way to get in touch with you. And besides, I actually didn't fully believe Ronnie when she told me all this shit. I mean, I read it and, at the time, would never have thought that it would have sold the way it did."

At a complete loss, Rich remained silent, rubbing his temples and chewing the inside of his bottom lip. It was too much to digest. If he accepted what Dennis was saying, it meant rethinking everything he had ever believed about the concept of hell.

He steadfastly believed in God and Heaven, and although it had been years since he had attended church, or for that matter prayed, he had never acknowledged the possibility that there might be a hell. Since childhood, it had been a thought too terrible to entertain. The mere idea of fire and brimstone, whatever brimstone was, set him awash in a fear so extreme that only an immediate denial would quell.

Finally, Rich muttered, "What am I going to do?"

"Well," Dennis asked, "what do you want to do?"

Rich shook his head, searching for the answer, "I have to do something. I can't just turn my back and let Volos get away with this."

"What's done is done, mate."

Rich looked up at Dennis, his eyes pleading, "I've got to do something. The book is still flying off the shelves!"

Dennis thought for a moment then said, "Like I said before, what's done is done. You might be able to stop more suicides, but there's nothing you can do about the ones that already happened."

"All those kids!" Rich moaned as he began to cry.

Offering him another cigarette, Dennis said, "You can't let yourself feel responsible for those deaths. That is purely on Seth, and Veronica."

Rich resumed biting the inside of his bottom lip. "I know," he said, "But I'm part of it, and if there's something I can do to stop it, I have to do it." He stopped for a moment and added, "This is unreal."

"Oh, it's real alright," Dennis confirmed. "Ronnie has told me stories that would keep you up at night."

He proceeded to regale Rich with stories Veronica had passed on to him, how Volos had played a part in such infamous calamities as the Lindberg baby kidnapping, the assassination of Martin Luther King and 9/11, to name just a few. He went on to warn Rich of Volos's power and influence, not only with the Devil, but in world politics. How Volos had called upon such notables as Idi Amin, John Wilkes Booth and Charles Manson, the way a neighbor borrows a cup of sugar.

Then, out of left field, Dennis asked, "Do you have a copy of the contract you signed?"

"I have my photo copied copy. Why?" Rich said.

Dennis groaned. "But you don't have an original? The one you said looked like parchment paper?"

"No. But Gwen might have it. Why?" He took to the edge of his seat with the prospect of Dennis having a plan.

"I'd like to see that contract."

Rich stood and reached into his pocket for his cell phone. "I'll call Gwen, maybe she can fax a copy of it to my hotel!"

Dennis nodded, "That's a start."

As Rich dialed, he asked, "What do you have in mind?"

"I just want to see the wording. You said it had Latin printed on it."

"Oh, it's ringing," Rich interrupted.

"Don't tell her why you want it just yet," Dennis said, rising to his feet. "And don't tell her I'm here or that we've talked."

"Hi!" Rich shouted nervously into the phone as he waved Dennis off. "How are things there?"

Rich was silent as Gwen told the story of her day. Then, answering her, he said, "Yes, I called him but I just got his voicemail." Then, changing the subject he asked, "Hey listen, do you have a copy of my contract with Volos?"

Rich tilted the phone so Dennis could hear the answer.

"Yes," she said. "What do you need it for?"

He stammered for a second and then said, "Well, you know. I just want to see how much longer I'm at his beck and call."

He was caught off guard when her tone was more agreeable than he had expected. "I don't blame you. The more I learn about him the more freaked out I become."

Dennis and Rich shared a puzzled glance. "What's going on?" Rich quizzed.

"I went to the office to clear out my desk and get the final instructions for your book deal, and you know that big mirror in the waiting room?"

"Yeah."

"He's been using it to spy on me! I was going to wait to tell you when you got home, but I've been really worried about it. I knew he was up to no good, but this mirror thing is the last straw!"

Without warning, Dennis snatched the phone from Rich's grasp and spoke. "Gwen, this is Dennis. Dennis Goodman? Do you remember me?"

"Yes! Yes I do!" Her voice was warm and genuine. "How have you been?"

"Never better," Dennis smirked. "Listen, Gwen, I have some information about Seth Volos that I never shared with you, and it sounds like you've discovered the tip of the iceberg. I'll let Rich explain as soon as possible, but for now, can I just get you to fax a copy of Rich's contract to us?"

"Absolutely! Just give me the fax number!" she chirped.

Dennis returned the phone to Rich who said, "Do me a favor and just call the hotel front desk and fax it to them."

"It'll be there in five minutes! Call me as soon as you can talk for a while."

"Okay, thanks Gwen."

"Say goodbye to Dennis for me."

"Will do." Rich flipped the phone shut and hailed a cab.

Twenty minutes later, they were sitting in the hotel lobby studying the copies of the contract. As Dennis leafed through the pages, he asked, "Where's the Latin you were talking about?"

Rich took the contract and flipped through once, then again. "I'm sure it was on the last page. Hold on."

He carefully scanned each sheet of paper, becoming more and more frustrated as he proceeded. "God dammit, I know it's here someplace," he snapped as he turned page after page.

Taking to the edge of his seat, he laid out each page on the top of a coffee table before them. As he scrutinized each paragraph, he complained, "It was just a few sentences, about this big." He indicated with his fingers.

"Let me call Gwen," Dennis said, reaching for his cell. "What's her number?"

Rich handed over his own cell for Dennis to use. He dialed. She answered. "Did you get it?"

"Gwen, this is Dennis. Did you send Rich's copy? Or did you send a copy of the original?"

"You're kidding, right?" she mocked. "The original is in Mr. Volos' office."

"Can you get it?" Dennis asked.

"See," she began, "that's another weird thing right now. I was telling Rich that I went to the office to get some things, and I needed to go into his office and it was locked! He never locks his office. I mean never."

"And you don't have a key?"

"I poked around my desk looking for one, but didn't find anything. What do you think is going on?"

"Look, Gwen," Dennis said, "I don't usually get involved with Seth and Ronnie's games, but Rich is," he paused and winked at Rich, "just so damned cute when he's nervous."

Rich shook his head and sighed.

"Seriously, though," he went on, "I need to see the original contract."

"Well, it's got to be in his office, but I don't know how to get in."

Dennis thought for a moment then suggested, "Can you break down the door?"

"I am not, repeat, not going into his office without a key. Even with a key, he'd turn me into a pillar of salt or something if he found out."

There was silence among all three of them. Finally, Rich asked, "Would Veronica have a key?"

Neither Dennis nor Gwen commented.

"I mean," Rich added, "Gwen, you said that she worked there before you came along, and Dennis, you said she's been his cohort forever. I'll bet she can get into his office."

"That's not a bad idea, Mate!" Dennis chimed.

"Dennis, put me on speaker," Gwen commanded.

Rich took the phone and did so. "Okay, you're on."

"Now listen, the both of you," she argued, "I'm not calling Veronica and asking her to let me in his office. I might as well call him directly."

"She's right," Dennis agreed. "Besides, she's in Paris with him."

"But wait!" Rich cried. "She and I share a fire escape!"

As Gwen protested from the speaker phone, Dennis added, "That's right! You live right next door to her!"

"Forget it!" Came the voice from over the phone.

"She could get the super to let her in my apartment again!"

"Perfect!" Dennis egged.

"No way!" Gwen squeaked.

"Then," Rich calculated, "she could go out of my bedroom window and onto the fire escape and go through Veronica's window!"

"But what about the super?" Dennis posed.

"I said forget it!" she cried.

"I could just tell him that she's going to be spending the night! He'll let her in and that'll be that!"

"That's great idea, Mate!"

"Are you listening to me? I said forget it! I'm burying my daughter day after tomorrow for Christ's sake! Why do you need that contract so badly in the first place?"

Rich and Dennis shared a knowing glance as Rich pressed a button, removing Gwen from speaker. "Here's the thing, Gwen," Rich confessed. "Dennis told me what Volos is up to."

"I know! I know! He's probably some kind of a crook. But I can't get involved! I did my time and paid him back for his help. Now I'm done with him."

"You don't understand. It's way bigger than you think." He paused for an instant and then went on. "He's responsible for Casey's death."

As silence echoed from Gwen's end of the line, Rich sat down on the lobby sofa, measured his thoughts and then continued. "In fact, the whole suicide thing that's been happening, it's all Volos."

After a few moments of silence she pled, "How is that possible?"

"Look Gwen," he dodged, "it's a really long story, and I promise I'll tell you as soon as we're face to face again, but I really need for Dennis to see the original contract as soon as possible. See, he's leaving for Greece in the morning and," he paused, then went on, "if he can see the original document, I might be able to stop what's going on."

Gwen remained silent, having learned that, at such an impasse, the first one who speaks loses.

Rich lost by saying, "Forget it. I'll come home tonight and get into Veronica's apartment myself."

"You can't cancel your interview tomorrow!" she warned.

"Big deal!" he mocked. "What's another interview?"

"I was hoping to keep this from you so you'd be able to have some plausible deniability during the broadcast, but I received a call from an Agent Crawford," she paused, steeling herself, "with the FBI."

"About what? Why do I need deniability?" he shrieked.

Passersby in the lobby stopped and turned in his direction, gathered themselves and went on.

He lowered his voice and repeated his question.

"Because," she added, "They're investigating the book, and if you cancel your appearance it's going to look really bad."

The blood drained from Rich's face as he leaned back into the sofa.

"What's wrong?" Dennis pried.

Rich shook his head and spoke into the phone, "Why are they investigating the book?"

Dennis took a seat across from Rich and blocked out the din of the lobby as he listened.

"They're actually investigating you, and Mr. Volos," she admitted. "They're trying to connect the rash of teen suicides to the popularity of your book. They think there might be a subliminal message somehow planted in it. And with what you just told me, I'm beginning to freak out just a touch."

"Oh my God," Rich moaned.

"So," she continued, "you can see why I'm not committing any breaking and entering any time in the near future."

Rich huffed for more than a few moments then said, "Okay. I'll handle this. I'm coming home right now. I'll find Veronica's key, but you've got to be the one who opens his office and finds the contract."

"That's right, Mate!" Dennis cried. "You've got plenty of time to get to New York and back by tomorrow morning!"

"Can you meet me outside of my apartment around," he checked his watch, then went on, "seven?"

"I suppose so," she relented.

"Dennis and I will find the key while you just wait in my apartment. Then you and Dennis can go to Volos' office and find the contract." Rich turned to Dennis and asked, "Are you down with that?"

"Am I down with it?" Dennis squealed. "It'll be just like we're the Mod Squad!"

Gwen could be heard groaning from the other end of the cell phone line, then said, "On one condition."

"What?"

"Dennis has to tell me the entire story too," she commanded, "from beginning to end."

Rich smiled and said, "I'm sure Dennis will be happy to. I'll see you at seven."

As Rich flipped the phone shut, Dennis asked, "What will I be happy to do?"

"I'll tell you on the way," he promised as they rose and headed for the street.

"No really," Dennis pressed, "what will I be happy to do?"

TWENTY FIVE

By nine o'clock that night, while Dennis and Gwen looked on in the darkness, Rich was unlocking and raising his bedroom window.

"I knew it," Dennis boasted out of the blue. "I knew that sooner or later I'd have you in your bedroom."

Gwen and Rich moaned in unison.

Dennis added, "I didn't figure on there being a lady present though."

"Will you please focus?" Rich whispered.

As he stepped out onto the fire escape, Rich steadied himself and offered a hand to Dennis. "I'll get her window open, but you're going in first," he ordered.

He moved to Veronica's bedroom window like an alley cat stalking a half eaten sandwich, and examined the lock. "Pass me that screwdriver," he muttered.

Gwen disappeared for a moment then returned, passing the tool through the window to Dennis.

"Let me do it!" Dennis begged.

"Be quiet!" Rich snapped. He grabbed the screwdriver and wedged it between the two window panes. Soon, with a little prying and jimmying, the lock slid smoothly to the side. With the screwdriver tucked into his back pocket he knelt, found purchase and slid the window upward. It scraped and grunted in protest before finally yielding enough for a body to slip through.

"M'Lady?" Rich said, breaking his own self-inflicted tension as he stepped back.

Dennis took the cue and moved closer to the window. He circled, like a dog in search of the ideal napping position before finally hoisting one extensive leg through the window. Ducking as best he could, he pulled his seven foot frame into Veronica's bedroom, his other leg following suit. From Rich's bedroom window, Gwen covered her mouth in silent revelry at the spectacle. A moment later, Rich too disappeared through the window.

Giddy with excitement over his successful break in, Rich's thrill soon gave way to pangs of guilt. As he gazed about the room, scanning framed photos, shelves of trinkets and memorabilia, and the lacey pillow ensemble upon her bed, a rush of warmth rose from his chest to his head.

"Come on, Mate!" Dennis whispered from another room.

Rich followed his voice and found Dennis elbow deep in the bottom drawer of a roll top desk. "Did you find anything?"

"Not yet," he answered. "Go over and look under the coffee table. There's a box under it where she keeps her weed."

Rich took heed and crept to the coffee table. "Can we turn a light on?"

"I don't see why not," Dennis said, opening another drawer.

"Do we even know what we're looking for?" Rich asked. "I mean, how will we know if we have the right key?"

Dennis slid shut the drawer and said, "Let's just see how many keys we can find first." He moved to the kitchen and began rifling through the pantry. "We'll worry about whether or not they fit after we get back downtown."

With the small wooden box in hand, Rich sat on the couch and popped the lid. Immediately, the syrupy aroma of marijuana wafted upward and taunted his senses. He reached in and pulled out a half filled baggie of the flakey, green manna and buried his face in the plastic. Inhaling, he closed his eyes and reminisced on how many months it had been since he had partook. After a few moments he placed the bag beside him on the sofa and dug deeper into the contents of the little box.

"Wait a minute," he recalled out loud, and returned to the bag of pot.

He once again held it to his nose and inhaled. Suddenly, a recollection assaulted him. He closed his eyes and it came to him. "The fuse box!" he shouted.

He fumbled, hurriedly stuffing the booty back into place, then shoved the box back under the coffee table.

"Keep your voice down, Mate," Dennis admonished from the bathroom.

Rich bolted for the dining room, heading straight for the tiny fuse box on the wall. As he stumbled his way through the darkness, he recalled how, months earlier Veronica had retrieved a key from inside of it. It came rushing in, clearer than ever, the night he had met Veronica, and Dennis. He had just finished reading his story to a group. Someone mentioned that Veronica should call her friend in the publishing business. Veronica opened the fuse box and clutched a key that hung on a shoestring, holding it close to her heart, making a mental note to call Volos.

In seconds, he came face to face with the painted metal door. He reached for the handle and tugged. Just as the door swung open, a key on a shoestring flung itself from inside the door, smacking Rich squarely on his left cheek.

"I got it!" he cried.

"Shh!" came from the bathroom, where Dennis was lifting off the top of the toilet tank.

Rich glanced around the room, certain he was being watched, and clicked the metal fuse box door shut. He made his way to the bathroom door and whispered, "I have it! Let's go!"

Taken aback by the revelation of Rich's apparent nefarious talents, Dennis froze then quickly returned the lid to its place.

As they headed back for the bedroom window, Dennis whispered, "Where did you find it?"

Rich said nothing as he climbed back out onto the fire escape.

"Seriously, Mate," Dennis pressed, "How do you know it's the right key? Shouldn't we keep looking? Just in case?"

"It's the right key. I know it!" Rich exacted, as he pulled Dennis through the window.

As Rich slid the window shut and the two crawled back into Rich's bedroom, he explained his revelation of the key's whereabouts to the other two thirds of the Mod Squad. Minutes later they were in a taxi, motoring over the 59th Street bridge, heading to downtown Manhattan, Rich parting company with Dennis and Gwen at Pennsylvania Station.

Leaving Rich to catch his train back to Washington, Dennis brought Gwen up to speed with regard to Volos' history with Veronica and their escapades over the years. After revealing himself to her and talking her off the same ledge that Rich had been on only hours earlier, she accepted his words as gospel, each new twist of the saga evoking one "ah-ha!" moment after another. Her longstanding suspicions of dirty dealings and shady backroom transactions however, paled by comparison to what she was now hearing. And although she was not completely surprised by the things she was being told, strange pieces of a frustrating puzzle were coming together and finally making sense. She could no longer dismiss Volos' schemes as the hobbies of a learned old man with too much time on his hands. Instead, she was now faced with the genuine likelihood that she herself had abetted Volos in his reign, and in fact had contributed to her own daughter's death.

It was a lot to digest, but the numbing affect of losing a child permitted ancillary matters to roll easily off her back, freeing her to focus on the task ahead, stopping more suicides.

As they exited the cab, steeling themselves for the surreptitious work ahead, the driver, now sweating in fear for his life, floored it and sped away to parts unknown.

Gwen ransacked her pocket book, finally retrieving her after hours security card. After swiping it through the magnetic slot next to the giant glass doors, a loathsome buzzing heralded them to enter. As they headed for the elevators, they passed an ancient security guard. "Hey Pete!" Gwen chirped, waking the old man from his slumber.

"Oh!" he rallied, nearly tumbling out of his chair. "Ms. Wright! You're in late tonight!"

"Yes," she complained as they boarded the elevator. "Always something urgent popping up."

With that, the doors closed and they began their ascent.

Once inside the reception area, Dennis handed over the key to Gwen and she made for Volos' office door. With an almost welcoming ease the key slid in and turned, yielding before them the dimly lit office. Gwen reached over to the wall on the left and flipped up a switch, lighting two table lamps that flanked a mighty leather sofa near the window.

As they crept in, Gwen said, "You never said what you wanted the contract for."

"It's the Latin," Dennis answered as he followed her to Volos' desk. "I need to see what the Latin actually says."

Gwen pulled out the desk chair and sat. For a brief moment she could almost feel the power and influence that seemed to emanate from this spot in the room. She slid open the top drawer only to find a miscellany of pens, paperclips and post-it notes. Moving on, she went through each massive drawer. There was a box of imported cigars, a coffee mug that was half filled with an assortment of colored crystals, an antique letter opener, a shiny brass ashtray, a white envelope that held a clump of black hair, wooden matches and a stamp pad, among other incidental items.

As Dennis snooped around the room, Gwen finally made it to the bottom right drawer. She pulled it open to reveal an array of hanging file folders. "I think I might have something," she whispered.

Dennis came to her side and peeked over her shoulder. "What is it?"

She leafed through the files until she came to a familiar red folder. "This has got to be it."

As she opened the folder, Dennis reached up and turned on the desk lamp.

"Right on top!" she said, separating the paper clipped contract from the folder.

"Let's see," Dennis said as she handed it off to him. "Shit, this is parchment."

"What does that mean?" Gwen fretted.

"It just confirms what Veronica told me. That it's a contract with," he stopped as he noticed the color draining from Gwen's face.

As he leafed through the pages, Gwen slowly stood and moved toward the liquor cart. On her way, she stopped and gazed in wonder at the newly acquired collection of boxes inside the book cabinets. "I wonder when he got all these," she said to deaf ears.

Dennis, after scanning the contract, sat at the desk, retrieved a sheet of paper and a pen and began writing.

Gwen pulled open the double doors of one massive cabinet and marveled at the uniformity and apparent care with which the boxes had been stacked. "What is this stuff?" she pondered aloud.

Dennis paid no mind. He scribbled with the zeal of a madman as he exorcised the Latin from the last page of the contract. The pen danced across the paper with ardor, tearing a time or two through to the desk blotter beneath.

Gwen caressed the stacks of boxes, stopping on one and sliding it out from its place. As she did, she heard the distant cry of children, the ghostly wail of an abandoned orphanage. Remaining still, she focused her attention, but could only hear the sound of Dennis scribbling. Yearning for the sound to repeat itself, she cocked her head and closed her eyes. Soon, though, she chalked it up to the misfires of a mother's overwhelmed brain, and returned the box to its place in the cabinet.

"Got it!" Dennis called out.

Gwen broke from her stupor and returned to Dennis's side. "What's it say?"

"I don't know yet," Dennis said.

"I thought you read Latin."

He chuckled and mocked, "Are you serious? Who the hell reads Latin?" He pulled the chain on the desk lamp and headed for the door, adding, "I need your computer."

She followed closely behind, nearly tripping on his heels. "What for? What are you going to do? What does it say?"

Plopping down upon her chair he said, "Will you just chill out for ten seconds?" He reached beneath the reception desk and turned on the computer. "I need to translate this."

As she crossed her arms in a huff and mustered the fortitude to stay silent, Dennis impatiently tapped out a rhythm on the desk, waiting for the system to boot up. Finally, with a melodic tune, the monitor came alive and Dennis began to navigate the screen. Deftly, he maneuvered the cursor over the internet icon, double clicked, then proceeded on to his favorite search engine. Moments later he began typing, filling an online text box with;

Exsisto is notus ut quicumque Ego dedi meus animus ut Omnipotens Diabolus pro plures donum Ego vadum suscipio per meus Terrenus existance. Insquequo vicis of meus Terrenus demise , meus professio vadum duco pallens, quod illud animus quoque vadum exsisto dedi ut Omnipotens Diabolus. Ex is dies porro , meus animus est forever reus hac consensio.

Gwen peered over his shoulder, grimacing at the unusual text, as Dennis moved the cursor and clicked "translate".

As the tiny hourglass revolved on the screen, Dennis championed, "This ought to do it!"

"So all of that was on the bottom of Rich's contract?" asked Gwen.

"Yup."

"I wonder what was on the bottom of mine," she worried.

Suddenly, a new page opened to reveal the translation from Latin to English. They silently read together,

To emerge this known when I to give my courage when All-powerful Devil for many more gift I ford to raise up very my Earthly existance. Until time of my Earthly set down , my monastic rule ford to lead on the march pale , and that courage also ford to emerge to

give when All-powerful Devil. Out of this day forward, my courage is forever defendant this side agreement.

Gwen peered down at Dennis and said wryly, "I don't get it."

"This must be a literal translation," Dennis carped. "But it's pretty clear that the Devil is involved. Look here." He pointed to the words, all powerful Devil.

Gwen wrung her hands and said, "Dennis, I'm scared."

"There's no need to be," he consoled as he clicked the print icon. "You better get things locked up and put away."

As Gwen returned to Volos' office to turn off the lights and tidy the desk, Dennis removed the sheet of paper from the printer and checked his watch. "Hey!" he shouted in to Gwen as she immerged through the doorway.

"I'm right here," she said in a hush.

"It's nearly eleven. I have to get home and pack. My plane leaves in six hours," he said, folding the paper and stuffing it in his shirt pocket.

"Well," Gwen quizzed, "What now?"

"I have to do a load of whites," he began, "Then..."

"I mean," she interrupted, "what happens with the contract? How are you going to get Rich out of it?"

As they covered their tracks and headed for the door, Dennis explained, "I have a buddy who can decipher this in to a more general translation. I'll fax it to him from the airport."

"What should I do in the mean time?"

"Don't do anything," he instructed. "You said yourself that your contract with Seth is complete. If I were you, I'd change my phone number and stay as far away from here as possible."

Gwen struggled with the possibilities, and on their elevator ride down to the lobby, she raised, "But what if he tracks me down?"

"Look," Dennis countered, "I told you before, he can't read minds. He can't track you down with demonic radar. You've got to be in his presence for him to hurt you. Granted, you could run into him on the street and he could probably turn you to dust, but trust me, he's content just knowing that you're afraid of him. And besides, he has no clue that you know anything more than you knew three days ago."

The elevator doors parted, and as they passed the security guard, Gwen waved a good night.

"For instance," Dennis went on, "how would he ever know that we just went through his desk? And if he ever did find out, I'd be more of a target than you."

"But what about Rich?" Gwen asked as they made their way onto the street.

Dennis ignored the question and headed for the curb where he waved for a taxi.

"I said, what about Rich?" Gwen pressed as a cab stopped.

Dennis opened the back door of the taxi. Handing Gwen in, he confessed, "Rich is in way over his head. I know from what I've translated so far that he's in big trouble. How he's going to fix it," he paused, thought for a moment then went on, "I don't know. Maybe something will present itself once I get a more thorough translation of the contract."

He slammed the door shut. As she rolled down the window, Dennis concluded, "I'll be in touch as soon as possible. You've got a lot to do over the next few days. Try to forget about this drama and go be with your family now."

Gwen watched as he turned, strolled across Broadway and disappeared into the sultry Manhattan night.

TWENTY SIX

The following morning, Rich sat quietly alone in the green room sipping a Diet Coke. Sleep deprived, he gazed blankly at the television monitor that hung in the corner and pondered the origin of the green room. He had heard the term before and had spent the last few months in one after another, and none of them had been green. He recalled having imagined that the walls might have been painted green, or that it was lit with green lighting to soothe the nerves of those waiting to go on the air, but in his experiences of late, none of those myths had proven true. Swishing the soda around in his mouth, he made a mental note to find the source of the legend.

His reverie was shaken when Marcie, an intern that couldn't have been older than nineteen, popped her head in the room and said, "Mr. Rossi, I'll be by to get you in about ten minutes. And by the way, my little sister is reading your book. We can't drag her away from it."

Rich smiled and nodded until she pulled the door shut, and then deflated with angst. As he paced the room, he rehearsed his responses. The customary answers such as, it came to me in a dream, and, yes there might be a sequel, would flow off the tongue as fluidly as ever. But if Stew Rosencrantz got wind of the FBI investigation, he was screwed. The interview would no longer be about promoting the book, but about suicide and subliminal messages.

He had spent the night tossing in his bed, predicting what questions he might be asked and how to answer them, how to evade, dismiss or even lie, not only to Washington's most notoriously determined morning news host, but to the millions of viewers that would be watching.

Going back to his spot on the couch, he returned his attention to the television set, this time to more intently study Rosencrantz's technique. But before he could garner any usable information, Marcie once again made her appearance.

"We're ready for you, Mr. Rossi," she said as she waved him forward.

He said nothing as he straightened his suit and tie and followed her down a featureless cinder block corridor.

"I'm not supposed to do this," she dithered as they moved on, "but if I go home without your autograph, my little sister is just going to kill herself."

Rich grimaced, both at the irony of her sentiment and the Diet Coke making its way back up his esophagus.

"I'm sorry," Marcie surrendered, noticing his discomfort. "I should never have asked."

"No, it's not that," Rich said, forcing a smile and patting his chest. "I just drank my soda too quickly."

"Oh!" she gushed, stopping dead in the hall. "Then you don't mind?"

She turned a few pages on her clipboard and, exposing a blank sheet, offered it, and a pen to him.

"It's my pleasure," he said, holding steady the clipboard. "What's her name?"

"Cindy."

"Cindy," he repeated as he scribbled a few words followed by his name. "How far along in the book is she?"

Just then, the stage manager rounded the corner and barked, "We got thirty seconds. Let's go!"

Marcie shrank backward as Rich followed the stage manager to the studio. "Sit right over there," he commanded as he pointed to a chair across from Rosencrantz.

As he made his way, Rich was met by a young man who promptly outfitted him with a body mic. At the same time, a lighting guy passed by, holding a dial of some sort up to the ceiling before disappearing behind a camera. As Rich stepped on to the stage, Rosencrantz arose from his seat, stretched over the massive table and grabbed Rich by the hand.

"How you doing, son?" the gray-haired television icon growled in his all too familiar tone.

As shivers of discord clawed their way up his back, Rich nodded and managed, "Hey," then was promptly shoved down into his seat by the sound guy.

A voice from somewhere behind the cameras began counting down as the stage crew scampered out of sight.

"We're back!" Rosencrantz heralded to the world. "I'm here with Richard Rossi. If you haven't heard of him by now, then you probably live in a tree. He really needs no introduction because his face has been plastered on every billboard in the country at least once this summer."

Rich squirmed as he always did when the light on his camera came on. Although he had been on more news and radio shows than he could now count, he had never gotten comfortable with the spotlight.

"I for one am getting sick of looking at him!" Rosencrantz howled at his own interminable wit. "No, but really," he went on, turning his attention to Rich, "you're actually better looking in person!" He chuckled.

Rich forced a smile that even he himself didn't believe.

"So, Rossi," Rosencrantz went on, "what's the deal with your book? I read it! It didn't make me jump off a skyscraper!"

Through a monitor next to a camera, Rich caught a glimpse of his own horrified face. As his posture stiffened, and his jaw went limp, the old man went on.

"I'm just messing with you, kid." He reached over and gave Rich a fatherly nudge on the arm. "But I will say this," he went on, "my researchers have told me that since the release of your book, three months ago," he scanned a paper before him, then continued, "there have been four thousand and twenty one suicides where the victims have been found to be either still holding on to your book, or your book was somewhere very nearby. They have jumped off their balconies, drowned themselves, jumped in front of moving trains and taken overdoses of Mother's little helpers" He looked up from his paper, leaned in and looked unflinchingly into Rich's eyes. "What do you make of that?"

Rich paused for what seemed like an eternity. As the world watched, a tiny bead of sweat hatched on his temple.

Rosencrantz went on. "Let me back up. What made you decide to end the story with the two heroes committing suicide?"

"Well," Rich twisted in his seat, "originally, the book had a more customary ending. You know, they all lived happily ever after."

Rosencrantz nodded.

"But," Rich continued, "after lots of advice, some of which came from my thirteen year old nephew, I..."

He froze in mid sentence. Suddenly, and with the force of a gamma ray burst from the center of the universe, the image of his nephew, Tommy, battered him senseless. Literally dumbfounded and motionless, he gazed past Rosencrantz's right shoulder at the clock on the wall, his mind incoherently measuring the seconds.

Rosencrantz, a seasoned veteran, knew stage fright when he saw it. And with the ease of reciting the alphabet, he took control of the situation. "So," he began, "you got a lot of advice and the consensus was to kick it up a notch."

Rich, nearly catatonic, still did not speak. As he watched the second hand on the clock glide smoothly around, he tried to calculate where Tommy might be at this exact moment.

"Well," Rosencrantz plodded on, "whatever the reason, it must've been the right thing to do. Your book, according to the latest tallies," he once again scanned the paper before him, "has outsold even the latest installment of the Harry Potter series."

The rest of the world vanished as Rich struggled to recall his last conversation with his sister. Tommy would be picked up by his father on Thursday, or was it Friday? They would be heading out to Ed's cabin, or was it to Niagara Falls? "Why am I thinking Niagara Falls?" he fretted to himself.

Rosencrantz, becoming annoyed, pressed on. "That's a pretty good accomplishment for your debut novel."

"He was in such a hurry to get back to the book," Rich thought. "Surely by now he's nearing the end." He drew an audible breath that skirted past his tongue emitting a sound that resembled a hiccough.

Snapping to, Rich answered, "Yes."

Somewhat relieved, yet still cautious, Rosencrantz allowed himself to ask an actual question. "Do you believe the book would have sold as well if the ending had been, as you say, more customary?"

Rich blinked a few times and fought to re-engage, "Well," he croaked, "I owe a lot of the book's success to my publisher."

"Indeed," said Rosencrantz. And without so much as a beat, added, "I understand he is being investigated by the FBI. My research says that they are trying to link your book to all of the teen suicides. What do you make of that?"

Rich made a lame attempt to laugh it off, then answered, "Yeah, I've heard those rumors too. It's kind of a waste of taxpayer money don't you think? I mean, subliminal messages? Come on. Didn't we put those to the test back in the eighties? I mean, my mother tried to lose weight using those subliminal message tapes back then. Trust me, they didn't work."

Rosencrantz leaned in. "So how would you explain all of those kids' bodies still clutching your book?"

Rich paused for a moment, looked up and said, "Why do I need to?"

Completely flummoxed by the audacity of his guest, Rosencrantz straightened in the seat and raised his eyebrows.

Rich went on to say, "Besides, the main characters in my book jump off a cliff." He turned to face the camera, "There, I said it. Now the ending is ruined for all of you that haven't read it." He turned back to Rosencrantz, "The suicides to which you are referring have been by every conceivable mode. You yourself confirmed it in your research, balconies, trains, drowning. I'm not trying to minimize the tragedy that those families must be going through, but to blame it on my book is ridiculous."

Convinced that the entire viewing audience knew he was lying, Rich turned his attention to Tommy. And with the motivation of a million fire ants nipping at his ass, he rose from his seat, pulled the body mic from his tie and bolted for the hallway, turning on his cell phone as he steamed forward.

This wasn't the first time Rosencrantz had been abandoned by his guest. He had been left in the lurch by heads of state, politicians, actors and even royalty. So, mustering his poise and grace, he looked into the camera and said, "We'll be back after these messages."

As he burst through the heavy steel exit door that led to the underground garage, Rich dialed his sister, Rachel. Just as she answered Rich hopped into the back seat of the awaiting limo.

"Back to the hotel!" Rich shouted. He then turned his attention to the phone. "Rachel? Is Tommy still with his father?"

"Yes," she answered. "What's wrong with your voice?"

He paused for a moment to catch his breath. "I'll tell you later. Where did they go?"

"Are you sure nothing's wrong?" she pressed.

"Listen! You've got to get a hold of him, or Ed, or Abby!"

"Why? What's going on?" Her voice began to quake with fear.

Conscious of the driver just feet in front of him, Rich lowered his tone and spoke as cryptically as he knew how. "You've just got to get a hold of them. You've got to get that book out of Tommy's hands."

"Okay, I'll call right now, but you've got to tell me what I should say!"

"Say anything!" he shrieked. Then, remembering the driver, added, "Just call them now and get the book out of Tommy's hands. I'll call you as soon as I'm back at the hotel."

Ten minutes later, Rich was in his hotel room, packing. As he sped about the room, tossing items in his suitcase, his cell phone rang.

"Hello?"

"I can't get through! It goes straight to voicemail!" she cried. "Now, do you want to tell me why you're so freaked out?"

Preparing himself for a difficult few minutes to come, Rich steeled himself, took a deep breath and began. "You're never going to believe me, so just listen and don't comment. I found out last night that my book is the cause of all the kids killing themselves." He paused, expecting some measure of protest, but heard nothing and went on. "Volos put some kind of spell on the book. The kids that read it get sucked into it and become the characters!"

Utter silence prevailed from Rachel's end of the line. Rich couldn't be certain whether she was in shock and disbelief, or quietly maintaining control over the inevitable explosion of condemnation that would surely ensue.

"Hello?" he peeped, wondering if perhaps they had been disconnected.

"I'm listening," she replied stoically.

Hopeful by her tone, he went on, "So, we've got to get that book away from Tommy! Where did they go? Did they go to Niagara Falls?"

"I don't know!" she cried, Rich's panic having caught her. "They were doing a whole road trip thing! They're supposed to call me when they're on the way back home!"

"Okay," Rich said, leaving his room and jogging to the elevator, "keep trying them. No matter what, they have got to get the book away from him."

"I will! But Tommy's such a well-adjusted kid! Are you sure about all this?"

"I'll explain everything when I get home. Just keep trying them."

An hour later, Rich was on the Amtrak heading north to New York City's Pennsylvania Station. In the three and a half hour trip, he heard from Rachel six different times. In each call she would further decry the irresponsibility of Tommy's father for not answering his phone, and in turn, Rich would disclose another revelation of Volos's past. From parchment paper and one-way mirrors, to FBI probes and Dennis's "side effects", Rachel found herself spared the tumult of learning firsthand the scope of Rich's troubles. Instead, she found herself piecing random puzzle bits together until it all seemed quite believable and real. And by two-thirty that afternoon, Rich found himself in Rachel's living room retelling the story from start to finish.

Φ

TWENTY SEVEN

Dennis' plane touched down in Athens around eleven, Sunday night, Athens time. Five PM New York time. As they taxied toward the terminal, and got the all clear from the flight crew, Dennis powered up his Blackberry and checked his email. Scrolling past the daily spam from Lands End and Personalization Mall, he stopped and clicked on the reply email from his friend in Haiti. Like a nine year old on Christmas morning, he squirmed with anticipation as the message opened. It read;

Dear Denny,

I promised you many years ago that I would never pry into your personal life, but the fax you sent has me a little concerned. Are you in some kind of trouble? If so, let me know if I can help. Anyway, I spent the day deciphering what you sent and here is what I came up with. The translation is as follows:

Be it known to all that I offer my soul to Almighty Satan in return for the many gifts I shall receive during my Earthly existence. Additionally, until the time of my Earthly demise, my art shall influence the weak, and those souls too shall be offered to the Almighty Satan. From this day and until my death, I am bound by this agreement.

Again, if you need anything else, let me know.
Regards,
Manny

Dennis' face clouded over in despair. For several months he maintained his disbelief in Veronica's story, but it was now clear that she had been telling the truth. That Rich had made a pact, albeit an unwitting one, with the Devil. And it stood to reason that, since she had been honest about the contract, she must have been telling the truth about the souls.

The weight of a thousand worlds collected upon his shoulders as a flight attendant uncorked the plane and he retrieved his carryon luggage. As he made his way past his fellow travelers to the baggage claim, he flipped open his cell and called Veronica.

Around that same time, back in the states, Rachel's phone rang. An irate Ed bellowed from the other end of the line, "Where's the goddam fire? What's with all the messages?"

Shushing Rich, Rachel bawled, "Did you do what I said?"

"I never even gave that goddam book back to him! We were unpacking and Abby found a lighter in his suitcase, so he's being punished!"

Leaning in and tapping into the conversation, Rich let out a sigh of relief as Rachel went on. "Oh thank God! Make sure he doesn't get a hold of it."

"Don't worry," Ed assured, "I hid it, and the lighter in the boathouse. He doesn't go in there. Too many spiders, he says."

"Good."

"Yeah," Ed interrupted, "I watch the news. I know what's going on with that book. Did they lock him up yet?"

"It's not what you think!" she protested.

"Of course not!" he mocked. "But the FBI has something altogether different to say about it. They were here at the cabin this morning asking all kinds of questions about your brother!"

"Did Tommy see any of that?"

"No," he snapped, "Abby kept him busy."

"Where is he now? Can I talk to him?"

"He's sulking in his room. You can talk to him if you want, but he's supposed to be packing." He paused for a moment, then changed his mind. "On second thought, no. It would be nice if you didn't undermine my authority for once."

Rachel couldn't think of a clever rebuttal. He was right. The moment she would hear Tommy's voice her instincts would compel her to stroke away all of his pain and misery.

"Besides," he added, "we'll be leaving here soon. By seven o'clock you'll be mothering the living shit out of him."

The ring of her brother's cell phone broke her train of thought, sparing everyone the ineffectual rant that was bubbling inside of her. Instead, she merely ended the conversation with, "I'll see you in a couple hours," and then flipped her phone shut.

She sat for a moment and lit a cigarette, her first in several years, as she quietly rehearsed the tongue lashing she would give her ex upon his arrival. As she gazed out the living room window, seething with ire, Rich emerged from his telephone conversation in the kitchen.

He was pale and deflated, as though the blood had been let out of him. Slack jawed, he stood for a moment and stared blankly at his sister. To her, he appeared mere seconds away from passing out. "Hey!" she yelled, rising from her chair. "What's going on?"

He slowly shook his head, braced himself on a dining room chair and sat.

"Who called?" Rachel probed.

Still, he didn't answer.

"Was it Dennis?"

He nodded, scratching the back of his neck.

"What did he say? Did he figure out what the Latin said? What do you have to do?"

He gathered his strength, stood and went to the living room window where he scanned the city skyline. As he drank in the scenery he recalled a moment not so long ago in Volos' reception office when he pondered how long it would be until the people on the street below would know his name. And how sixty seconds earlier there was still a chance that he could rectify his predicament and maybe even parlay it into the finest career a writer could ever dream of. But irony impaled him as he faced his reflection in the window, until finally he turned to Rachel and said, "I can end this."

He gathered his keys and cigarettes and headed for the door.

"Wait!" Rachel cried. "Where are you going? What do you have to do?"

He went to his sister and grasped her shoulders. "I'm going to put a stop to everything."

"Rich, I'm begging you!" she sobbed, "Please tell me what's going to happen!"

He pulled her closer and hugged her with resolve. When he let go he said, "I'm going to Volos's office. There's a lot I have to do."

As he turned to go, Rachel stopped him. "Wait!" she ordered, as she disappeared into her bedroom.

Seconds later, she returned. "Here, take this," she said, as she took his hand and shoved in a holstered pistol. As she closed his hand around it she added, "It's the last thing Ed gave me before leaving."

He opened his mouth to protest but she shook her head and decreed, "You need to protect yourself."

Still, he shook his head.

"If you don't take it with you," she added, "I'll call the cops on you myself."

They shared a moment of silence until Rachel grabbed him by the shoulders, spun him around and said, "Now go tie up those loose ends."

He tucked the pistol and its leather housing into his trouser pocket, and as he made his way from his sister's apartment, down the elevator and sixty blocks downtown, he recalled his conversation with Dennis.

"I'm telling you, Mate," he had said, "she feels really bad. She was thinking of that night we all first met. And how she regretted getting you involved with Seth. You've got to go to his office. Break in if you have to. Go to the cabinets and open all the boxes. Break every glass vial inside every box you can. It's going to release every soul your book has given him."

Rich couldn't bring himself to replay the final task Dennis had given him. It was too unnatural. And although inevitable, he placed his own suicide on the back burner and rehearsed how the next few minutes might go.

Soon, however he was standing in front of the office building on Broadway. Collecting himself, he made his way through the gigantic plate glass doors and past the security desk without incident. As the elevator doors parted and he stepped on, his mouth became devoid of spit. His hands quaked as he pressed the 24 button, and as the doors closed and he ascended, he began an assault on his fingernails.

It was an eerily quiet ride up, but he imagined Sundays might always be this way here. When the door finally opened, he poked his head out of the elevator like an inept spy. Finding no one in sight, he stepped out. Now, only feet away from the front door, he took several deep and cleansing breaths. Then, with a brute force that stunned even him, he hurled his body forward, slamming his right shoulder into the door. Impressed with himself when it gave way on the first try, he took a quick glance about the hallway then stepped inside and heaved the door upward, closing it behind him as best he could.

Once inside, he sized up the door to Volos' office, puffed out his chest and charged. This time however, he overestimated his masculine dexterity and managed only an ill-maneuvered body slam that left him seeing stars. Rearranging his pants and rolling up his sleeves, he once again accessed the door. He took a few steps farther back, curled his frame like a professional linebacker and exploded from his feet, slamming into the door. As it tore away from the hinges, shards of wood trim flew in every direction. Finally, the door landed on the office floor with a crash, Rich tumbling over in kind.

Confident that he hadn't hurt himself, Rich mindlessly jumped to his feet, dusted himself off and examined his surroundings. It had been many months since he had been inside the old man's lair, and as his eyes adjusted to the near pitch black environment, he stumbled over the fallen door and reached for where he remembered the desk to be. Instead, he came in contact with one of the leather chairs that sat opposite the desk.

Slowly, he could begin to make out the outline of tables, shelves and paintings, and before many more moments, he could see, in full detail, the cabinets of which Dennis spoke. As he made his way to the wall of cabinets, he reached for the lamp that sat upon Volos' desk. Giving the chain a tug, he afforded himself just enough light to notice the liquor cart. The crystal decanters sparkled, reflecting what little light there was in the room, beckoning him. Numb with the idea of the finality that was to come, he stepped toward the cart and grabbed a bottle. He unplugged it and, surveying the wall of cabinets before him, took a mighty chug. The bittersweet flavor of Rye brought the hair on the back of his neck to attention, stinging his throat as he swallowed.

Many more gulps later, he carefully grasped a pair of cabinet knobs and gave them a swift and decisive yank. The doors clicked as they parted and squeaked only slightly as he opened them to capacity. There, he found row after row, column after column of stacked wooden boxes. They seemed to hum with energy, and as he ran his hand over them, he was sure that he could hear the distant cry of longing and despair.

He fought hard to dismiss it all as a bad dream. Evil words in a book, vampires casually walking the streets among us, deals with the Devil and souls trapped in little brown boxes. None of it seemed to completely register as real. But as he peered about the office, to the chair where he had first met Volos, the corner credenza where Gwen had written his first check, and the door that lay on the floor, ripped from its hinges like a casualty of a bad cartoon chase, he once again resolved that it was indeed all for real. And that it might someday make a hell of a book.

He turned back to once again face the stacks of boxes. He popped his cuffs, planted himself firmly on the carpet and, like a Jenga master, carefully slid a box from its place. Gazing down through the clear glass top he saw what Dennis had described, dozens of tiny vials, each containing what appeared to be samples of colored gasses. But in truth, Rich knew he had the captured souls of innocence in his hands.

He retrieved the Rye and moved with the box to Volos' massive desk, placed it carefully down and opened the lid. Removing one tiny vial, he held it up to the lamp and studied the churning red cloud that danced inside. Fully immersed in the surrealism of the moment, he imagined it to be the essence of a boy, maybe from Ohio, or California. His eyes welled up as he descended into the misery that this child's mother might feel, and took another healthy swallow of Rye.

As the sting of tears ran down his cheeks, he gently placed the vial upon the desk blotter and plucked another from the box. This one, a sort of neon yellow, seemed to come alive, ricocheting off the inside of the glass as he cradled it in his palm. He pulled out another, then another, until he found himself in Volos' chair weeping uncontrollably over a test tube classroom of lost potential.

Finally, when the salty taste of his lamentations reached his lips, he awoke from his despair, sat up and returned to task. It was now or never. The bottles had to be broken. He placed a single vial squarely in the center of the desk, careful to keep it from rolling away, then scoped the immediate area for something that would break it. A pair of heavy marble bookends caught his eye, and without hesitation he grabbed one, letting the books domino to the floor.

It wouldn't take much, he thought, so he moved in closely, braced himself and tapped the glass, allowing the weight of the bookend to do the work. Immediately, the vial imploded and the tiny puff of pink mist shot upward with the squeal of a hot tea kettle. It raced throughout the room, expanding and contracting, circling and dancing, emblazoning the walls with shards of bright pink light until it finally evaporated.

At that moment, an indefinable sense of wellbeing enveloped him. He felt stronger and more purpose driven than ever before. He reached for another vial, placed it next to the crushed glass of the first, and tapped it open. This time the room awoke with a pulsating brilliant Kelly green. It too waltzed about the room with a joy that seemed to tease his heart.

Thrilled and alive, he reached into the small wooden box, this time coming back with a fistful of the tiny young spirits. He laid them side by side and began striking them two, three at a time. And the room came alive with whistles, hoots and even laughter. The colors circled overhead, entwining, hop scotching and tumbling. As one by one they evaporated, Rich dug deeper into the box, finally dumping its contents atop the growing pile of fractured glass, smashing open every imprisoned essence.

As the colors and sounds transformed the office into a carnival of elation, Rich dashed to the cabinets with his bottle and began pulling out boxes, two, three at a time. As they fell to the floor, he danced with abandon upon them, crushing the mountain of wood and glass beneath his feet, releasing a veritable rainbow of sights and sounds. Like a madman, he stomped, kicked and staggered, all the while clawing and dragging every box from its place and onto the floor. As he tripped and stumbled over the rubble, the laughter of a thousand liberated souls filled the air. Giggling, chanting and sighing, the playful apparitions seemed to tickle and pinch, eliciting from him a melody of delight he had not known since childhood Christmases of old. And although his fingers bled from the errant shards of glass that glanced up from the floor and down from the cabinets, he was too enrapt, too drunk to notice the pain.

ℋℛ

TWENTY EIGHT

At about the same time Rich's shoulder hit the office door, give or take a minute or two, Ed and Abby were back at the cabin powering down. Dinner had been served, which Tommy had refused, electing instead to remain in his room and brood. The pickup had been packed, the cellar door reinforced, the well disconnected and the windows shuttered.

As Abby carried the last box of staples to the pickup, she passed Ed on the porch. "Can you holler for him? He's completely ignoring me."

Ed sighed and headed for the foot of the stairs. "Come on, Tommy! You've proven your point! You're pissed!"

Not hearing so much as a footstep from above, Ed went on, "Goddamit Tommy! Get your ass down here! We're leaving!"

Joining him at the foot of the stairs, Abby volunteered, "Let me go talk to him."

"Well we don't have all night!" Ed barked, retreating to the front porch.

As he took to the edge of a rocker, Abby came bolting down the stairs two at a time. "He's not up there!" she cried, bursting through the screen door onto the porch.

"What do you mean?" Ed said, standing and heading inside.

"He's not up there!" she repeated, grabbing his arm.

"Well where the hell could he be?" Ed snarled.

They both stood for a moment, mentally retracing their steps, trying to recall when last they had actually seen the boy. As they groped their own consciences, they indicted themselves for their weak parenting skills until, in near perfect unison they both chimed, "The book!"

They exploded from the front porch, sprinting past the pickup truck and down the grassy hill that lead to the boathouse. As they gained momentum and their bones rattled in protest, the little red shack came closer into view. Finally, from his vantage point Ed could see that the normally padlocked door was gaping wide open. "Oh shit!" he cried, his voice trembling with each step.

As they came to the wooden decking, Ed, sweating and gasping for air, stopped in the doorway and brushed his hair out of his eyes. As he stepped inside, his gaze turned immediately to the shelf where he had hidden Tommy's book. Noticing an empty spot, he dashed to the shelf and climbed up, hoping beyond hope that the book was somehow still there. But it wasn't.

Agonizing over the prospect that Tommy had run off to finish his book, Ed hadn't noticed, until Abby brought it to his attention, that the boat too was missing. With mounting horror, Abby and Ed raced to the water's edge and scanned the horizon. But the lake was dead calm, reflecting nothing but clear white sky. Nearing panic, they split up, Abby taking to higher ground, calling out for the boy, and Ed skirting the shallows, searching for any sign of his son's past few minutes.

As the shadows grew longer by the minute, Ed finally climbed the knoll back up to the cabin. "Abby!" he called as he passed the pickup.

As she appeared from inside, Ed surrendered, "Call the Sheriff."

While most little boys relish the fantasy of their parents ruing the day they ever invoked punishment, Tommy was indifferent. For weeks he had longed to complete the story his uncle had written. He had dodged school yard blabbermouths, avoided the nightly news and had waited more patiently than any thirteen year old boy should. Now, oblivious to his father's worry, he would at last have his time alone with *The Keeper of the Key*.

He had known from day one where his father had hidden it, and over the past 48 hours had devised a scheme to get it back and snigger in the face of his father's cruel and unusual punishment. So just before dawn he padded his way into his father's bedroom, carefully lifted the keys from the hook next to the light switch and crept to the boathouse. There, he opened the padlock and left it to hang. After returning the keys to the hook, he crept back to bed, falling asleep as he anticipated the next morning.

Just after breakfast, he had returned to his room to sulk, making sure that his tantrum-like stomps could be heard ascending the entire length of the stairs. Then, in a final act of drama, he slammed the bedroom door shut, punctuating for all to hear that he was indeed confining himself to his room.

Then he waited. With his prize branded firmly in his mind's eye, he waited. He paid strict attention to the sounds coming from the house below him, the squeak of Abby's sneakers, the folding of the his father's newspaper, the twang of the screen door, until all audible signs pointed to one definable conclusion. The adults had left the house, talking their grownup talk together as they headed for the orchard just beyond the property line.

This was it. With the stealth of a Ninja he opened his bedroom door and crept down the stairs as the grownup voices became more distant. Slowly, he pried open the screen door and scanned the periphery. Then, with almighty haste and agility, he sped down the hill, nearly airborne, until he reached the cover that the boathouse provided. As he peered around the corner, keeping his eyes in the general direction of where the grownups had last been seen, he unlatched the old wooden door. Once inside, he tossed the padlock on a nearby shelf. Moments later he was sitting in the row boat, his book tidily in front of him upon a bench as he shoved off with one heavy oar.

As he drifted out from under the boathouse he made a hard right turn and, opting for a stealthy getaway ignored the motor and paddled along the shore line. After a hundred yards or so, he abandoned the shady cover of the tree line and paddled toward open water. As the cabin shrank in the distance, the exhilaration of defying his father peaked. And although he knew that the consequences would be dire, he relished this purest form of independence.

Now, nearly a mile from the cabin, he drifted in absolute solitude. Not a rustle from a tree nor a bark from a dog could penetrate his senses at this distance. So he kicked off his shoes, grabbed his book and stretched out on the deck. As he settled into position, the boat leveling out, even the lapping of the miniscule waves against the boat's hull waned. Now, nearly motionless, he carefully opened the book, and leafed forward to the dog eared page where he had left off so long ago. As he smoothed back the pages, the familiar warm glow beamed outward from the book, welcoming him back into its world.

It would be several hours before his father would discover he was missing.

TWENTY NINE

His elation at full tilt, jumping and skipping maniacally upon a heap of glowing rubble, Rich didn't notice when Volos entered the room. In fact, Volos had stood quietly for a full three minutes, observing, seething while Rich gleefully destroyed all he had worked so hard for.

At first shocked by the sight of the office doors torn from their hinges, the old man scanned the room in disbelief. His desk had been ruined, ravaged by splinters of glass and wood, his two imported leather chairs had been upended and slashed up the backs, and the entire North wall of the office appeared to have been the casualty of an errant bulldozer.

He watched with sheer contempt as his children escaped, vanishing into thin air as this unwelcome savior whistled, hooted and danced about this sacred space. Still, he said nothing, opting instead to let Mr. Rossi finish his work.

As the souls became fewer and farther between, Rich, now breathless from his unrestrained forty-five minute looting spree, stumbled about the debris kicking and digging for stragglers. Sweating and gasping for air, he made his way back to Volos' desk where, wiping the sweat from his brow, he sank into the massive swivel chair and let out a jagged sigh.

Then, from the corner of his eye he spotted a figure. He had to look twice, for the old man stood with such disciplined stillness that he nearly blended into the décor. In the nanosecond it took to realize he was not alone, Rich was once again on his feet. The glare of the desk lamp now below his line of sight, he could now identify Volos standing mere yards away.

The old man limped toward Rich, the sound of glass crunching beneath his feet. Rich froze in his spot as Volos stopped at the desk, the lamp casting up an eerie pall from beneath him.

"So," the old man growled, "you think you're pretty smart huh?"

Straightening his posture, Rich held his ground but said nothing.

"Well, let me tell you this," Volos added, "I've been betrayed by better men than you!"

Rich had the words, but fought to get them out without his voice cracking. "I would think that betrayal would be a way of life for you."

"Touché!" Volos replied, as he turned and headed for his liquor cabinet. "Obviously," he went on as he poured himself a snifter of brandy, "you're on to me."

He turned, and with his brandy, motioned toward the wreckage around him. "Why else would you be here destroying everything I've made?"

"You're right," Rich slurred. "I am on to you. I know everything. I know how you manipulated me, and I know what the contract is all about. Everything."

"Sounds like you've got it all figured out," Volos quipped. "But do you really think coming here and ransacking my office is going to do any good?"

"It's a start," Rich said defiantly.

"Not really," Volos smirked. "You see, this week that pathetic piece of garbage you call a novel is making its European debut. By this time next month I'll have a thousand times more than what you've destroyed here today!"

"Well," Rich confidently crossed his arms and swaggered around the desk, "what you don't seem to understand is that I know how to stop it all. The contract, the one that you, in your infinite wisdom constructed, clearly states that," he paused and looked to the sky, mocking, "let's see, oh yes, that the weak shall be influenced by my art until the end of my Earthly existence."

"And?" Volos baited.

"And," Rich said, removing the pistol from his pocket, "my Earthly existence ends today."

Volos casually sipped his brandy, then placed the snifter upon the desk. "Now Son," he whispered, hobbling toward Rich, "your Earthly existence is just beginning."

Rich backed slightly away, unwrapping the gun from its leather holstering.

Volos went on, slowly and deliberately, "Haven't you been paying attention? Have you checked your bank balance lately? Haven't you everything that I promised you? The celebrity? The prosperity? Remember the day we first met? Remember what your response to me was when I asked you how badly you wanted this? Mr. Volos, you said, as long as I can remember, nothing has felt as right to me as when I was witnessing the expressions on the faces of those who were listening to me tell a story. I will do anything it takes to spend what time I have left on this planet feeling that joy. Do you remember saying that?"

Rich began to shiver as he raised the gun and pressed the barrel against his temple. "I didn't want it like this," he croaked. "If I end it here and now, if my Earthly existence stops today, no more children will die from reading my book."

"You're right," Volos concurred as he inched still closer to Rich. "If you pull that trigger, your book will no longer influence the weak. It will instantly become just another book. And your young life will be over."

Volos reached for Rich with the comforting arms of a father. "If that's really what you want," he murmured, "let me help you."

As tears streamed down Rich's face, Volos leaned his cane against the desk and moved still closer, until he was holding Rich in his arms. "Do you want me to help you Son?" he consoled.

Rich hesitated, then nodded his head and allowed Volos' grasp to join his own, both now holding the gun against his head. The two men held on to one another as Rich closed his eyes.

"It's all going to end now," Volos comforted. "Are you ready?"

Rich nodded with a quiver.

§

THIRTY

His eyes fixated on some unknown point in space, Tommy closed the book and placed it gently upon his lap. With blissful calm he reached into his pocket and grasped a shiny orange disposable lighter. His tiny thumb began to compulsively flick the wheel as he pulled it in to view. As he held it out before him, his gaze turned to the glittery blue and yellow sparks that issued forth from its top. Mesmerized by its beauty, he lowered it to just below the bench in front of him, and holding the flame against the gnarled wood, his thoughts turned to Cassandra and the pact they had made. As the flame devoured the ancient wooden bench, Tommy sat quietly and dreamt of the reunion he would celebrate with her.

As the fire spread, consuming every bit of fuel in its path, Tommy, now wholly spellbound, closed his eyes and let the smoky warmth envelope him.

THIRTY ONE

Grimacing, Volos tightened his grip around Rich's hand squeezing the trigger. Then, with almost no effort at all, he turned the pistol toward himself and with one horrific bang a single bullet pierced his forehead.

Rich jumped, his eyes snapping open just in time to see Volos sinking to the floor. Time seemed to stand still, and for one liberating moment, he had forgotten why he was where he was.

With the sound still reverberating in his ears, he watched as Volos smiled and tried to speak, knowing the old man had kept him from ending his own life. For a brief second, an horrific premonition jolted him senseless. The European launch, skyrocketing sales, a readership of millions. And as Rich looked on, and the old man unceremoniously passed from this Earth, he couldn't have known that in that same moment, his nephew, Tommy had succumbed to an inferno on a lake nearly a hundred miles away.

But his stupor was broken when he heard an approaching ruckus from the hallway.

"Shots fired!" a man's voice harkened. "Shots fired!"

As Rich turned toward the voices, he was confronted by two well-dressed men wielding firearms much larger than the one he still held.

Squatting in the doorway, pointing their weapons, one shouted, "FBI! Freeze!"

"Drop the gun!" commanded the other.

"Don't shoot!" Rich cried, raising his hands in surrender. "It's me! Richard Rossi!"

"Drop the gun!" the first agent repeated.

Keeping his hands up, Rich released the gun, letting it fall to the floor with a thud.

As the first agent stood his ground, the second broke his stance and crept cautiously into the room. "Put your hands on you head and turn around!"

"You don't understand!" Rich cried.

"Hands on your head!"

Rich fearfully complied, linking his fingers together atop his sweaty mat of hair.

"Now turn around!"

He obeyed, pivoting to face the ruins. "You don't understand!" he repeated.

"I'm agent Crawford," the man behind him said as his arms were pulled down behind him. "You're in big time trouble Mr. Rossi."

As the cold steel of handcuffs closed around his wrists, Rich pleaded, "You don't understand! I was trying to..."

"Shut the fuck up!" Crawford barked. "Yates," he said to his partner, "do we need a bus?"

Agent Yates looked up from Volos' lifeless body and shook his head.

Without hesitation, Agent Crawford began, "Richard Rossi, you're under arrest for the murder of Seth Volos. You have the right to remain silent. Anything you say can and will be used against you in a court of law..."

Rich didn't hear much else as he was being shoved past the doorway and out to the elevator.

THIRTY TWO

A trial was held to determine Rich's guilt or innocence, and predictably, not one member of the jury bought the defense's story. They didn't believe the testimony of Gwendolyn Wright, or Rich's sister, Rachel Downs, the prosecution objecting that their statements were hearsay. They didn't buy Rich's story of a contract with the Devil, souls of suicidal children being scooped up by Volos, or spirits being imprisoned in little glass vials. And while Rich clung to the hope that Dennis Goodman would appear at the last minute, flash his pearly white fangs and blow the lid off the whole case, he was nowhere to be found. Nor was Veronica Hall.

It was easier, and far more practical for the jury to believe what the prosecution had held all along, that Volos and Rossi had struck a deal that had gone sour. That greed, revenge and perhaps jealousy over Ms. Wright had poisoned their business relationship, and that Rossi had gone to Volos' office to confront him and put him out of the picture. And that Rossi had trashed the office in an effort to stage a break in.

But for all that was brought to the table, during a trial that lasted exactly 1 day longer than his book tour, Rich's fate was sealed by the testimony of Agents Crawford and Yates who had found him standing over the victim quite literally holding the smoking gun.

Richard Rossi was sentenced to life imprisonment with the possibility of parole in the year 2036. Upon his arrival at the Cape Vincent Correctional Facility in Northern New York, he was processed and led to his cell where he would begin serving his time.

As the weeks and months passed, the popularity of *The Keeper of the Key* swept throughout Europe. And as it did in the states, it's hold over the children there became the topic of many fruitless debates.

And with not much else to do with his time, Rich kept tabs on the book's repercussions. Daily, he amassed newspaper clippings, timelines and statistics, imagining that one day, the story of his last year of freedom would make an extraordinary novel.

Several months into his incarceration, now the most famous inmate in Cape Vincent, Rich was offered an assistant to aid in reading and responding to the hundreds of letters he would receive each week. Hate mail, prayers and marriage proposals would mingle together in a dirty canvas sack until they were poured out onto his bunk and sorted.

One Friday afternoon, while his assistant autographed glossy black and white photos, Rich opened and dumped the contents of a dingy old bag onto his bed and began the ego-stroking task of arranging the envelopes by size. As the pile dwindled, he spotted a small package, already opened, scrutinized and then resealed by prison security. Like a boy on Christmas morning, he held it up to his ear, shaking it, wondering what it could be before turning it to inspect the return address. 18 Rue de la Roquette, Paris, France.

He ripped through the packing tape, pulled open the cardboard flaps and found wads of crumpled tissue with an envelope tucked neatly within. Balancing the box upon his lap, he ripped open the envelope, retrieved the slip of paper and unfolded it. It read, *Just the second of many more editions to come.*

He became lightheaded with helplessness, the dismal grey prison walls seeming to close in around him as he dug through the tissue paper to reveal a brand new copy of *The Keeper of the Key*. As he opened the front cover, his eyes became transfixed on the thick black ink that scribbled out the words, *Congratulations on your best seller. V.*

THE END

EPILOGUE

After burying her son, Rachel Downs left
Manhattan and returned to her hometown of West
Reading, Pennsylvania, where she now works in a local
drycleaner. She has had almost no contact with her
brother, Richard, or her ex-husband, Ed.

Ed Downs sold his cabin and is living on the
streets of Phoenix. Since the death of his son, he has
medicated himself by whatever means available,
alienating his fiancée, Abby Taylor. Having lost
everything dear to him, he survives by panhandling
and visiting charitable organizations.

Gwendolyn Wright remains in New York City
where she now runs a successful literary agency from
her home office. About once a month she takes a
weekend trip up to Cape Vincent, New York where she
visits Richard, then returns home with another
installment of whatever current manuscript he is
working on.

Dennis Goodman remained in Greece until the storm of Rich's trial blew over. He has since changed his name and is living in Port Elizabeth, South Africa where he is putting the finishing touches on a novel of his own.

Veronica Hall has spent most of her time in Europe, defending herself from the allegations that have swirled around *The Keeper of the Key*. And while she still mourns the death of her beloved Seth Volos, she keeps the torch alive, wreaking as much havoc as her soulless body will allow.

Made in the USA
Lexington, KY
29 November 2013